COWBOYS

A BOYS BEHAVING BADLY ANTHOLOGY BOOK #6

DELILAH DEVLIN   JAMIE K. SCHMIDT
ELLE JAMES   MARGAY LEAH JUSTICE
REINA TORRES   CINDY TANNER   KELLY VIOLET
JANUARY GEORGE   JENNIE KEW   MEGAN RYDER
MICHAL SCOTT   IZZY ARCHER   NATASHA MOORE
AVA CUVAY   SUKIE CHAPIN

Daniel,

Happy reading!

Kelly Violet

XOXO

TWISTED PAGE INC

Cowboys

A Boys Behaving Badly Anthology
Edited by Delilah Devlin

Dedicated to readers for their love of great stories!

STORIES INCLUDED

Sweet Home Cowboy – Jamie K. Schmidt
Free Rein – Elle James
Eight Seconds to Love – Margay Leah Justice
Sweetgrass Summer – Reina Torres
Cowboys & Zombies – Cindy Tanner
Carry Me Home – Kelly Violet
East of the Rift – January George
Tying the Knot – Jennie Kew
Second Chances – Megan Ryder
The Patience of Unanswered Prayer – Michal Scott
Something to Talk About – Izzy Archer
The Scoundrel – Natasha Moore
Solar Flare – Ava Cuvay
Hunk of Burning Love – Delilah Devlin
Thoroughbreds and Thermodynamics – Sukie Chapin

SWEET HOME COWBOY

Jamie K. Schmidt

WYNN CAMERON TRUDGED out of the airplane, wishing she had tried to fall asleep on the flight instead of binge-watching episodes of *Sex in the City* for the tenth time on her laptop. Dragging her beat-up carryon with the wonky wheel, she stepped off the escalator leading to the exit and blinked at the brightness of the Texas sun that was streaming through the floor-to-ceiling windows.

"Over here."

That unmistakable voice cut through the weary haze of her travel-plagued brain. After all this time, Wynn's body still turned to obey the curt command. Digging in her heels, she stopped in the middle of the corridor to look at the man she'd left at the altar two years ago.

What the hell was Leo Anders doing here?

And why the hell did he have to look so damned good when she felt like a crumpled-up paper bag stained with potato chip grease?

Leo wore a black Stetson and crisp blue jeans with a tucked-in tight T-shirt. She tried not to stare at his muscled chest or the curve of his biceps that were accentuated by the way he crossed his arms over his chest.

"Move it, lady." A man pushed by her, and she stumbled, banging her knee against a wobbly steel gate. To her horror, Wynn's eyes filled with tears. It hadn't hurt. It was just a reaction. Exhausted from the plane ride, strung out from worry about her father, and then facing Leo Anders again, was too much for her to bear. Straightening up, she glared at the rude man's back.

Leo pushed through the crowd towards her and, at the last minute, dropped his shoulder. The rude man got plastered into a column as Leo plowed through him.

"Hey," the rude man snarled, shaking his head to clear it.

Leo just stared at him, eyes as flat and cold as a rattler's. The rude man adjusted his jacket and walked away from whatever he saw in Leo's eyes. Without a word, Leo reached down and grabbed her carryon bag. Wynn opened her mouth to protest but saw he wore a wedding ring.

The tears came back, this time with a dizzying nausea. Luckily, he was striding away from her without a backwards glance. She wasn't sure what was worse, that he'd gotten married or that he was wearing the wedding band they'd picked out together.

This wasn't how their storybook romance was supposed to have ended. Once upon a time, there had been an Oklahoma ranch girl who'd dreamed of leaving the dusty, sweaty countryside to live in a modern apartment in Manhattan. Every day, she was told her duty was to keep the ranch in the family and work backbreaking chores from sunup to sundown. One day, a handsome older cowboy, that all the women had been trying to catch, asked her to marry him. The girl threw out all her dreams of New York to be with him. Then she found out he was just marrying her to get the ranch. The girl left Oklahoma and never saw him again.

Until today.

Wynn had to hurry to keep up with his long-legged stride. She was irritated that he thought she would follow him blindly, doubly so because that's exactly what she was doing. "Leo, why are you here?"

He didn't answer her. When they got to a dusty Ford F-250, he tossed her carryon in the back. "Get in."

She really wanted to tell him no, or at least, go to

hell, but what was the point? He was here, and her bag was already in the car. She might as well save the taxi fare to the ranch. After hauling herself into the massive cab of the truck, she was barely buckled in when Leo pulled out of the parking spot.

"How's Dad?" she asked.

For a minute, she thought he was going to continue with the strong silent treatment, and she was content to stare at the outline of his jaw and wonder if his lips still felt the same. He turned his gaze to her, and she flushed, wondering if she had been tired enough to say the last bit aloud.

"He's not going to be able to walk for a long time. His right leg was shattered. When the horse threw him, he hit the ground at a bad angle."

Wynn closed her eyes and sank back into her seat. Her proud father would hate that. He would hate not being able to work on the farm, and he would despise being the object of pity, both real and imagined. It was going to be a tough road to recovery.

Leo didn't say anything else until he pulled into the town hall parking lot.

"Why are we here?" she asked.

"We're getting married."

Leo left Wynn gaping at him, with those luscious red lips parted in shock. He got out of the truck, walked around to her side, and opened the door.

"Have you lost your mind?" she asked.

Reaching in, he unclicked her seat belt, and then held out his hand for her to take so he could help her down. He thought he was behaving rather civilized, but she still stared at him like she didn't know him. Like she had forgotten about him while she'd been fooling around in New York City. Maybe she had. That thought didn't sit well with him. Hooking his arm around her waist, he tugged her off the seat and into his arms. She fit like she belonged there, and if he held her against him for longer than was necessary, it was because she smelled like honey and roses. A silky wisp of blond hair strayed from the messy ponytail she wore and tickled his cheek.

He remembered how they would lay in each other's arms after making love for hours. With a shuddering breath, he set her on her feet before he did something stupid and kissed her. They'd wind up back in the truck, risking everyone in town seeing them going at it.

She looked up at him with dazed eyes. Leo couldn't resist rubbing his thumb over her bottom lip. It was past time she was his wife. He'd been waiting two years for her to come to her senses. He wasn't going to waste a moment longer.

"Leo," she whispered, sounding so lost and helpless that he pulled her against him again in a fierce hug. "I can't marry you."

Stiffening, he put her at arm's length. "Is there someone else?" He hoped that had come out calmly because the thought of her in another man's arms made him want to punch his truck.

"What? No."

"Good." That solved that. Leo took her by the upper arm and walked her up the stairs to the town hall.

"Leo, damn it. Stop. What is going on? I need to be at the hospital with my father. Not here."

"Before his accident, your father signed over the ranch to me." Her sharp intake of breath was all the proof he needed that she hadn't known.

"And the catch was that you had to marry me?" Wynn said bitterly.

"No." He tried to go through the door, but the stubborn woman refused to move, and short of carrying her, he didn't know what to do. "He hoped, of course, that I would."

"Is that why we're here?" Wynn tried to struggle out of his grip, but he wasn't having any of that.

"We're here because you and I agreed to be married. I've waited long enough."

"We ended things."

"You ended things."

"Because you didn't love me."

Leo cursed himself for being all kinds of an idiot. He wasn't the type of man who bought roses and candy for a girl he liked. He had bought Wynn a palomino with a hand-tooled leather saddle because he'd seen how her face lit up whenever she saw something like that. He had watched her watching him, but had never felt it prudent to ask the boss's daughter out on a date—until her father had dangled the ranch in front of him. Leo had thought it was the perfect opportunity to get everything he'd ever wanted in one neat package. But it had been too easy, and as their wedding day had gotten closer, Leo hadn't felt like he'd earned the ranch or the girl of his dreams.

He cleared his throat. "I handled everything all wrong. I'm sorry my cruel words hurt you. I didn't mean them like you took them."

"You've said that before. I've heard your apologies. It didn't change my decision then, and it doesn't change my decision now. I came back for my father. Not for you."

Her words felt like a gut punch. Even though he knew all of that already, he wasn't ready to admit defeat. "Yes, I wanted the ranch. Yes, I was willing to marry you to get it. But that has never changed the fact that I wanted you, too."

"You told your best man that you didn't want a wife."

"I didn't." Leo wished he had looked around before blurting that out in the church two years ago, because his casual words had hurt Wynn and had kept them apart all this time. He hadn't wanted to get married, not because he hadn't wanted to settle down like Wynn had thought. He'd wanted to have something to bring to a marriage, but all the explaining in the world hadn't been able to convince Wynn of that.

She had heard what she'd wanted to in his careless words. He'd have given anything to take back those words.

"And now you want a wife?" she sneered.

"Yes," he said.

"Why now?"

"I've been running your family's ranch ever since you left. I earned the right to buy it. I no longer have to marry into the family to get it."

"Then why marry me?"

He drew a deep breath and gave her a steady glare. "No woman has ever come close to making me feel like you do. Is that love? I don't know. I haven't had a lot of experience with love. But I know regret and loss, and that's how I know I can't let you get away from me this time. Wynn, be my wife."

WYNN MANAGED to pry herself loose from Leo's grip before her body betrayed her and launched itself at him. This couldn't be happening. His words were demolishing her very carefully laid plans. The ones that involved being a sophisticated New Yorker who didn't shovel hay and horse manure.

"Leo, I have a life in Manhattan." So what if she hated her job and every penny went to paying rent. "I can't marry you. Please, just take me to see my father."

Leo set his jaw, and for a minute, she thought he was going to toss her over his shoulder and carry her inside to the justice of the peace. Wynn's heart thumped in anticipation, and she caught her breath. He could always make her crazy like this.

Instead, he gave her a curt nod and strode back to the truck. He didn't say a word until they got to the hospital. But he made it a point to place a hand on her back to guide her down the hallway. Every time he touched her, a sizzling frisson of desire coiled inside her stomach until she was shaky on her feet. She kept hearing his words over and over in her head. If he had said them two years ago, would she have left?

When they got to her father's hospital room, Leo pulled her aside. "I need you to do something for me."

Swallowing hard, Wynn forced herself to meet his steely grey eyes. "What?"

Taking her hand, he pushed her wedding band on her finger.

"Damn it, Leo," she said, trying to pull her hand away. Too late. It was there. It was heavier than she remembered it being and more beautiful.

"Your Dad is confused. He asked me the other day why I wasn't wearing my wedding ring."

"What?" Wynn said, frowning.

"He got real upset. That's why he demanded to see you. If you're not wearing your ring, it might set him off again."

"But we're not married," she hissed at him. "We were never married."

Leo shrugged. "It surprised the hell out of me, too. But the doctors want to save him from any trauma."

"This better not be a trick."

"It's not a trick."

"Why didn't you tell me this before?"

"Would you have gone through with the civil ceremony if I had?"

"No," she said.

He shrugged. "It is what it is. Pretend that you're married to me and try not to upset him."

"Isn't he going to be even madder when he finds out we've been lying to him?"

"You could always marry me."

Wynn pushed by him into the hospital room. Her father's gaze flickered over to her. For a moment, she didn't think he recognized her, and her heart sank. But then her mother rose from her chair by the hospital bed and gave her a hug. "I'm so happy you came home," she whispered. "He's been asking for you."

She hugged her mother back, and then sat down in the chair. She held her father's hand. He looked so old and frail. He was covered in black and blue bruises.

"How do you feel, dad?" Wynn asked.

"Like I've been run over by a train," he said, his voice raspy.

He turned her hand over and looked at her ring. "I had a terrible dream. I dreamed you went away."

Wynn cleared her throat. "Well, I'm here now."

"Get me some water, would you?"

There was a pitcher of ice water on a table, and she poured him a glass and helped him drink it with a straw.

"I'm having problems remembering things," he said.

She exchanged looks with Leo, who leaned against the far wall with his arms crossed. "That's probably to be expected, Dad. You had quite a shock to your system."

"I'm not going to be able to be much help anymore," he said.

"It'll be fine," Wynn soothed him. "Don't worry about that now. Concentrate on getting stronger."

Her dad gave a small, tight smile. "I'm glad you have Leo. He'll know what to do."

"Mom knows what to do, too," Wynn said, her throat tightening.

Her mother laid a hand on her shoulder and squeezed. She looked up at her. Her mother's eyes shone with unshed tears. "Leo has been a big help. I know your father will rest easy if the two of you manage things while I'm here with him."

Now, Wynn felt like she had been hit by a train.

AFTER A FEW HOURS, the nurses kicked them out. Wynn had offered to stay to give her mom a break, but her mother didn't want to leave her husband when he was so confused.

11

"Don't worry about me," her father said, as Wynn kissed him on the cheek. "I'll be all right."

Wynn managed to hold it together until they reached the truck, and then everything just hit her all at once. She was dimly aware of Leo hauling her onto his lap and cradling her against his chest as she cried herself out. It felt so good to be comforted. He rubbed large circles on her back. After she thoroughly drenched his shirt, he handed her a stack of napkins to blow her nose.

"I'm sorry," she said. "I don't normally lose it like that."

"It's been a long day," he said. "I bet you're hungry."

"I couldn't eat a thing." Wynn rubbed her aching stomach. "I just want a hot shower and to sleep for twenty-four hours."

"I can get you that."

She might have dozed off a bit on the way back to the ranch because they were there in minutes. When she opened her eyes, he was pulling up to the ranch house.

"Do you need anything?" he asked as he let her in. "Your room is just as you left it."

"Thanks, Leo," she said. She turned to look back at him from the doorway. "I know things didn't end well for us, but I'm glad my parents had you these past few years."

"Things haven't ended between us," he said. "But that's a conversation for tomorrow. In the morning,

I'll save a stack of pancakes and sausage for you from the ranch hands' breakfast."

That brought a smile to her face. She'd always loved Miranda's blueberry pancakes. She had been the ranch's cook ever since Wynn had been a little girl.

"That would be nice."

"I can be nice," Leo said, leaning in to give her a quick kiss on the mouth.

She felt the electricity zing through her at the small contact and hurried up the stairs. Her room was exactly as she'd left it, but she didn't have time to get nostalgic. Peeling off her clothes, she staggered into the bathroom. Turning on the shower, she gratefully sank under the spray. Even her favorite soap, shampoo, and conditioner were fully stocked. She could have stayed in there for hours, but she settled for a quick scrub and washed her hair. Wrapping a towel around her hair and winding another one around her body, Wynn stifled a yawn.

She was surprised that Leo had brought up her suitcase and had chosen a night gown for her to wear. It lay spread across her comforter. She wasn't sure if she was happy he hadn't rifled through her bag for a pair of underwear, or if the absence was on purpose. Either way, she was too tired to do anything more than slip the nightgown over her head and slide under her robin's egg blue duvet.

· · ·

THE MOONLIGHT DRIFTING through her window woke her up. Her phone said it was one-thirty in the morning. She tried to roll over and go back to sleep, but after tossing and turning for ten minutes, she gave up and decided to go downstairs and raid the pantry for a peanut butter and jelly sandwich to tide her over until breakfast. Wynn paused by the front door, which was open. Only the flimsy screen door kept out trespassers and bugs. Before she closed the door, she peeked out and was surprised to see Leo seated on the wicker sofa that her mother loved.

"You don't have to stay here," Wynn said, her voice loud in the night.

Leo poured more whiskey into his glass. "I live here. Your parents moved into the cottage last year."

She stumbled out to the porch. It was a chilly night, and as the night air passed through the flimsy nightgown, she remembered she wasn't wearing anything else.

Leo's face was in shadows, but she could feel his gaze on her like a caress. "I'm in your house? You should have brought me to the cottage."

"Want a drink?"

She shook her head. Not on an empty stomach. She shivered again. "I should go. It's getting cold."

Leo stood up. "You should've stayed in bed."

"I was wide awake," she protested, backing up a step.

Pressing her against the door, he opened it up and she nearly fell. "Careful." He grabbed her to him and walked her back inside. While he closed the door and locked it behind him, she took a few steps away and pressed her hands to her burning cheeks. It had felt good to be held against him. Her body remembered how it felt to be loved by him.

Love? That shook her out of her fog. It had always been business and good sex with them. Yet, they were both still wearing their wedding rings. She could stand there and stare at him all night, but that would get them nowhere. Wynn headed into the kitchen, not really surprised when Leo followed and eased his bulk into one of the chairs.

She gathered the makings of a peanut butter sandwich and asked him if he wanted one.

He shook his head. His gaze was still riveted on her.

"What are you doing up so late?" she asked. She knew he had to be up before dawn to get an early start on the day's work.

"I was thinking about sneaking into your bedroom, unwrapping you from the covers, spreading your legs, and licking you awake."

The knife fell on the counter from her nerveless fingers. "Leo," she said shakily.

Then, he was behind her, and his breath was hot on her neck. "Two years, Wynn. I waited two years for you to come to your senses."

Her thin nightgown was no protection against the soft denim of his jeans, and his hardness pressed into her backside. She leaned back against him when his teeth grazed her neck and his stubble rasped on her sensitive skin.

"And accept it was a business deal with benefits for us?" she said, trying hold on to her sanity. She gripped the counter, but she could feel her self-control slipping away with each brush of his body against hers.

Leo reached around and cupped her breasts with both hands. Wynn bit back a moan but was unable to stop herself from rubbing her ass against his hard cock. She had slept with him on their first date. Their goodnight kiss had erupted into her wrapping her legs around him and him carrying her into the barn where they'd scared the barn cats. Afterwards, she had snuck him up to her room for a quiet round two, desperate not to wake her parents even though they were on the floor above them.

Tugging on her nipples, Leo went back to torturing her neck while she raised up on her tiptoes so she didn't miss any little bit of him. He nudged his leg between hers, spreading them. Then lifting up her nightgown, he slipped his fingers inside her.

"Leo," she gasped when he began to rub her intimately.

"I hurt your feelings with my careless words. I apologized. I explained my feelings. You left anyway. You should've stayed. We would've made it work."

She caught her breath, his words almost over-shadowing the sweet play of his fingers tickling her into what was working toward an explosive orgasm. Wynn squirmed in his arms, but Leo held her tight.

"Do you want me to stop?" he asked gruffly in her ear.

Her entire body shivered in denial. He flicked his fingers faster through her slick folds. The wet sound of her arousal was loud in the night's silence.

"Tell me," he demanded, stopping what he was doing.

"No," she protested and wiggled on his fingers, dying for him to hit the spot again.

"Tell me what you want," he said kissing her shoulder.

Wynn took a deep, shuddering breath. Whatever their problems had been, this hadn't been it. "I want you to make me come."

"And then what?" Leo found her spot again, and her knees wobbled. He fingered her slowly, while his other hand teased her nipples.

"Leo…" she said, trying to get him to stroke her faster.

"And then what?" The bastard stopped again.

Groaning in frustrations, Wynn said, "Then I want you to fuck me. I want you to fuck me until we can't move."

"About damned time," he grunted. Picking her up, he carried her up the stairs to her room. When he dropped her on the bed and started pulling off his clothes, it was like no time had passed at all. Leo ripped her nightgown down the front as she kissed him desperately. Her hand wrapped around his cock, and she jerked him fast with eager strokes.

"I'll come all over your hand," he warned against her mouth.

"Okay," she said, not able to stop.

Kneeling on the bed, they rubbed each other, kissing and moaning. She felt like the naïve twenty-one-year-old she'd been, trusting Leo to make everything all right. There hadn't been anyone else for her. No one had come close to making sex feel so dirty, so right, and so damned good.

He came first, and she cackled with glee until his sensuous growl of satisfaction turned her into goo. "Thank you for that," he said lowering her down on the bed. "Now, I can last more than ten seconds once I'm inside you."

"Now," she begged.

He chuckled. "Not even close."

Leo covered her mouth and trapped one of her thighs between his. He was still hard. He went back to playing with her, using his fingers until Wynn's body shook with a pent-up orgasm that had her screaming his name. It was a good thing they had the house to themselves this time.

"I missed the taste of you," he said, kissing down to her chest.

He lovingly licked her nipples while she still quivered through the aftershocks of pleasure. He trailed kisses down her belly until he reached the juncture of her thighs. "You are so damned beautiful."

Then he traced his tongue everywhere his fingers touched. Her hands twisted the sheets as her hips rose to meet the flat strokes of his tongue. The tension was building again inside her. She was still shaking from the buzz. How had she gone two years without this? Wynn closed her eyes. Because she had loved the jerk, and her pride hadn't let her settle for anything less than love. But right now, this was a close second. Her toes curled as he lapped at her clit. Wynn thrashed on the bed, but Leo held her exactly where he wanted her.

"Leo," she sighed and rode his face to another limb-shaking orgasm.

"Now," he said, breathing hard. "Now."

Leo moved up to ease inside her, and Wynn wrapped her arms around him. The fit was still tight. Her fingernails dug into his shoulders. When he began to move, the friction was almost too good to bear. He rocked into her fast and hard. Excitement tore through her. The anticipation built as he pounded into her. She twisted and pushed back, eager for every inch of him. The slick drag of his body against hers felt like coming home.

The bright lights of the big city paled against the streaming moonlight in her childhood bedroom, while the only man she'd ever loved fucked her into oblivion. Wynn lost count of the number of times she came, and when they finally slowed down to catch their breath, she wrapped herself around him and fell asleep. She was home. Oklahoma might not be her dream place to live, but right now, she'd take being held in Leo's arms over all-night takeout and her cold, lonely bed in Manhattan.

LEO WAS GONE when she woke up. Her phone said it was half past ten. He'd be in one of the back pastures with the cattle by now, making sure the herd was taken care of. Her body felt sore in all the right places, and when she stretched her arms over her head, the diamonds on her wedding ring sparkled in the sun.

How would her life had been different if she hadn't gone to Manhattan? She probably would've always wondered what she was missing. As Wynn took a quick shower and got dressed, she thought about what she'd been running away from. Barn chores were at the top of the list, along with long hours of working the land and falling into bed exhausted at the end of the day.

Miranda was waiting for her in the kitchen, wearing a big smile on her face and holding an even bigger plate of pancakes.

"We missed you so much," Miranda said, enveloping her in a hug. "Your daddy needs you more than ever now."

Wynn sat down at the kitchen table and dug in, pouring thick maple syrup over the buttery blueberry pancakes. No one needed her in New York. No one really cared one way or another. She still worked hard and still fell into bed exhausted at the end of the day. And working in a PR firm, she was just shoveling a different set of horse manure every day.

"And Mr. Leo needs you, too. You broke his heart when you left," Miranda chided softly.

Wynn almost choked on her pancakes. "It's not like that between us."

Miranda arched an eyebrow at her. "Everything he's done these last few years has been for you. He kept this ranch going. He supported your mom and dad when they needed him." She pointed upstairs. "Your old room was kept like a museum, your bedding changed every week, just in case you decided to come home." Miranda folded her arms over her ample chest. "When are you going to put that man out of his misery and marry him?"

Twisting her wedding ring, Wynn sighed. "I thought he was only marrying me for the ranch."

"The ranch is his now." Miranda cleaned up the counter while they talked. That was true. He had every reason to let her be if he didn't want her, but he had made it abundantly clear that he still wanted to marry her.

"He never said that he loved me," Wynn said quietly.

"Do you love him?" Miranda asked.

Wynn heard his bootsteps behind her, but she didn't turn around. "I've loved him since the first time I saw him on his horse, riding in covered in trail dust and barking orders."

His hands fell on her shoulders, and still, she wouldn't look at him.

"I've got to get the laundry," Miranda said, hurrying out of the kitchen.

"Is it so hard to say the words?" Wynn asked. "Or is it that you don't feel them?"

Leo took a deep shuddering breath. "If I say I love you, will you stay?"

Wynn got angry. She tried to get up, but he held her down. "This isn't emotional blackmail. It's not a negotiation. Let me go."

He immediately released her, and she popped up. Spinning towards him, Wynn said, "I know you feel something for me. Is it just sex?"

Leo winced. "Keep your voice down."

"Like Miranda doesn't know we're sleeping together," Wynn scoffed. "She knows everything that happens on this ranch."

"Do you hate it here? Would you rather live in New York?"

"Why?" she asked, narrowing her eyes at him.

He hauled her back against him. "I'd hate it, but we could have a long-distance marriage. I love this ranch, and I love you. But I understand if you don't want to be a rancher's wife. You can still be my wife, though."

Gripping his shirt, she tugged him closer. "Say it again."

"I love you, Wynn. Be my wife."

She kissed him fiercely. They could figure the rest

out later. Right now, her family needed her in Oklahoma, and she needed Leo.

"We should get to the courthouse before they close," she murmured.

"About damned time," he said, scooping her up in his arms and taking her back upstairs.

FREE REIN

Elle James

"DEVIN LAYNE? Or should I call you Daredevil?"

As the voice sounded behind him, Devin turned, a frown forming on his forehead. Daredevil was a moniker he no longer attributed to himself. Not since his last deployment. The mission that had taken the lives of some of his best buddies in the 10th Special Forces and had gotten him a one-way ticket out of the military. He flexed his aching leg and faced a man with black hair, black eyes, and military haircut. "I'm Devin."

The man stuck out his hand. "Jake Cogburn. My colleague, Max Thornton, asked me to talk with you."

Max Thornton? Devin remembered Max Thornton. He'd been a member of the 10th Special Forces a couple years before Devin. Max had been on a mission with him at some time in the past. Then Devin hadn't heard or seen anything about Thorn—the callsign he'd gone by—for several months. "So? Am I supposed to be impressed?"

Jake gave a quick grin. "No. But he said you were a top-notch Green Beret."

"Past tense," Devin said, turning away. "If you'll excuse me, I'm working."

"I know. I don't want to take too much of your time here. But I'd like to buy you a drink and talk."

Devin shook his head. "I'm busy."

"How about tomorrow…Gunny's Watering Hole…seven o'clock?" Jake persisted.

Irritated, Devin gathered his horse's reins. "Like I said, I'm busy."

"At least, think about it. I have a job opportunity you might be interested in." Jake touched his arm. "Just hear me out over drinks. I think you could be an asset to our organization."

Devin snorted. "I doubt it." He stood for a moment by the fence overlooking the arena where the Fool's Gold, Colorado, annual Gold Rush Rodeo was taking place. This was the first job he'd landed since he'd come home to Colorado, and it was only for the duration of the rodeo. Yeah, he had some money coming in from his medical retirement from the Army, but his dissatisfaction wasn't so much the money as the need to work. The problem was there weren't too many opportunities for a man who could barely get around. Unless he settled for a desk job. He frowned. "How did you know I'd be here?" No one but his immediate family knew he'd returned to Fool's Gold.

"I ran into your sister, Laurel, in town." Jake Cogburn leaned his elbows on the rail, watching as a contestant lowered himself onto a huge bull in the chute.

Seconds later, the gate opened and the bull leaped out. The man held on to the rope around the bull's middle for four seconds before he was thrown by the frenzied beast.

"Laurel has a big mouth," Devin muttered.

"Laurel cares about her brother," Jake countered. "Besides, I asked about you. She didn't want to lie, so she told me you'd come home."

"So, I'm home." Devin shot a narrow-eyed glance at Jake. "How did Thorn know to ask about me?"

Jake gave a hint of a smile. "He has his connections in the Special Forces like I have mine from my time in the Navy SEALs. We belong to an organization called the Brotherhood Protectors. We recruit former military, who are highly trained for Special Operations, and put them to work."

Devin's frown deepened. "Look, I don't know what Thorn thinks, but I'm not the same guy who fought with him in Afghanistan." He took a step away from Jake, demonstrating the decided limp. "I didn't quit the Army; they processed me out because of this." He patted his leg.

Jake lifted the leg of his jeans, displaying a prosthetic. "I get it. This civilian life is new to you, and you're trying to figure out how you fit." He shook his head. "I was where you are not long ago until an old buddy of mine, Hank Patterson, pulled my ass out of the bottle I was trying to drown myself in and gave me purpose. I didn't think I could be of any use to anyone when I was one leg short of a pair." He lifted his chin. "Hank proved me wrong. And I'm here to offer you the same deal he offered me. Come to work for the Brotherhood Protectors. We need men like you."

Devin wanted to believe what Jake was saying, but it all sounded too good to be true. "I don't need anyone's pity or handouts."

"We aren't handing out either. You have to work for your pay on our team. Some of our assignments are dangerous. Tell you what, don't say no right now. Think about it. I'll be waiting for you tomorrow at The Watering Hole. I'll buy you a drink."

"I have to get to work." Devin said.

"You don't have to commit to anything." Jake held out both hands, palms up. "What can it hurt?" He grinned. "See you tomorrow." And he left.

As soon as Mallory Watts drove up to the arena, her horse trailer in tow, she could sense something was different. She'd been to the Fool's Gold arena so many times in the past twenty years, she could find her way around blindfolded. Hell, she'd cut her teeth riding barrels and had fallen in love with a bronc rider.

And that was another story she'd just as soon forget. That bronc rider had chosen to join the military with the promise to come back and marry her someday.

She snorted in a very unladylike way as she parked the truck, climbed down, and strode to the back of the trailer. Jazz pawed the floor of the trailer, more anxious than usual.

"I get it," Mal soothed. "I feel it, too." She unlocked the gate, swung it open, and stepped inside. She untied Jazz's lead and backed her out onto the hard-packed dirt. "Let's just do what we came to do and go home to a warm stall and a bucket of sweet feed, all right?" She rubbed the horse's muzzle and patted her neck.

Jazz tossed her head as if ready to do her part and get back to the Lucky Star Ranch.

Mal's edgy feeling didn't go away and must have transferred to Jazz because she tugged against the lead and danced sideways.

"Whoa, girl," Mal whispered. "We have to wait our turn." She glanced over the top of her horse's neck at a man on a horse, wearing the polo shirt of one of the arena's security staff. His hair was rich brown, cut short on the sides and barely longer on top. The guy sat straight in his saddle, his hips swaying with the steady gait of the horse as if he'd been born to ride.

A memory tugged at Mal's heart. If she didn't know better, she'd think it was...

No. It couldn't be. She'd know if he was back. Surely, he would've called her if he was coming home. At the very least, Devin would've called his sister Laurel to let her know he was home. And Laurel was her friend. A friend let her friend know when a certain former fiancé was in town. Mal shook her head.

She moved around her horse to get a better look at the man. Her pulse kicked up a notch, and she found herself breathing a little erratically. If she wasn't one of the most down-to-earth women she knew, she'd think her mind was playing tricks on her.

Then again, Devin had been gone far too long. His sister had mentioned he'd been injured and was in rehab at Walter Reed Hospital in Maryland. When Mal had asked for details, Laurel had insisted Devin hadn't wanted any visitors. She'd gone out to Maryland anyway, only to be turned away. The man *really* hadn't wanted visitors. Not even her.

That had hurt. A lot. And she hadn't heard from Devin for several months. It was as if he'd fallen off the face of the earth. Had he lost interest in her? Was he blowing her off?

"Mal!" a voice called out, pulling her back to the task at hand. Laurel Layne hurried toward her. "Whew. I'm glad I caught you."

Mal's eyebrows drew together. "Hey, I didn't

think rodeos were your thing now that you have your own florist shop?"

Laurel beamed at her. "When my bestie is riding, and it's in town, I'm there. Besides, I have a good helper now. She's manning the store today. And isn't it a glorious day to be outside and riding?"

"It's okay, I guess." Was it her imagination, or was Laurel overly upbeat? Mal glanced back toward the man on the horse, wishing her friend had waited a few more minutes to find her. Surely, the guy would've turned his head just enough to reveal he wasn't Devin, and she'd have gone on to do her ride free of curiosity. Distractions made her lose focus. If she didn't have focus, she'd lose the race. She'd been training hard with Jazz. He deserved her attention and commitment after all he'd put up with.

"I've been meaning to call you," Laurel said.

A flash of guilt tugged at Mal's gut. Laurel was always the one to call or keep in touch, up until about a week ago. "No worries. I've been busy out at the ranch. We got a new quarter horse to train. I've been working it pretty steady for the past few days, and I figured you were busy with the shop."

"Yeah," Laurel glanced away. "We've been busy, but I meant to call and let you know—"

"Stay tuned, folks," an announcement blared out. "Next up is the barrel racing competition. You don't want to miss the event. You might want to empty what's full and fill what's empty before the fun begins."

Mal's head shot up. "That's my cue. I'd better check in before they think I'm a no-show."

"But Mal—"

"Can we talk after my ride?" Mal asked as she slipped the bridle over Jazz's head and buckled it in place.

"It might be too late, by then," Laurel muttered so low Mal wondered if she'd heard her correctly.

Mal reached for the saddle horn and looked over her shoulder. "What did you say?"

Laurel gave her a weak smile. "Nothing. You go do your race and show them how it's done. I'll be here when you get back."

Mal nodded, her frown deepening. "Is there something you wanted to say?"

Laurel shook her head. "Nothing that can't wait. I know how you like to focus. So, get in your zone, or whatever, and we'll talk when you've won the race." She winked and stepped back.

Mal swung up into the saddle, still frowning. Laurel was acting weird. However, she didn't have time to figure out why. "We'll talk after," she said and rode toward the staging area to wait her turn.

As she stood in line behind the other riders, she glanced around. No sign of the man on the horse. Good. She could focus on the race ahead. Mal leaned over and scratched behind Jazz's ears.

The first barrel rider came in at just over twenty-one seconds.

Mal gave the woman a nod as she rode out of the

arena. Good, but not great. She and Jazz averaged closer to eighteen seconds. Nineteen on a slow day, and seventeen and some change on good days.

The next rider burst into the arena.

Movement out of the corner of Mal's eye drew her attention away from her competition. The security guy in the polo shirt rode around the corner of the concession stand into full view.

Mal's heart leaped into her throat, and then pounded hard inside her chest. Joy filled her, sending a rush of warmth to every part of her body.

It was Devin. He was home. Sweet Jesus.

A smile spread wide across her face. Without thinking about it, she nudged Jazz and turned him toward the man who'd held her heart in his hand from the moment they'd met at this very arena fourteen years ago.

No sooner had the horse started toward him, then a thought edged its way through her euphoric haze. How could he have a job as arena security the day he got back? Unless he'd been back for several days, maybe longer. If he'd been back for more than a day, why the hell hadn't he contacted her? And why had he insisted he didn't want her to come out to Maryland after he'd been injured? Isn't that what fiancées did for their true loves?

A thousand questions rushed through her head. She pulled back on the reins, a frown pulling her eyebrows together.

At that moment, Devin glanced her way. His

gaze met hers, and his eyes flared. But like a flame blown out, they grew shadowed, and he looked away.

"Oh no, you don't," Mal muttered beneath her breath. She pressed her booted heels into Jazz's sides, urging the horse forward.

When Devin turned his horse away, Mal sent Jazz into a trot, catching up before he could get away.

"How long have you been back?" she demanded.

He refused to meet her gaze again. "What does it matter?"

"What does it matter?" She sputtered, anger building deep inside and bubbling to the surface like lava about to spew. "I haven't heard from you in months. You refused to let me come to Maryland when you were injured, and then you show up at a rodeo in our hometown as if nothing is wrong."

Devin's lips pressed into a thin line. "Nothing is wrong."

"The hell, you say." Mal was just getting revved up. "What happened to talking with the woman you promised to marry? You cut me off without any idea of what's going on. You didn't even let your family in on your condition, your prognosis. All they knew was that you were alive and back in the States. At least, they got word. I got nothing."

"I didn't want to bother you," he said.

"Didn't want to bother me?" Mal's anger turned cold. "Well, it didn't work. I was bothered. I went to Bethesda to find out what was going on. They wouldn't let me in to see you. They said you had specifically told them no visitors, even family."

"I didn't want anyone there," he said.

"Why? Did you ever think that people who love you could've helped with your recovery?"

He shook his head. "No. There was nothing you or anyone else could do to help."

"Why?"

"I'm not the same man who left Fool's Gold."

Mal's gaze swept over him. "You look like the same man."

"Looks are deceiving." For a brief second, his gaze met hers. A shadow crossed his face, but then he looked away. "I've changed."

Her breath caught and held in her throat. "Or is it that you've changed your mind about us?"

"Fine," he said, his voice harsh. "Yes. I've changed my mind about us. There is no us. There. Now, will you leave me alone?"

The rodeo announcer chose that moment to say, "Next in the arena is Miss Mallory Watts, a five-time winner of this event, here in this arena. Hold onto your hats, ladies and gentlemen, she's fast!"

Mal stared into Devin's eyes, hurt pulling so hard on her heart, she could barely breathe.

"You're up." Devin tipped his head toward the arena gate. "You better hurry before you forfeit."

And that was it. He'd dumped her.

Mal lifted her chin, spun her horse around, and entered the starting gate.

The gate flew open, Jazz leaped out, and the race was on.

Moisture filled her eyes, making it hard for her to see the barrels. She made it around the first one thanks to Jazz and the hours of training. When they rounded the second one, she was completely blinded by tears flowing down her cheeks. Her knee clipped the barrel, knocking it over, giving her an automatic five-second penalty. Jazz skittered sideways and kept going. Somehow, they completed the event and raced out of the arena.

Jazz came to a stop twenty yards past the gate, no thanks to Mal. The reins hung in her hands, and the tears streamed down her cheeks, dripping off her chin. Yes, she'd known something was wrong with her relationship but had held out hope that Devin would come back to her and make it right. She loved him with all of her heart.

Her broken heart...

"Mal," Laurel's voice broke through her misery. Her friend, the sister of the man who'd just dumped her, touched her boot. "I'm so sorry," she said. "I tried to warn you, but..." She sighed. "I'm sorry."

"We're through," Mal whispered, and more tears slipped down her cheeks. She'd never felt this empty in her entire life. She sat on her horse, unable to function, barely able to breathe.

"He's not the same," Laurel tried to explain. "He's angry at the world. I've never seen him this way."

"He's not the same?" Mal flung her hand in the air. "What does that mean? He's Devin, for godsakes."

"His injury…" Laurel looked past her.

Mal turned to see Devin on his horse, looking their way. "He never let me in to see him when he was in Bethesda. It hurt then. But this…" She looked away from Devin, afraid he'd see the tears he'd inspired.

"Damn him," Mal said through her teeth. "Why did he have to come back at all?"

"He had nowhere else to go," Laurel said.

Mal brushed the moisture from her cheeks. "He can go back to his beloved Army for all I care."

Laurel shook her head. "He can't. They medically discharged him, based on his injury. He's without a job for the first time in his adult life."

And he hadn't bothered to let her in on any of his pain, his status…his freakin' life. He really was done with her.

"Tell me the truth, Laurel," Mal pinned her friend with her stare. "Did he fall in love with his nurse during his stay at Walter Reed?"

Laurel shook her head. "No way. He's only ever loved you."

Mal fought back more tears, swiping away those that came anyway. "I call bullshit."

"You have to give him time. He's trying to process his life without the military. He's seems kind of…" Laurel raised her shoulders and let them drop, "lost. Like he has no purpose, no direction."

"He had enough direction to tell me to leave him alone."

Laurel snorted. "If it makes you feel any better, he's told everyone who loves him to leave him alone."

Everyone? Mal turned again.

Devin was in the exact same spot, still seated in his saddle, looking toward her, a haggard expression on his face.

Something tugged at her heart.

No. She wouldn't feel sorry for the man. He'd done the dumping, not her.

Still...he did appear, like Laurel said...lost.

Her instinct was to turn Jazz around and confront Devin, calling him out for dumping her. What injury could be so bad that he'd be kicked out of the Army? And what could be so bad that he'd push away all those who loved him?

He appeared to be the same Devin who'd left nearly a year ago, promising to come back and marry her after his deployment.

Well, almost like the same Devin. Those shadows beneath his eyes and the gray tinge to his skin weren't normal.

Three boys ran past her laughing and playing tag. One of them raised his hand in the air, holding something in his fingertips. He laughed and slammed his hand down. A sharp pop sounded, like a hand-held firecracker.

Jazz reared.

It was all Mal could do to keep the horse from

landing on the kid. She pulled hard on his reins while trying to stay in the saddle.

When the horse came back down on all four feet, he took off, bit between his teeth, and ran like the wind.

No amount of hauling back on the reins or shouting *whoa* got through to Jazz. He was scared, and he was getting away from the noise that had spooked him.

And he was heading straight for the busy highway that fed tourists into Fool's Gold at sixty miles per hour.

Mal had to get him to stop before he reached the road, or she and Jazz would become roadkill or cause a massive and deadly pileup.

DEVIN HAD WATCHED as Mal ran her race. It was as if she didn't give a damn or couldn't see what was in front of her. When she blew out of the arena, he'd been on the verge of swallowing his pride, riding up to Mallory, and telling her he was wrong, and he didn't want her to leave him alone. She was the last person he wanted to leave him alone.

He'd just nudged his mount forward when a kid set off a firecracker beside Mal's horse.

Jazz reared up on his hind legs.

Devin sucked in a sharp breath.

As experienced as Mal was, the surprise of a horse, rearing like that, unseated even the best riders.

38

Mal held on, struggling to bring Jazz down without taking out the culprit who'd been stupid enough to set off fireworks near the horses.

When Jazz dropped down, Devin almost breathed a sigh, but the horse wasn't done. He took off with Mal on his back, racing faster than he'd seen the animal move in the arena. Hell, if he didn't slow down, he'd make the highway in less time than it took to run a barrel race. Horses and speeding vehicles didn't mix well.

Devin slapped his mount's hindquarters with the reins. "Gitup!" he shouted and raced after Mal and Jazz.

They were well ahead of him and widening the distance.

He dug his heels into his gelding's flanks and leaned forward in his saddle. The only saving grace was that Mal was leaning back on her reins, pulling hard enough to slow the animal. Unfortunately, it appeared Jazz had the bit between his teeth. No matter how hard Mal pulled, she wouldn't stop him.

With his heart in his throat, Devin pushed forward, gaining on the runaway horse. They were withing fifty yards of the highway when he finally caught up. With his horse abreast of Jazz, he edged closer, reached out, snagged Mal around the waist, and pulled her out of her saddle and onto his lap.

The frightened animal kept going.

Mal refused to let go of Jazz's reins and almost yanked herself and Devin out of his saddle.

Devin dug his boot heels into the stirrups and pulled hard on his horse's reins.

Mal held on to Jazz's reins, turning him as Devin slowed his mount.

A few short yards from the highway, the horses came to a halt.

Winded, Jazz heaved air in and out of his lungs. Lather covered his chest and neck, and he foamed at the mouth.

Mal struggled in Devin's arms. "Let go of me."

"I can't." Devin tightened his hold to keep her from falling to the ground.

But Mal wiggled so much Devin was losing his grip. "If I let go, you'll fall," he warned.

"I don't care," she said. "Let go."

He didn't have a choice. Mal slipped from his grip and fell to the ground at the horses' feet.

Jazz reared again and would've run out onto the highway, but Mallory hung onto his reins even though she lay flat on her back. The horse dragged her with him.

Devin dropped down from his horse before he remembered his leg wasn't strong enough to hold his weight on impact with the hard-packed dirt. He fell to his knees and groaned as pain shot up his leg. He fought to rise, managing, only by holding onto his gelding's stirrup. When he was finally up, he hurried around to where Mal was being dragged toward the highway, shouting, "Whoa!" to her spooked horse.

Limping heavily, he managed a shuffling run. He

caught up, snagged the reins, and brought the horse and the woman to a halt.

Then he dropped to his knees on the ground beside Mal, grimacing at the pain it caused. "Oh sweetie, are you all right?"

"I'm fine, except for the scrapes across my backside." Mal stared at him, at the leg he was favoring, and then up into his eyes. "Is this why you're pushing people away?"

He frowned, his back stiffening. "I'd rather not talk about it." He pushed to his feet, fighting hard not to show how much it hurt to straighten.

When he reached down to offer his hand, she stared at it, her eyes narrowing.

"I call bullshit," she whispered as she laid her hand in his.

When he brought her to her feet, she didn't let go of his hand. Instead, she held on tightly and pressed her chest to his.

The warmth of her hand and her body flooded through Devin. After the explosion, when the medics had carried him into the chopper and airlifted him to the field hospital, all he'd thought about was this woman and how much he wanted to hold her again.

The surgeon at the field hospital had told him he was lucky to be alive as much blood as he'd lost. He'd told the doc he had a girl back home he wanted to see, joking that he'd had to get blown up for the chance to go home.

When it was all said and done, and the doctors at

Walter Reed had taken a look at the damage caused, they'd said he'd be medically discharged. That's when it had hit home. He was jobless, with no skills other than he was a really good shot and had great skills in a battle. How useful would that be in the civilian world?

As useless as lipstick on a pig as his father would've said, if he were still alive. No. He couldn't go back to Fool's Gold and expect Mallory to marry a man who didn't have a job and had no prospects.

Mallory wrapped her arms around his neck. "Did you hear me?" She raised her eyebrows. "I call bullshit."

"I don't know what you mean," he said, his voice hoarse, the effort of remaining stiff and remote straining his control. He was exactly where he'd wanted to be. "You deserve more."

"More what?" she challenged.

"More of a man," he said, his tone gruff with anger at himself, his shortcomings, the situation…hell. Angry at his life.

"So, you get to make all the decisions in this relationship? I don't get a say?" She laced her fingers at the back of his neck. "Tell me that you don't feel anything for me. That you don't love me, and I'll walk away."

Devin's anger bubbled up. He gripped her hips, his fingers digging into her soft flesh. "Damn it, Mal."

"Say it," she demanded.

He stared down at her, fully intending to tell her

that he didn't love her, but when he opened his mouth, he said, "I never stopped loving you."

Then his arms came up around her, and he crushed her to his chest. "Thinking about holding you in my arms was the only thing that got me through that first night, the surgeries, and the torture of physical therapy."

She cupped his cheek in her hand, her eyes filling with tears. "Then why didn't you let me come to you?"

His jaw hardened. "I didn't want or need your pity. I didn't want you stuck with a washed-up guy who was only half a man. You deserve more."

"Again, are you the only one making decisions in this relationship? There are two of us." She leaned up on her toes and brushed her lips across his. "I choose you."

"But I'm not me, anymore," he insisted. "I'm not fit to fight. I'm not good behind a desk. I used to know exactly what I wanted to do in life and had a plan on how I'd get there. Now, I don't know who I am."

She held his face between her hands, forcing him to look into her eyes. "You're Devin Layne. The man I fell in love with at this rodeo fourteen years ago."

He stared into her beautiful gray-blue eyes, and his heart melted all over again. He loved this woman with all his heart.

"You're worthy, and you're strong. You wouldn't have made it this far if you weren't," she said.

Recalling the grueling pace he'd pushed himself to

learn to walk again on his damaged leg, he couldn't deny her words. A lesser man would've given up. Even when he'd wanted to quit, he'd pushed through the pain, knowing he had to get back to Colorado to see Mallory, even if he couldn't be with her.

"I love you, Mallory. I always have."

"And that's all that matters." She leaned up and captured his lips. "The rest will come. Job, home… children." On that word, she leaned back and raised an eyebrow, challenging him to disagree.

"How can I keep up with a child, much less a beautiful wife?"

"You'll figure it out." She smiled up at him. "Just like you'll find work. You're a Layne. You'll land on your feet."

He remembered Jake's invitation and nodded. "Damn right, I will—even if I land a little wobbly."

She laughed. "See? You're the same man under all that bullshit you've been dishing out. I love your sense of humor."

"And I love your tough love and patience."

She leaned her cheek against his chest. "Mmm. Patience isn't one of my strong suits."

"And losing isn't easy, if I remember correctly."

Mallory winced. "You saw my race?"

He nodded. "Not like you to knock a barrel over."

"I've never cried over a man before."

He frowned down at her, his gut knotting at the thought of Mallory so upset she'd thrown a race. "You were crying?"

"Look, cowboy. You have free rein on my heart." She poked him in the chest. "Don't make me cry again."

He held up both hands. "I'll do my best not to. It hurts me to hurt you."

Devin gathered her into his arms and held her close She fit perfectly against him, and he loved the way she smelled of the outdoors. Hell, he loved everything about this woman, and he'd do anything to prove to her she wasn't making a mistake by choosing him.

"What are you doing tomorrow night?" he asked.

"Spending it with you."

He chuckled. "How would you like to have a beer at The Watering Hole?"

"I'm in." She looked up at him, her brow furrowing. "Any special reason?"

"Maybe." He thought about Jake Cogburn. "Ever heard of the Brotherhood Protectors?"

"Sure have." She grinned up at him. "And you'll fit right in. See? Things will fall into place. Before you know it, we'll have half a dozen kids running around our feet."

"I'd be so lucky." And he kissed her, anxious to get started on that brood.

EIGHT SECONDS TO LOVE

Margay Leah Justice

Sela

How long does it take to fall in love?

An hour?

A day?

A month?

A year?

For me, it only took eight seconds. Eight mind-blowing, heart-stopping seconds, and I was a goner. How did it happen so fast, you might wonder? It went something like this:

One second… I saw him.

Two seconds… he saw me.

Three seconds… our eyes met.

Four seconds… my breath caught.

Five seconds... my heart raced.

Six seconds... he slayed me with a rakish smile.

Seven seconds... time paused.

Eight seconds... I fell.

Now my world will never be the same...

"Hey, sweets, whatcha writin'?" my cousin Denise breaks into my thoughts, scattering them to the far corners of the earth with her pure country twang—it's thick with this one, but I love it. She shoots a quick look at the notebook in my lap as she sits down beside me with a cold beer and plateful of barbecue. "I swear, you carry that thing with you everywhere —" she's not wrong—"so it must be good, huh?" She leans in for a closer look despite my attempts to hold her off. Her pert little nose scrunches up in confusion. "Well, that's something, isn't it?" Her tone has a slight edge of confusion. "Looks like some of that fancy poetry you took a shine to in high school"—she makes a sound halfway between a scoff and a laugh; neither is very complimentary—"or the lyrics to a really bad country song."

Ignoring the sting of those last words, I mutter, "It's called haiku."

"What?"

"The fancy poetry," I say a little louder, holding the notebook against my chest so she can't get a better look at it—or find any other fault with it. To think, she's my favorite cousin. Why is that, again? "It's called haiku."

"Oh, right." She nods as if she already knew that.

She didn't. I'm surprised she even knows what poetry is; she's not exactly the scholarly type. Not that she ever wanted to be. Oh, no, she's a beauty queen through and through—as evidenced by the way she literally waves me off and says, "Well, whatever it is, I'm sure it can keep 'til later." She shakes her head in disbelief, the gesture making her hair skim along her shoulders like a beautiful blond waterfall. "I mean, *seriously*, girl, how can you sit there writin' in that book with all these yummy men millin' about just waitin' for the takin'?" Yeah, another thing about my cousin Denise...? She's what my mom would call "boy crazy"—and she makes no apologies for it.

And wouldn't you know it, just as if they planned it that way, the crowd parts to reveal the subject of my "fancy poetry" in all his good ol' cowboy glory, standing a mere five feet away. Oh, lord, he's so pretty. Even more so this close than he was the first time I saw him, clinging to an animal aptly named The Beast for the most thrilling, heart-stopping eight seconds of my life. And I'd only just begun to breathe easier, having caught all of my emotions from that ride on the tip of my pen and transferred them to my journal. A moment in time captured in writing. I never thought I'd see him again—at least, not this soon. And certainly not at my grandparents' ranch, chatting with my Uncle Stan and his cronies. Now, I'll have to start all over again.

Why is first love so hard?

I guess I could ask Denise. She's been "in love"

enough times to really know the ins and outs of it, so she'd probably have some good advice for me. Trouble is, she's a hearts-in-her-eyes kind of person. And impulsive. That's a bad combination. With my luck, she'd probably want me to do something radical. Like make me go talk to the guy and…

No. Not gonna happen. I'd rather sit here and take notes on life than take a chance at *living* it, thank you. Less chances of getting hurt that way, and after what my mom went through with my dad, I think I'd like to keep it that way. So, instead of jumping on the yummy-guy bandwagon with my cousin, I try to put her off the scent with, "I really don't see anyone I want to take."

"Bull!"

At first, I think she's calling me out on the big fat lie I just told, and I hold my breath, waiting for the rest. But then, I realize she's not even looking at me. Oh no, her attention is cast forward.

Right at the guy I can't get off my mind.

And now, because of her—

He's coming this way with a big ol' knee-weakening smile on his pretty face.

Thank God, I'm already sitting down.

I might just faint.

BEAU

I love what I do for a livin'. Tamin' bulls ain't for the faint of heart, and if there's anythin' I'm *not* it's faint of heart. Some say I'm kind of a risk-taker, and to some extent, I guess that's true. Every time you get on a bull, you're takin' a risk. One small misstep could be deadly. Still, it's a risk I'm willin' to take for the sport I love.

What I don't love? The politics behind the sport. And the assholes who think they know everythin' tryin' to tell you how to do it better. Like this bunch I'm currently—reluctantly—jawin' with. Just another bunch of wannabe rodeo stars tellin' me how I coulda done this better or shoulda tried that instead. Like they know what the hell they're jawin' about. The only bull they come close to is the shit they sling at the real riders, myself included. What I wouldn't give to get away from them right now.

"Bull!"

Who says the big man isn't listenin'? He just answered my own damn prayers with that shout from one of my adorin' fans. Okay, so it's the daughter of my main sponsor, but still. She loves me. Not in the hearts and flowers kind of way, more like the annoyin' big brother she never wanted to have kind of way.

Sucks for her, though. She's stuck with me. Her daddy asked me to keep an eye on her whenever she shows up at one of our events, and I owe him big for helpin' me get my start, so I take that shit seriously. I know what kind of assholes run around on the PBR circuit—hell, I am one—and the last thing I wanna see is her gettin' hurt by one of 'em. So, I keep 'em all at bay with threats I'd be only too willin' to deliver on, if any of 'em dare cross the line I drew in the dirt.

The trick is keepin' her from findin' out I'm doin' it. She might be tiny compared to my six-three, but she's a fierce little thing. And if she ever finds out I've been runnin' interference on her love life at her daddy's request, she'll have my balls on a skewer roastin' in the BBQ pit.

It's an epic clash of wills in the Calhoun clan, to be sure. On the one side, there's Daddy Jim, wantin' to keep his little girl a little girl forever. On the other side is Denise, just wantin' to find somebody to love her like her daddy does her momma.

Too bad she's lookin' for it on the PBR circuit. That ain't no place for love. If all you want is a good roll in the hay with some chump you'll probably never see again after, then have at it. But love? That's not what any of these guys're lookin' for after an event. We're like the rock stars of rodeo, and a lot of these guys party like 'em, too. Don't get me wrong, there's some good dudes on the circuit but a lot of bad ones, too. I'm just protectin' her from the bad ones.

When she calls for me again, I plaster on a fake smile for the self-important assholes still tryin' to schmooze me, sayin', "Sorry, boys, gotta go answer this call." And I leave 'em in the dust of their unrealized dreams in pursuit of more pleasant company. Yeah, I'd rather let Denise roast my nuts than spend another minute here listenin' to these chumps showboatin' about somethin' they've never done and know nothin' about. Don't care if it seems rude; I've been listenin' to these dudes go on for the better part of an hour now, and that's fifty-nine minutes too many. I don't owe 'em anythin' more.

With a genuine smile for Denise, I swagger my way to her—but nearly stumble over my own damn boots when I see who's sittin' with her at the table under the trees near the patio.

Well, hell, it's her.

The girl from the stands.

The sweet little thing that nearly made me lose my grip on The Beast—and the prize money—for goin' the full eight seconds with him.

The one who made me question if I was losin' my damn mind. Because it hit me hard, square in the chest like a mule kick—that sense I'd just met my fate.

That my life would never be the same again.

And damn, it hit me so fast, I was a goner before I even knew I was goin'.

Now, I'm not a man of words so I can't rightly describe it, but it was like the wildest ride on the orneriest animal of your life. And I was hangin' on for my life as I tried to ride it out.

One second… I was settin' in on the bull.

Two seconds… I was released from the cage.

Three seconds… I saw her in the stands.

Four seconds… I felt the punch of… *somethin'*… in my chest.

Five seconds... I nearly lost my grip on the bull. And other things.

Six seconds... I couldn't rightly breathe; the air just wouldn't come.

Seven seconds... the world slowed down to nothin' and it was just us, alone in a streak of blurred images and muted noise from the crowd.

Eight seconds... the crowd roared as the ride ended and I jumped off the beast, not the same man I was when it started.

And not because it was a life-changin' ride, either. Hell, I don't remember much about it—just the beginnin' and the end. Everythin' in the middle was just gone, lost in my vision of *her*.

The girl.

This girl.

The one I couldn't get off my mind then, and surely won't be able to get off my mind *now*. Now that I've seen her up close and felt that punch in my gut again. Yeah, I guess that wasn't a one-time thing, after all. Nope, it's happenin' again, and I can't rightly say it's just pure lust I'm feelin'. As to what it *is*... Well, I can't rightly name that either.

See, I've never been what you might call a romantic, so I've never given much thought to it—not even when my sister Hailey would try to match me up with one of her friends who had a crush on me. I'd just politely decline (my momma raised a gentleman) and go find me a woman who was down to fuck and nothin' else 'cause I wasn't interested in anythin' else with any*one* else. Still ain't.

So, I don't understand what's goin' on here now, why I'm so twisted up over this sweet girl with hair the color of molasses and those big doe eyes that look at me with some kinda wonder like they are now. Like I'm some kinda hero from one of her favorite stories. And damn, if I don't wanna be one for her, if only for a night. Too bad I'm more sinner than saint —don't think her sweetness can handle my bad.

Not sure how to approach her and the need shinin' in her eyes, I slow to a crawl, my mind racin' through possibilities. I discard each one as pathetic or useless until I'm left with nothin' but my swagger and the smile on my face. Let's see how she likes that.

"Ladies," I grin broader as I reach 'em, tippin' my dusty ol' black hat to them in the traditional country boy greetin'. "How y'all doin'?" Without waitin' on an answer, I direct my next question to the pretty little fawn at Denise's side. "You enjoy the show today?" And before she can answer, I qualify the question with, "Don't think I've seen you in the stands before."

"Um, it was my first time, actually," she says so softly, I have to lean in to hear her over the chatter of the rowdy gatherin' behind us. And damn, even her voice is sweet. Is there anythin' about her that *isn't*? Shit, now I'm thinkin' about what else about her might be as sweet.

And my thoughts are fuckin' *dirty*.

"That right?" I say, tryin' to keep my mind on the

conversation and not the things I want to do to her if I can get her alone. "They don't have PBR where you're from?"

"Well, I'm from Boston so...no."

Hitchin' a leg over the bench this side of the table, I take a seat across from her, Denise all but forgotten in the gravitational pull between me and her friend. "Funny, don't sound like you have that kinda accent."

"Well, I'm not actually *from* the city," the girl says, dippin' her head in a way I know is real shyness and not that fake bullshit some chicks use to get your attention and make you think they're one thing when they're the total fuckin' opposite. Not this girl, though. This is the real McCoy right here. "Just a small town in Massachusetts."

"Well, why didn't ya just say that?"

"Because when I tell people I'm from Mass-achusetts, they usually think I'm from Boston anyways, so..." She ends the statement with a shrug like that's explanation enough, and I guess it is. Even I think Boston when someone says Massachusetts.

"Makes sense." Stickin' my hand out across the table, I say, "I'm Beau Calloway, by the way. And if Denise had any manners, she woulda told ya that already."

"Hey!" Denise protests. "Y'all didn't give me a chance with all that jawin' ya done."

"Sela Ford," the girl says, slippin' her delicate little hand into mine.

And once again, I get a mule kick to the chest.

What is it about this girl that's got me so twisted up?

Sela

The cowboy has a name, and it's so country, I kind of love it.

Beau Calloway.

And it's so perfect for him, too. Somehow, he even *looks* like a Beau, if a name could have a certain look. It just fits him. I don't know how to describe it. There's just something about the way he looks at you with those mossy bedroom eyes and that sexy tilt of his pillowy lips, and when he tips that well-loved hat at you, it just completes the image.

He's a country boy to the bone.

And I suddenly want to go country.

With him.

That's how I find myself sneaking off with him sometime after dark, just hours after initially meeting him. And I'm not that kind of person. Some of my friends back home tried to sell me on the pleasures of one-night stands, but I always balked at the idea. I mean, what's so fun about having sex with a stranger in some grungy bathroom at a nightclub, anyway? I'd rather get to know the guy—at least a little—before I have sex with him. It's not just about the act; it's about the connection. And how much of a connection can you get in just one night?

Yet here I am, climbing into the hayloft of my

grandfather's old barn with a virtual stranger while the "barbecue" rages on at the house.

But I can't seem to stop myself.

It's like he's got some magical hold on me, and I'm so mesmerized I'll blindly follow him anywhere.

Like up into the hayloft.

Is this too cliché of me? I wonder how many other girls he's brought up here. Well, maybe not *here*, in particular, since this is my grandparents' place, but to a different hayloft someplace else. I watch movies and read books. Isn't this always where the cowboys bring their girls for a "quick roll in the hay"? Oh God, is that really all this is? What am I *doing* here?

I'm so caught up in my own thoughts, not many of them good, that I don't realize how close he is in the near-dark of the loft until I *feel* him, not even a breath away from me. I also don't realize how badly I'm gnawing on my lower lip until he rescues it from my teeth with a thumb tip, murmuring, "Hey, now, don't go chewin' up that pretty little mouth of yours... I might be wantin' to kiss that later."

Startled, my mouth goes slack. "You want to *kiss* me?"

He moves closer to me, hips snug to mine, arms draping loosely around me. "Well, yeah, darlin'," he whispers into my left ear, "I wanna do a lot of things to you." He withdraws enough to look into my eyes. "But we can start with that if ya like."

Overcome by the potency of his nearness, I stammer, "S-start with?" I gasp as he nibbles at my earlobe, clouding all my other senses with sensual delight. "W-what do you want to e-end with?" Yeah, I'm kind of having trouble thinking beyond this. Beyond what he's currently doing to my ear and my neck with his mouth and tongue.

"Your legs wrapped around me while I make you come."

And all I can do is swallow hard at the image his words invoke and whisper, "Oh. My."

Beau

Oh, my.

What a cute response to my promise to fuck an orgasm out of her. That's proof right there the girl's too damn sweet, 'specially for what I have planned for her. But is that gonna stop me from takin' her? Hell, no. It's just gonna spice up the takin' and make it a helluva lot tastier. Sure, she's not my usual type. Don't usually go for the sweet ones with all the complications—*expectations*—that come along with them. But, damn, if I can resist the siren call of this one. There's just somethin' about those pretty doe eyes that lured me in and that shy smile that kept me there, soakin' in her presence like some lovesick pup. And anyone who knows me will tell you I don't do that shit. I'm more of a love 'em and leave 'em kind of dude. But man, do I love the shit out of 'em—physically, at least—before I leave. Same as I'm gonna do to Miss Sela Ford from back east.

At least, that was the plan before I got a taste of her sweetness. Fuck, I wonder if other parts of her taste as sweet.

Damn, I can't wait another fucking second. I gotta find out.

With my hands restin' lightly on her curvy hips (fuck, I like that there's a little somethin' to hold onto, not just a bony ass—that'll come in handy in so many ways soon), I ease her back where I want her, all the while distractin' her with my mouth ravishin' her skin. Earlobe, neck, jaw, chin. And when she gasps as her calves come up against a hay bale...finally, her mouth. I devour it. Plunder it. Lay siege to it. Make it *mine*.

Just like I'm gonna do to the girl.

"Is this too fast?" she rushes out the words as I start to ease her down onto the bale, one delicate little hand pressin' against the hardness of my pecs. "Are we moving too fast?"

"Seems 'bout the right speed to me, darlin'."

"You ride bulls for eight seconds. I don't think that's a good measure for time."

Though I don't think she meant it as a joke, I can't help but chuckle at that. "What can I say? I like things fast. "If we're not on the same page, we can head on back to the party now, no offense taken."

"It's not that," she's quick to reassure me. "It's just the speed thing. And the danger." She scrunches up her nose in a cute way that makes me wanna kiss it. So, I do. But that doesn't stop her from tryin' to have a real conversation before we get to the main event. "Why bull riding, anyway?"

I growl low in my throat to release a little sexual tension as I humor her with an answer. "It's kinda like how I like my sex, I reckon." I give her hips a little jostle with my hands still restin' on them before slidin' 'em down to cup those two perfect ass cheeks and bring her closer to me. Yeah, right there. "Hard, wild…and a little bit dangerous." She makes a sound of disbelief, and I capture it in my mouth as I go in for another kiss, saying, "Reckon you could say I fuck like I buck."

Sela

   I fuck like I buck.

I gasp at his words, at his hands running up and down my body in increasingly intimate caresses with each pass. I don't know what to say to that so I guess it's a good thing I can't even formulate words at the moment. One thing is certain though, I don't know what to make of him. Beau Calloway, quintessential country boy and star bull rider. In the one respect, he seems a world apart from me, like I'm totally out of his league. But then he does something like kiss me like I'm the only woman he ever wanted and tells me I'm the "sweetest thing" he ever tasted and he "can't wait to have more", and it makes me feel like maybe I *am* special. Maybe I *do* deserve to be with him. And that maybe, just maybe, I am actually in his league, for once.

Take that, you nasty bitch, I say to the hyper critical voice in my head.

"Take what, darlin'?" Beau whispers against my skin as he trails a lazy path down my neck to my collarbone.

Well, crap. I guess that wasn't just to the voice *inside* my head. But maybe that's okay. Maybe this is my chance to just put it all out there and take a risk on something for once. Take a risk on *me—for* me. So, I do. "Everything," I tell him with more boldness than I have ever felt in my life. "Take everything."

And he does.

The words are barely out of my mouth when, flashing me a wolfish smile, he flips me onto my back on the hay bale, following me down soon after. Then there's a flurry of frenetic activity as clothes are dispersed, skin is laid bare, and he begins to show me just how he likes to "fuck like he bucks".

Beau

Take everything.

Now if that ain't a fucking greenlight, I don't know what is.

And what a sweet submission it is—of course, it is. As I'm discoverin' about this girl at every turn, everything about her is sweet. So why wouldn't her submission be?

Not one to squander opportunities, I plunge right in, barely takin' the time to strip away clothes and sheath the beast first 'cause I'm afraid that, if she has enough time, she'll come to her senses and put an end to this before it even gets started.

But she's not stopping me.

Or putting up a fight.

She's opening up to me both in the figurative sense and the literal, her shapely thighs parting to make way for my hips, my dick. Yeah, she wants this as much as I do, and the slickness that greets me as I start to slide in is proof of that. Still, she's a little tight, a little tense, so I slip a hand between us to coax her into relaxin' for me. "Shit, babe, you're so tight." And then a thought strikes me, and I pause for a beat to frown down at her. "You've done this before, right?"

I'm not too encouraged by the way she hesitates, bitin' down her lower lip before she answers me. "Well… once. But it was a while ago and not that great, so I wasn't all that eager to try it again, you know?"

"Did you get off?"

"What?"

"Did he at least make you come?" Again, she bites her lip and hesitates, and that's all the answer I need. "Well, hell, darlin'," I mutter as I bottom out inside her. I groan at the sheer fucking pleasure of being so deeply seated inside her. Fuck, this right here is what sex is all about. I lick my lips as I set a rhythm, picking up the pace with each thrust of my hips until I'm bucking madly within her. And she's matching me thrust for fucking thrust. Yeah, she might be inexperienced with her lackluster first time, but she's a fucking natural at this. And I'm the lucky bastard that gets to reap the rewards of it. So, I make damn sure I bring her right along with me every damn step of the way. And if her screamin' orgasm is any indication, she enjoys it every bit as much as I do.

Well, damn. I think I just met my match. And I am more than fucking okay with that. I just hope she's on the same page as me 'cause I want more of this— more of *her*. It's kinda funny when I think about it. My daddy always told me when I fell, I'd fall hard. And quick. "It's just the way of the Calloway men," he used to always say, and I'd laugh right at him, never believin' it'd ever happen to me. But, hell if it didn't.

Sela

So how long *does* it take to fall in love?

I don't know about anyone else, but for me and Beau, on that day, it only took eight seconds.

SWEETGRASS SUMMER

Reina Torres

Silas Witten walked into the Sweetheart Diner and stepped up to the register with cash in his hand.

The cook in the kitchen lifted his head and gave him a nod through the window. "I'll be right there, Silas. Just waitin' for the chicken to cool enough for the box."

It wasn't anything Silas had to worry about. He was always early for the pickup and didn't mind the wait.

He did mind the curious looks that turned in his direction. The diner was appropriately named, as it was smack dab in the middle of the town. Some towns were centered around a church or a town hall, but Sweetgrass was centered around the diner.

Looking down the line at him were the preacher and his wife, the mayor and her husband…and his aunt.

His aunt raised a curious brow at him before she spoke. "Going somewhere special, Si?"

She didn't have to ask. No one did.

Everyone knew what everyone else was up to in Sweetgrass, and they all knew where he was going.

"I'm heading over to the Parish place."

Every head in the place nodded as looks were exchanged around the room.

"That Juno," the preacher started in, "she's a fine girl, son. A fine girl."

"A fine woman," his wife said with a nod. "It's about time for you to put down roots, young man."

At five and twenty years, Silas had roots enough in Sweetgrass soil. He was the fourth generation of Wittens who had lived and worked with the same Montana soil under their fingernails. He'd also had the reins of the ranch for a good year since his mother had moved back to Boston to take care of her sister who had entered hospice. He had roots, but he knew exactly what the preacher's wife was thinking. What everyone in the diner was thinking.

It was time for him to settle down with a wife.

And everyone knew that woman was Juno Parish.

The cook came out of the kitchen with a big grin under his mustache and above his beard. He set the picnic basket down on the counter and gave Silas a nod. "Big day, son?"

The room went silent at the older man's words,

and Silas fixed a steady gaze on the cook as he handed over his money. "Thanks, Jack."

Without another word, Silas lifted the basket off the counter and walked back out to his truck. He had a date with Juno, and he wasn't going to be late.

JUNO PARISH WAS ready to combust.

Sitting out on the porch of her childhood home, she crossed and uncrossed her legs, trying to ignore the ache between them. It was Friday and the end of the week for most people—but not for her. In her life, since she'd come back to Sweetgrass, Friday was the beginning of her week and the highlight, too.

Ever since she'd move back to town, her Friday nights were full of love. With Silas.

Silas Witten. Her childhood sweetheart. Her middle school frustration. Her high school temptation. And the aching hunger of her adult life.

He had been a good boy, and by everyone's account, a fantastic man, but he was also a perfect gentleman. Perfection to the point of driving her crazy.

He'd kissed her on her sixteenth birthday.

Dared to touch her breast on the night of their graduation.

And the night before she'd moved to Missoula for college, he'd pulled her onto his lap and let her ride his thigh to orgasm.

A swirl of dust up the long dirt road toward town

told her he was on his way, and that was enough for her body to react. Her breasts swelled, and her nipples tightened into peaks. The ache between her thighs drew a breathy sigh from her lips, and she crossed her legs, trying to ease the building need that thinking of him always caused, but instead of easing it back, it just made her need him more.

It was torture really. Every weekend, he'd take her somewhere private and hold her close. He'd talk about the future and what he hoped for between them. And then, he'd kiss her, doing things to her mouth that she'd begged him to do to the rest of her body.

But he'd always stop those kisses.

Stop before the clothes came off.

Stop before he made her his in the only way you can't take back.

He'd made her wait, and she was still waiting. But that was going to stop.

As Silas' truck came to a halt at the base of the stairs, she didn't even wait for him to get around to her side before she pulled open the door and climbed up inside the cab. She knew her brother and his wife Abbie were inside, watching through the gap in the curtains. She knew that Jake would shake his head because she hadn't waited for Silas to come around, but she'd had her fill of waiting, and she'd told Abbie so.

She looked at Silas as he made it to her door and saw the red flush under his skin, saw the narrowed look he gave her, but she just smiled at him. "Hello, Silas."

"'lo, Juno."

She almost shivered at the rough tone of his voice. "Is that our supper I smell?"

"You know it is, Juno." His voice crawled up her spine. "Just like last week and the week before."

"Ah," she sighed and leaned back against the seat, "nothing different today?"

He looked up into her eyes and raised a brow at her question. "You won't find out unless you put on your seatbelt, sweetheart."

She wanted to feel that word deep down inside, but "sweetheart" was just what Silas Witten called her. He'd done it so often in their lives that, in the grand scheme of things, he'd probably called her sweetheart more than he'd said her actual name.

Feeling, and yes, acting a little more petulant than she'd intended, Juno gave him a haughty look. "Then you put my seatbelt on me, Si. Take care of me."

She'd felt the growl in her own voice and swept her tongue over her bottom lip. She'd put an edge to her words and given him the thinly masked challenge, but Silas was nothing if not steady.

And solid.

And instead of raising, or lowering, himself to her challenge, he put a boot up on the step and stood up in the open doorway of his truck. With a quick pull, he extended the seatbelt from the frame of the truck and all the way across her body. She heard the soft click as the tab fit into the lock, and then she sighed as he backed out of the cab with a satisfied nod. "Let's get going."

While he walked around the truck, she let out a soft, almost wistful groan. She'd waited for Silas to "get going" for long enough. She knew he liked to be in control of things; he certainly did well running the ranch.

Still, she wasn't going to sit still and wait any longer. Nope. Silas was about to have an awakening. What kind? Well, she'd just have to wait and see how he reacted.

Juno knew she couldn't just keep waiting.

Not anymore.

When they were a good ten minutes from the main gate of the Witten Ranch, Silas slowed the truck and turned onto a dirt road. They didn't go more than a mile before they reached a gate that Juno had never seen. Before she could say a word, Terry, one of Si's men, swung open the gate and tipped the brim of his hat to her as the truck rumbled by.

Still pinned to the seat with the belt, Juno could only duck down and look in the side mirror as Terry locked the gate and swung up onto the back of his horse.

When she turned back around to look at Silas, he was staring straight ahead through the windshield with a big grin on his face.

"All right," she folded her arms and gave him a narrowed look, "what's going on?"

"Just a little change of plans."

"A change of... What's going on, Si?"

The sound of his laughter shocked her into silence.

"If I tell you everything, sweetheart, then where's the surprise? I thought women liked surprises."

"Women," she scoffed. "How many women are you planning to surprise?"

The warmth of his hand settled on her knee, and Juno about jumped out of her skin. How she loved the warmth of his touch. And she craved it like her next breath.

"I'm only interested in you, Juno. You know that."

She sat in the passenger seat quietly, taking in the sound of his voice and the message in his words.

She must have taken too long to respond because he asked, "Don't you, sweetheart?"

His thumb swept over her cotton-clad thigh, and she felt every inch of her skin tingle in response.

Juno unfolded her arms, trailed her fingertips over the back of his hand, and felt the stutter in his movements. With a deep-indrawn breath, she turned her head to look at his handsome profile. "I know that I love you, Si. I know what and who I want to be to you, but the rest of it? I can't say I do know."

His hand stayed where it was, but his thumb lay still beside her knee as he continued to drive across the field, tracing an old and almost faded path.

It wasn't until they stopped that she realized where they were.

Sitting up, straining against her seatbelt, Juno looked out the windshield with a wide-eyed gasp. "No!"

He dropped his hand. "It's been a while since I brought you here."

Hearing the happy tone of his voice, Juno rolled her eyes and gave him a sassy look. "Years, Si. I'd almost forgotten it was here."

"Any chance you'll wait for me to come around and help you down?" The look in his eyes said he knew the answer before he'd asked the question.

"Nope." She saw the way his smile grew, and she dropped her hand to the seatbelt clasp, opening it with a click. "Are you setting up the picnic in the *bed*?"

She knew he heard the edge she put into the word when she saw the rise and fall of his Adam's apple in his throat.

"Yeah."

She gently scraped her lower lip between her teeth and reached for the doorhandle. "Then you better hurry up before I decide to go in without you."

JUNO WAS a breath of fresh air.

And a swift kick in the pants.

She could make him feel warm all over with a look or a touch.

And she could make him so hot and hard that he couldn't think straight.

In a word, she was heaven.

Keeping his hands, and the rest of himself, from touching her was hell.

Silas knew that he'd pushed her almost to her breaking point.

All of his life, the people of Sweetgrass had told him that he and Juno were meant to be together. They were an expectation and a promise of the future.

He'd heard the words so often that he'd started to believe them.

In that belief, he'd also started to accept their destiny so much that he'd forgotten that Juno couldn't see straight into his heart.

That, and he'd never been all that good at speaking his mind either, so he had his challenges.

Pulling the basket out from behind the seats in the cab of the truck, he walked it around to the truck bed and got to work. He'd laid out the thick pads across the hard surface and covered it with quilts and blankets from the chests in his attic. Quilts sewn together by generations of Witten women. Quilts from weddings and hope chests, baby showers and christenings. Whole life cycles of love that had worked their way down to him.

To that very moment. He left the tarp in place over the quilts and set the picnic basket on top. They'd have their meal, and then he'd ask Juno the question he should've asked her the moment she'd come back to Sweetgrass.

Instead, he'd set it in his mind to do things the "right way." He'd been told to court her and give her time, but he was starting to believe he'd waited too long and held too tightly onto the antiquated ways of the people who surrounded them. Advice, it seemed, wasn't always the smart thing to listen to.

His heart had been arguing with him for weeks, months actually. He was done waiting and wanted Juno to know the place she had in his heart and where he wanted her in his life.

The sudden silence of his surroundings turned his head. When his sweeping gaze found Juno, she was standing at the edge of the swimming hole, her gaze fixed on him.

It was a strange sensation. Being watched with such intensity.

Dropping down to the ground, Silas moved toward her, his gaze fixed on Juno in return. He'd meant to talk to her anyway. This might just be the time.

And then she reached up and gave the top button of her sundress a twist.

That's all it took.

Hard to believe, really.

One button springing free of its confinement loosened the neck of her dress, and it slipped to the very edges of her shoulders.

All it would take would be a stiff wind, and it might just fall to her hips.

And damn if he didn't wish for a stiff wind.

He was stiff enough for the both of them.

"Juno…"

She toed off her slippers and took a step back toward the pond.

"Juno, we need to talk."

Her shoulders slumped, and the straps of her dress slipped dangerously low on her arms. The only reason the top of her dress remained in place were the soft swells of her breasts. "I don't want to talk, Si." She shook her hair to make it feather around her shoulders, and then took another step back.

He could hear the soft squish of wet soil beneath her heels. "I have something important to say."

"And we have time, Si. I don't think you brought me out here to the pond so that you could talk. This was our favorite place to swim when we were kids."

"Yes," he said, having to agree.

"See?" Another step and her foot sank down into the water. She let loose a gasp. "I really should look where I'm going."

He heard the chiding tone in her voice and wondered how much of it was for him.

"I hope you're a better swimmer now than you were when we were kids, Juno." He ground his back teeth together when she laughed at him. "It's not funny, Juno."

"If you were so concerned," she leveled a look at him that had his heart pounding in his chest, "then why did you bring me out here?"

"Because I wanted…" he sighed and let the frustration building up inside of him leech into his voice, "to talk to you."

She seemed to think over his words, even nodding once before she moved. "Well, then," she grinned at him, and he swore her eyes were full of challenge, "you're going to have to catch me first."

One more twist of a button and the top of her sundress fell open, exposing the bare skin she'd hidden beneath. A quick push of her hands sent the dress rushing past her hips and down toward her feet.

Juno Parish stood before him, dressed only in a pair of white cotton panties that had him aching as his gaze sought every inch of her skin.

She was no shrinking violet. No, Juno didn't even need to lift her chin to look him in the eye. She held herself still under his curious, searching gaze and let him look his fill, and she did as well. He swore he could feel her gaze as a physical touch on his body.

"Juno..."

"Silas," she shot back at him, "I told you that you'd have to catch me."

He hadn't actually expected to chase her down. He'd thought she'd stay right where she was and torture him some more.

He'd been wrong.

Turning around, Juno gave him a look at her spectacular backside before she waded into the pool. A few seconds later she was gone.

Completely swallowed up by the water.

It took Silas half a heartbeat to shuck his shirt and jeans as he ran to the pond. There were bubbles on the surface, and with a running jump, he threw himself in just short of the disturbance on the surface of the water.

He may have gone in to save her, but he was the one who ended up swallowing a big gulp of water when he felt her hands on him.

As graceful as she was on land, it shouldn't have surprised him that she moved just as easily underwater. Sliding along his body, he was treated to a teasing graze of her breasts against his chest before she wound her arms and legs around him long enough to kiss him and literally steal his breath.

When she released him and kicked up to the surface, he followed her, and not *just* because he was dangerously close to being out of air. He was chasing the feeling that she aroused in him.

He needed it just like he needed her.

As his head broke through the surface, he watched her rise out of the water, her hands braced on solid ground at the water's edge and her lush backside pale and perfect in the late afternoon sun.

SHE HEARD the soft splash that told her Silas had pulled himself out of the water just a moment or two behind her. Juno hoped it meant that he was as ready as she was to move their lives forward. Being a gentleman was all fine and dandy, but couldn't he be a gentleman and fuck her senseless, too?

Turning over on her back, Juno hooked her thumbs into the thin waistband of her panties and wiggled them over her hips. A few kicks, and the garment hung from her toes. She turned her gaze to Silas and saw the stilted rise of his chest as if breathing was something he'd forgotten how to do.

"Did you still want to talk?" she asked in a teasing tone.

He met her gaze with a rumbling growl in the back of his throat. "This isn't funny, Juno."

"Is that what you think I'm doing, Si? Making fun of this?" She didn't give him a chance to answer because she was ready to snap. "I love you, Silas. I know that you love me. I just don't want to wait any longer for our life together to start."

"There's an order to how this all happens." His voice sounded tight, and she could see the way his boxers pulled against him, restraining the heavy curve of his cock.

He reached out a hand, and Juno thought he was going to touch her, but he pulled a handful of sweet grass from the ground. And as the sun warmed their skin and dried the lingering drops of water from their over-heating bodies, he worked with the blades.

Brow-furrowed and tense, the soft green medium took form, and when he finished, he held up a small, perfectly braided circle.

She looked at the ring in his fingers, and it stole

her breath away. "I... I wasn't... I wasn't serious. You don't have to—"

"I want to." He held the ring out to her, and crazy enough, her eyes were fixed on that simple circlet of green, which meant a hell of a lot considering the feast of flesh that lay behind it. "I've got my grandma's ring to give you, and then we've got a wedding to plan."

She sat up and felt his gaze caress her body, and yes, she instinctively preened before him. Arching her back, she set her hands on her thighs. "You don't have to give me a ring to get me to have sex with you, Silas. I want to."

He shook his head and sat up, drawing his knees under him as well. "I want you for my wife, Juno. I need you beside me every day like you're meant to be."

She rose up on her knees before him, her breasts inches away from his face. "I'd rather be under you. Over you. Just put me out of my misery, Silas."

She'd meant to cajole him and push him into action. Yes. That's what she'd meant to do.

What happened filled her with shock and wonder.

Silas removed what was left of his clothing and took her into his embrace. He pressed her down in the grass, his hard, muscular body settling between her thighs... his hard length pressing deep against her belly. His face above hers, he held the ring where she could see it—clear in her line of vision and just as real as the man between her legs. She felt the touch of something more against her skin.

Or maybe under it.

"I want you for my wife, Juno. Wear my ring. Live in my home, under my roof—and yes, under my body —and I will fill your nights with love. I'll give you what you want again and again."

She arched against him and felt his cock slide against her belly, its head caressing her and leaving a wet streak against her skin as if it was his tongue, tasting her.

Her eyes closed in a long, languid movement as she lifted up her hand, holding it in the air between them as if she was making a vow, hand to God.

And when she opened her eyes to see the tumbling clouds in the bright blue sky, she felt Silas slip the ring over her finger. It brushed against her skin like a lover's touch and fit at the base of her finger, snug, secure. Her head filled with the feeling of fullness and those thoughts settled lower, deeper in her body.

"I need to know what it feels like," she murmured the words, almost in a dreamlike state as the tips of her swollen nipples grazed his chest, "for you to fit inside my body, for me to be filled with you."

Juno heard him groan. Felt his belly quiver against hers, and the slick wetness against her skin wicked away with the gentle breath of air surrounding them.

She moved her hand, folded their fingers

together, and met his gaze with an unerring one that looked into their future.

"I'll be yours, Silas. I'll take you inside me and warm you with my body. I'll be there for you for the rest of our lives."

He shifted, pressing their joined hands into the grass and taking more of his weight onto his knees. And as he held her eyes, he pressed his fingers to her folds and stroked her slick opening from top to bottom and back again.

She felt like she was hovering off of the ground, laying on a cloud, as his fingers slipped over her flesh, coating her folds with her own need.

The clouds in the sky tumbled and swept across the blue as he fitted himself at the entrance of her sex.

"Yes... yes..." She was unable to breathe, her body tense and waiting for his intrusion.

"You'll stand before the preacher with me."

"Yes..."

His weight pressed down, and her folds stretched around his engorged head, but he still held back.

"You'll wear my ring."

"I'm already wearing it, Silas. Don't make me wait any more."

"And you'll be my wife."

Every inch of her body felt electric, as if the air surrounding them held too much of a charge, and she was waiting for lightning to strike and burn them alive. Quick, shallow breaths were all she could manage. She pulled in one after another and pushed them out. She finally found the energy to make a sound, and what a sound it was.

"I'm yours, Silas. I'm wearing your ring and your body. I'm your wife."

He sank into her with a shout as if the very sensation of filling her hurt him, cut him deep, and made him ache.

Lifting her knees, she wrapped her legs around his waist and fitted their bodies together as if she was the ring he'd placed on her finger.

"So perfect," she sighed and felt a tear course down here cheek, "you and me."

"You and me." He repeated her words with a soft, reverent tone. "Yes, Juno. The two of us together."

HE LIFTED some of his weight from her body and heard the soft needy moan that fell from her lips.

"Hold on, baby. Hold on."

She tightened her hold on his body. Her legs encircled him, while her hands held tight to his shoulders.

And when he felt like he was just about to slip out of her body, he plunged back inside again.

"Just like that." Her voice held a smile, and he gave her another deep thrust.

Over and over, deeper and ever deeper, he plunged in and felt her body, not only welcome him, but cling to him.

How he'd ever thought he could wait for that moment, he didn't know. Juno had been his temptation for years. The looks she gave him, the tender touch of her hands on his skin. And still, he'd tried to hold out.

He slipped his hand under her back and tilted her hips to meet his next thrust. "You're mine."

Silas heard her gasp of pleasure and watched as her eyelids fluttered closed.

"Say it." He pushed in and felt her walls tighten around his cock. "I need to hear you—"

"I'm yours, Si. It's all I've ever been. It's all I've ever want—"

Her nails bit into his shoulders, and he felt lightning arc through her into him.

Her orgasm threatened to pull him over the edge, but he wasn't done with her yet. He had heights that he wanted her to reach before he found his own release.

She shook beneath him, and he continued to push inside her, not the same fervent thrusts from before, but a slower, gentler rhythm to draw out her sighs and the fluttering pulls that her body made on his cock.

He'd never get enough of her.

"Never."

He felt her fingers moving over his shoulders and heard her sigh again.

"I'll never have enough of you, Si."

He didn't know what to think. Had he spoken

aloud? Or was she inside his head like he was inside her beautiful body?

"Even when we're old and gray," she wrapped her hands behind his neck and pulled him down for a kiss, "I'll never tire of holding you inside me, Si."

"You say that now," he murmured, his voice gruff to his ears, "but years from now…"

"I've held you in my heart for years." He heard the soft tone of her voice, as if she felt she had to whisper it to him. "Dreamed of you in my bed. Dreamed of our children. And yes, growing old together. Come, Si. Let me feel you come apart inside of me."

He took her lips in a searing kiss, mating their tongues together as if it might satiate some of his hunger. But the way her tongue battled with his as she tried to copy his movements made him ache hard inside her luscious body.

He broke away, looking down at her face, noting the rosy blush on her cheeks and high on her breasts. He could almost see the rounded perfection of her body protecting their future child.

That was all it took to bring him painfully to the edge of sanity.

He pulled out of her.

Felt the heavy pull of his hardened erection straining toward her.

He saw the delicious pout of her lips and the pink petals of her sex as she sat up, reaching for him.

Silas almost gave in, but he fought off the urge to

plunge right back into her, and instead, put his hand on her hip.

"Turn over, Baby. Hands and knees. For me. On your knees."

He felt her tremble at his harsh tone, or maybe it was his words, but he didn't see her hesitate. No, she turned over and placed her pale hands on the ground, folding her fingers into the grass like she had done earlier, holding his hand.

He heard the hitch in her breath as he placed a kiss on the curve of her lower back. He felt her shiver when he took hold of her hips with his hands, holding her steady.

And when he braced himself behind her and fit the tip of his aching cock into the wet warmth of her body, he felt his body tense and his balls pull up tight between his legs as she tried to press back against him.

"I love you, Juno."

"Oh God, yes." She lowered her cheek to the ground as the tip of his cock slipped into her welcoming heat. "Love me... just like that."

What else could he do but give in to her request, since it was exactly what he wanted, too.

He drove his cock home and felt her take the pressure, using her folded arms to absorb the brunt of his thrust as he bottomed out inside of her body.

From that moment, he let nature drive him. The sound of the wind whispering through the grass mingled with her breathy moans. The distant burble from the creek was a counterpoint to his soft grunts as he filled her in a relentless rhythm.

Her slippery walls tantalized him and sucked him in.

And as they heard the soft lowing of a nearby calf, he felt his entire body tense and release, drifting on the rolling wave of his orgasm from his heart down into his hips.

Juno was swept along with him. He heard her call out his name as her walls contracted around him. Her hips shook and her back bowed as her hands grasped at the sweet grass, pulling handfuls from the ground as he emptied himself inside of her.

WHEN IT WAS OVER and he could hear beyond the rush of blood in his ears, he drew her closer, encircling her sated body with his arms, eager to keep her close.

"I can hear your heart beating in your chest."

Tilting his head to the side, Silas nuzzled the soft curls loosened near the top of her head. "When do I get to listen to your heart?"

"Any time you like," she laughed softly, "but it might be faster than yours when you do." She wiggled against him until she could wrap an arm around him. "Having your lips so close to my... I mean—"

He brushed her hair back from her face. "We have the rest of our lives to be together," he assured her.

"Before long, I'll know everything about your body. Which touches make you hot and which ones drive you wild."

Juno laid her left hand against his chest and touched her ring with a gentle sweep of her finger. "The rest of our lives. I like...no, I love the sound of that."

Silas picked up her hand and pressed a kiss to the knuckle just above her braided ring. "I still have my grandmother's ring to give you."

She shook her head. "I like the look of this one, Si. This is the ring you put on my finger. The one that joined us together. I don't want another ring."

He held up her hand, and they both looked at it in the warm light of the sun setting in the distance. "Then I'll have a ring made like this, Juno. A ring to remember this moment."

"And to celebrate everything we'll discover in the future."

He kissed her then, as he would do a million times over the remaining years of their lives. As he made love to her again, he felt her beautiful body against his, heard her soft needy sighs, and smelled the pure, natural scents surrounding them of a sweetgrass summer.

COWBOYS & ZOMBIES

Cindy Tanner

"Worst apocalypse ever," I grouse as I try to tamp back my frustration and ignore the hunger pains.

"Sorry, darlin'." Lane's hand moves to tip his hat only to come up short. His hat, along with the rest of our gear, is currently surrounded by the horde of, for lack of a better word, *zombies*.

Dammit. Guilt sears through me as he runs his calloused hand through his hair. One thing. This entire time Lane has rarely asked me to do anything, but this time he asks one thing, and I manage to royally fuck it up.

"No, I'm sorry. I shouldn't have left the truck." I shut my eyes. "I was stupid." And the truth was, stupid, these days, usually got you dead or "undead" as it were.

"They'll tire out, eventually, and venture off." Lane smiles like it isn't a big deal we're currently hiding in a cramped ladies' room with a seat for one inside an abandoned coffee shop. My mouth had watered when I'd thought of freshly ground beans with a few pumps of vanilla. Power had still been on in other buildings along the street. I'd thought I could be in and out with a fresh bag of coffee with no problem. I hadn't expected the noise to draw such a big crowd.

I'd been so excited and confident in my abilities to slip in and out, I'd left my bag in Lane's old pickup. Right next to his. Meaning we could be stuck in here for who knew how long with no food or weapons. Hopefully, no one would happen along our truck and decide to take it. The camper shell on the back wasn't fancy, but it kept the supplies we'd been gathering for the last three days dry and safe.

"Thank you." I glance at him, too ashamed to keep eye contact. "For saving me." I don't say *again*. Neither of us needs the reminder that Lane has been saving my ass since he drug me out of work days ago.

"Rebecca, you don't even need to say anything." His voice is gruff, making me wonder, yet again, if he thinks I'm a burden, or worse yet, a liability.

Silence falls between us interrupted by the groans and thumps from the things lingering outside.

He had been a regular for the last six months at the coffee shop where I'd worked. One a lot like this one, only with a bigger bathroom. At least, this one seemed clean and smelled faintly of bleach and citrus.

Every Friday morning, he'd come in with some ridiculous order and a cheeky grin like he was hoping to stump me with a triple-pump-vanilla-soy-eight-scoop-matcha-green-tea-latte, with no foam, or something over-the-top fancy like an affogato. No matter what the order, it was never what I would've expected from someone in scuffed cowboy boots, work-worn jeans, and a cool, careless vibe.

Never mind that most customers ordered straight off the boring menu. Lane had never once glanced at it, preferring to swagger up to the counter and order something he seemingly pulled out of nowhere. I used to look forward to Fridays, not as the start of the weekend but because it was the day he came in. I'd dubbed him "my cowboy" after the first time he'd called me "darlin'" and had stopped writing his name on the side of the cup. That day, he'd given me a smirk that had drenched my panties.

I'd lived my whole week for the twenty minutes he'd be in the cafe.

I'd started reading up on new drinks. Spending my free time testing new recipes at home. It had been dumb luck I'd come across the recipe for espresso over vanilla ice cream the week before that had been his order. I'd even brought a pint of my favorite ice cream to work, planning to impress him with a recommendation.

That seemed like another lifetime ago. A week in apocalypse time felt like years.

"I wanted to use my barista skills to impress you and to finally be useful. But I think it's time we can officially say my skillset is useless." I'd majored in political science with absolutely no aspiration of what to do with it. My work history included babysitting and making coffee. Neither were assets for the current state of the world.

"Your skill set is just fine." Lane eased down on the floor, the room barely wide enough for him to extend his legs out and cross them at the ankles. I bet if he still had his cowboy hat on, he'd dip it down over his eyes. "Might as well use this time to get some rest."

"Rest?" I'm looking down at him and my voice makes him pop an eye open. "We are one flimsy door away from being eaten alive!" Panic fills my tone as the truth in my words hit me.

"How is this any different than sleeping in the truck?" He smiles, showing off the dimple hidden under days' worth of scruff.

"That truck is metal. A beast of a thing, and we always park somewhere not full of zombies!" My voice rose enough to draw them closer to the door. A loud thump makes me jump as Lane pats the empty space beside him.

"Relax, Rebecca. I've got you. Sleep if you can. Try to relax and rest if you can. Worrying right now isn't going to help." Lane yawns. Not panicking seems like the least I owe him. My options are limited to reliving my college days and hugging the toilet or taking the space next to him. It isn't a choice I need to think about. Settling thigh to thigh with Lane, I inhale. He smells like leather and dust. An odd combination that is both uniquely him and soothing.

"Hey, Lane?" I ask quietly, chewing on my lip as I wait for him to respond.

His answer is a deep chuckle.

"I'm not going to be able to relax right now, and soon, I'm going to start to fidget, which I know in this tight space will drive you nuts." I'd drive myself insane without a distraction. There was barely enough room for us to sit. If I'm left to my own devices, I know I'm going to start to panic over the tight space. "Tell me something I don't know. I need to think about something else."

"I've wanted to kiss you since I first laid eyes on you." Lane's voice is deep. His words make my stomach flip.

I open my mouth, but nothing comes out. Did he mean that, or is it just a means to get me speechless? If so, job well done, cowboy.

"I mean it," he says reading my thoughts. "My farm is nowhere near your coffee shop."

"What?" The air leaves my lungs.

"The first time I came into your work, there was a detour that brought me through. I stopped at your little shop needing to stretch my legs and grab something to drink." Lane tilted his head back and closed his eyes again.

"You can't just say that and expect me to relax now," I whisper-shout at him. "You came in every week." Lane was by far my favorite regular but never had I thought he'd been anything other than a wet dream. In the days we'd spent together, sexy time had been far from my mind, what with evading zombies, looters, and just trying to stay alive. Plus, it will be a terminal blow to my ego if the man I'm spending the end of the world with isn't interested.

"You were always there on Friday. If I took the detour each week to pick up supplies, it was on my way." He shrugs, crossing his arms over his chest.

"How did you know what kind of drinks to order?" I'm on my knees now, facing him. Panic forgotten.

"Google."

I'm going to strangle this man. "Did you even like any of them?"

"Some were good. I was a coffee purist before you corrupted me with your come-fuck-me eyes and sexy smile."

My mouth falls open just in time for him to open his eyes and catch my stunned expression.

"The last time you came in was a Wednesday." Not that I wasn't grateful he'd shown up just as I'd started the first brews for the day. No one else had bothered to show up to open. In fact, I hadn't really questioned why that was when he'd said it wasn't going to be safe to stay at work. It had been impossible to miss the news stories of increasingly bizarre events. It was incredibly sad that it took no time at all for society to fall apart.

"I needed to gather supplies, and I saw an opportunity to take what I wanted." His heated gaze stole my breath, making my pulse race. I'd always fantasized Lane as a bad boy who would fuck me rough and wild, leaving me blissed out and content. The look he gave me now was a promise to make my dream a reality. "I figured I could use the time to give you a reason to trust me, so you'd accept my place is safer than some apartment in the middle of a city." He sits up straight, closing the small space between us.

"And if I hadn't come with you?" I ask, my voice a whisper as anticipation fills me. Lane says nothing but his silence tells me everything I need to know. I would've gone with him whether I'd wanted to or not. A small sliver of fear tangles with my building desire. There may have been months of flirting between us, but Lane is a stranger. A stranger I'd known nothing about but had instinctively trusted with my life. Even now. Even if I shouldn't.

"I trust you." My gaze focuses on his lips, twisted up in a cocky grin.

"Then it looks like we're heading North from here on out, darlin.'" His lips crash down onto mine, the stubble from his face biting into my skin, a contrasting sensation to the passion of his kiss.

Without breaking contact, I'm in his lap, grinding against the thick erection filling his jeans.

Never in my life have I hated pants as much as in this moment. I want nothing between us. Nothing keeping him from thrusting inside me. Calloused hands brush my stomach before slipping under my cotton bra to graze my nipple.

Moaning at the contact, I arch my back, our hips' movements causing a glorious friction that has me needing more. I'm desperate for release.

Under me, Lane shifts, moving us so he can pull down my leggings. One finger grazes my entrance, making my hips buck up.

"Yes," I moan against his mouth as my hips rock against his hand.

A shrill beeping jolts us.

"Fuck," Lane sets me aside and is on his feet before I can blink the lust from my vision.

"Smoke." I see the alarm on his face as the grey white tendrils waft in under the door. "We've got to make a run for it." His hands are pulling me to my feet and yanking my pants back into place before he kisses me again. "We will pick up where we left off, I promise."

Lane is all business, while I'm still trying to focus on the present threat and not mourn the orgasm lost to the new danger.

Pulling off his flannel shirt, Lane rips off the sleeves and runs them under the tap to soak them before handing one to me and putting the other over his face. It's a freaking tragedy there isn't time to admire him in the tight-fitting black tank top that highlights his chiseled muscles. I'd spent many nights wondering what he looked like naked. If this is any indication, my mind lacked creativity and did him a serious injustice.

"Do you remember the direction to the front door?" he asks waiting for me to nod. "I'm running the opposite way toward the back, so I can lure them away. Give me a ten-second lead then you head for the front. We meet back at the truck to ride off into the sunset, where I'm going to make you come so hard you forget your name. Got it, darlin'?"

"Got it," I mumble into the damp flannel, fighting against the lump in my throat. This might be the last thing I hear anyone say so I focus on the next words out of Lane's mouth, enjoying the smooth timber of his voice.

"Count of ten, stay low, but move fast. I'll be waiting at the truck for you." Lane's lips brush my forehead before he has his makeshift mask back in place. Faster than I'm ready for, Lane darts out of the door. Smoke billows in as panic fills my chest. Alone, the room seems so much smaller as I count. Crouching low as I open the door, I hesitate. The smoke makes my eyes water as I force myself to move toward the front door, heat from the flames all around me.

My progress is slow as I move forward on one hand and my knees as I keep the flannel pressed firmly against my mouth and nose. For a brief moment, the dancing flames are mesmerizing. As they move closer, I realize it isn't dancing flames that is drawing my attention but a zombie now weaponized with fire.

"Shit!" I mumble hoping I'm close enough to the door as I jump up and run. I run past the tables I think are near the exit. Adrenaline and fear make it hard to focus as my hands fumble for the door. Breathing in a sign of relief, I realize I dropped the flannel as smoke fills my lungs, making me cough as I tug hard against the handle. Heat presses against my back as my watery eyes see the word PUSH. It occurs to me that I'm about to be done in by my inability to open a door. With a jerk, I dart to my freedom, dragging in lungfuls of fresh air, coughing as I stumble toward the ancient pickup parked down the block.

After a quick scan of my surroundings, I walk as fast as I can, my lungs continuing to cough in protest of the smoke I've inhaled. Relief brings a smile to my face when I see Lane, as promised, already waiting beside the truck.

Only the hair is too dark for Lane's sun-bleached blond. Further, the outline of the man is too short, the shoulders too narrow to be my cowboy. The smile falls from my face when I realize it's not Lane waiting for me.

"What are you doing?" My voice sounds gravelly, making the man freeze.

"It's not what it looks like." His hands instantly go up in surrender as he ducks his head.

"What does this look like?" I ask, wishing I had a weapon. The man in front of me straightens when he realizes I'm not a threat. At least, not a threat to anyone other than myself.

"You were in the coffee shop?" His eyes are wide. "Was anyone with you?" There's an urgency to his voice, one that I feel as I realize Lane could still be inside there.

"Yes. Lane, whose truck you're trying to steal." I narrow my eyes because, really, what else could he be doing? Now, it's time for me to size him up. He's smaller than Lane. Still an inch or so taller than me, but skinny. Maybe I can take him if I have to. Probably not, but I'd try.

"Your friend is still stuck inside? I saw a bunch of zombies around back."

My heart drops. "Lane was going out the back. Oh my God. We've got to help him."

"Let's drive around to pick him up."

In a rush, I turn, thinking only about Lane. It never occurs to me that I'm being naive until pain explodes in my head. My vision goes dark as my knees buckle. I struggle to stay conscious. I have to stay awake.

"Up we go," a mumbled voice breaks through the haze, filling my head as I'm shoved onto the worn leather bench seat of Lane's truck.

"Hey!" I realize too late my wrists are being handcuffed to the 'Oh Shit' handle before the passenger door slams shut. I give my head a shake, wincing as pain flares and clears the rest of the haze from my mind. Watching as the man walks around the front of the truck, I know that, if we leave, I'm as good as dead. So is Lane, and I'm not about to let that happen.

With panic settling in, I try to pull free with the cuffs biting into my wrists. What would Lane do right now? With a smirk, I stretch, hitting the door lock with my foot just as the man reaches the driver's door. A look of disbelief crosses his features, making my smirk widen into a smile. *Take that, Jackass.*

"Unlock the door," he shouts, spit flying from his mouth and hitting the window. *Gross.*

"No," I shout, letting my gaze drop to the keys still hanging in the ignition.

"Calm down and unlock the door—unless you want to be trapped in there and surrounded by the same zombies that ate your friend."

Pain rips through my chest. He's lying. Lane made it out. He had to have. I can't imagine going on without his smirks and the way his eyes light up when he calls me darlin'. Plus, he still owes me an orgasm I intend to collect on.

"No." Despite the throbbing in my head, I keep my smile in place. The one I've perfected with years of working in the service industry.

"Open the door!" He pounds on the glass. The force rocks the truck before he steps away to search the ground. The look of victory on his face turns my stomach as I watch him walk around the truck to grab a paving stone that has come lose from the sidewalk.

"Oh, shit." I realize he intends to bust the window as I brace my feet against the passenger door frame and grip the handle. "Please, please, I'll never make fun of you again if you just pull apart!" I grunt a promise to the powerfully made truck as my muscles strain.

The sound of the brick hitting the window makes my heart jump as I work to free myself, knowing I'm screwed if he breaks the window first.

With a soft pop of the handle pulling free, I fling onto my back hitting my head against the steering wheel and honking the horn. The sound of breaking glass makes me scream as I push the driver's door open.

A hard grip on my ankle halts my escape. With my free leg, I start kicking, my heel making a satisfying crunch against his face.

"You're going to regret that." The menace in his tone is filled with a dark promise, leaving me frozen. Time seems to slow as my brain screams for me to escape, but my body stays in place as he lunges forward. Pulling up my knees, I kick, hitting nothing but open air. A familiar set of broad shoulders fill my vision, making my heart leap.

Ignoring the broken glass all across the seat, I rise to my knees to watch as Lane lands a combination of hits that leave the kidnapping, car thief sprawled unconscious on the ground.

"You can't win against crazy, Jackass. Ha!" I shimmy in the seat, happy to have Lane alive and well in front of me.

"You all right, Rebecca?" I love the way my name sounds on his lips.

"Are you?" His clothes are disheveled and sooty. His shoulder is stained red with blood. Has he been bitten? Leaning in for a better look, I give the wound a poke.

"Easy, darlin. I cut it on some glass sneaking out a window." Lane put his hands on my shoulders studying me so he can look me over, too.

"He said you were dead." And a part of me had believed it even when if I hadn't wanted to.

"It'll take more than the apocalypse to keep me away from you." The possessiveness in his tone should scare me, yet it doesn't. Instead, it excites me.

I hold up my wrists. "Any chance you can find the key?"

"I'll check his pockets, but we should probably hurry." Lane's gaze flicks behind me, and I turn to see a few corpses stumbling into the street, coming our way.

"I don't mind leaving him here. You sure you're okay with that?" Lane asks, searching the still unconscious man's pockets. A week ago, I wouldn't have killed the spider that kept making webs at the corner of my closet door. But a week ago, this man in front of me had been nothing more than my bad boy fantasy and the world hadn't been thrown into chaos.

"He started the fire that could've killed us both and kept me from a nice cuppa. So long as you make good on your promise to pick up where we left off, I'm good with almost anything." I meant every word.

"I may be a lot of things darlin', but I'm always a man of my word." Lane's eyes are full of heat as he pulls a key from the man's pocket.

"If you had told me about the view, we could've been here days ago." I'm not talking about the view out of the window where the horses graze in the pasture against the gorgeous backdrop of the Teton Mountain Range. It's Lane's reflection in the glass that hardens my nipples. Turning to face him, I envy the stray water droplets running down his bare chest.

I'd been disappointed when I'd showered alone as Lane had tended to his horses, but I'm not feeling anything but right, now. I pull off the shirt I took from Lane's closet over my head, leaving me naked. I raise an eyebrow with an unspoken challenge. *It's time to pay up, Cowboy.*

The towel around his waist drops to the floor, giving my gaze full and unrestricted access to his body, but it isn't my eyes I want to use to fuck him.

Our bodies collide. His hands on my hips move down to my ass and lift me off my feet. Without hesitation, I wrap my legs around his hips, feeling his dick, hot and hard against my sensitive wet opening.

"If you aren't inside me in the next minute, I'm going to go insane," I mumble against his lips.

"I aim to please." I feel his lips turn up in his cocky grin as he lowers me to the edge of his kitchen table before kneeling down to bury his head between my thighs.

A cry leaves my lips as his tongue licks my folds. Gripping the table, I arch my back, muttering my appreciation to God, the Fates, *Cthulhu*, and any deity my blissed-out mind can remember that this man happened to cross my path. His calloused hand finds my breast, pinching the nipple to bring a jolt of pain that mixes with the pleasure his mouth is delivering.

"You taste just as sweet as I knew you would." Lane's words barely penetrate the fog of my lust.

"Yes." Time stops existing. Everything but the solid feel of the wood under me and the man lapping at my core fades away.

He pinches my nipple again, harder this time, as his tongue increases its pace. Bursts of colors explode as the tension he's building finds its release. I'm still riding the waves of my orgasm as Lane enters me in one hard thrust. Pain flares as my body stretches to accommodate him, increasing the pleasure as he fills me.

Lane is still for a moment until I can no longer take it. My body needs friction, demands movement, and my hips start working against his, searching for another release.

"You feel amazing," he moans, keeping his thrusts fast and hard, making the table under me rock.

Wrapping my legs around his waist, I take his mouth, the taste of my orgasm still on his lips, sweet like vanilla syrup.

Digging my nails into his back, I feel the slow build of another climax as hands grab my hips and he thrusts into me harder.

"Your pussy is so tight I could fuck you forever." Lane's voice is deep and husky. Exactly what I hadn't known I needed to send me speeding over the edge of another orgasm. Only this time, I'm not alone. With a final thrust, Lane tenses, saying my name like a prayer.

BRIGHT RAYS of sunlight filter in as I burrow my face deeper into the pillow. My body is still aching in all the best ways from the long night before. Lane's rough fingertips gently trace up and down the curve of my lower back.

"So, do you have chores I can help you with this morning?" My words are broken up with a yawn. I was never a morning person, and I have every intention of tempting him to stay in bed.

"Already done. Made a pot of coffee, too."

I'm definitely keeping this man.

"How did you manage that without waking me up?" I turn my head to face him.

"My momma taught me not to lie, but she also told me a woman never wants to be told she snores, so why don't we skip the questions this morning and do something else instead?" He lets his bare leg brush against mine. A quick exploration with my hand confirms he's naked and hard for me.

"Three times last night wasn't enough, Cowboy?" I laugh, suddenly forgetting about being sore. I'm more than ready for him.

"I said last night I could fuck you forever, and darlin', if you haven't learned it by now, I'll just have to remind you. This cowboy always keeps his word."

CARRY ME HOME

Kelly Violet

WHAT HAD POSSESSED me to get in the car? I'd lost my damn mind making the drive from New York to Kansas in the first place. *That's it.* What else explained the crazy idea that had taken root and wouldn't leave my brain over the last couple of weeks? But I needed a change.

By the time some common sense returned, I was already halfway to my destination. I convinced myself not to turn back. The GPS gave me the occasional notification to stay focused as interstate after interstate stretched ahead of me.

I was bone-tired after two days of driving, but my mind wouldn't settle. Not without doing one last thing. Curiosity bested me, and I had to know.

Aunt Sarah and Uncle Tony, college friends of my parents, spent more time traveling nowadays, so any gossip they shared with me was limited at best. For all I knew, the man was happily married with several adorable kids running around the farm. I'd never stopped thinking about him, though. The summers spent in the wide-open spaces of Pierceville, Kansas were some of my most cherished memories, and that had everything to do with Jake. The Davidsons were my aunt and uncle's closest neighbors, and I remembered spending my days following their son around while he'd completed his chores.

This has disaster written all over it.

Still, the absence of loud honking, blaring sirens, and the constant buzz of the city came as a welcome relief. This trip was already working its magic on me. I hadn't realized how much I'd missed the open air and quiet.

Before I knew it, I made the turn into the Davidson farm. This needed to be a quick stop, a way to appease the ball of guilt and nerves churning in my gut. Lights were on in the main house. As late in the evening as it was, Mr. and Mrs. Davidson had likely finished their supper.

I'd pop by to say hello to the sweet couple, satisfy my curiosity about Jake, and then head back to my aunt and uncle's place. No more, no less. This trip was all about kicking back for a while.

A slower pace would do me some good. Peace and quiet and a bit of clarity might go a long way toward giving me a little perspective while I figured out my next chapter.

The publishing house where I'd started my career as an assistant editor had completed their plans for downsizing after a recent merger. My position had been one of the last on the chopping block.

Becoming unemployed had blindsided me. Not one to stay down, I'd immediately gone back on the job market. After three weeks of countless applications, there had been no bites. It was time to reassess and regroup. The universe seemed intent to knock my ass to the ground and pin me there, even though I've had my fair share of hits lately. My father's passing two years ago had been the most gut-wrenching one of all. It had left a gaping hole in my heart. Since losing my mother before my ninth birthday, it had just been the two of us. Dad and me against the world.

After his death, new hurdles had taken center stage, and I'd found myself floundering in a city flush with activity and opportunity. In subtle ways, life in the big city had started losing its appeal. With no job prospects or concrete tethers keeping me in New York, I'd packed up my apartment and rented a storage unit.

A break from my dismal circumstances should do the trick. So, when my aunt and uncle had offered up their home while they traveled, I'd jumped at the chance to get away for a fresh perspective. Now, I only had room for positive vibes during this spur-of-the-moment road trip down memory lane.

Accepting anything less defeated the purpose behind the journey.

Plus, I looked forward to seeing the Davidson family again. *They'll be happy to see me too*, I hoped. *Two of them will at least.* Mr. and Mrs. Davidson had always treated me kindly during my visits to their property, inviting me to stay for lunch more often than not. I remembered hardly batting an eyelash before agreeing with a "thank you" as my stomach had fluttered with butterflies. Thinking back on those days, I realized I hadn't been fooling the older couple in the slightest.

I focused on a reunion, with them, while I continued up the long driveway. However, those same pesky butterflies reappeared, taking flight the closer I drove to the house.

Finally, I stopped and turned off the car. Twilight captured my attention with its mesmerizing blue and purple hues coloring the sky, stretching over the land as far as my eyes could see. I remembered being in awe of the size of this farm, even while Jake had tried to convince me it was small in comparison to others. This place had always felt vast and magical to me. So different from the fast-paced culture of the city where I'd grown up.

After taking several calming breaths, I exited the car and took my first steps toward the two-story farmhouse. The evening air felt crisp and refreshing on my flushed skin. Spring was fast approaching. Even though I'd love to stick around for it, my life was completely up in the air right now. I wasn't sure where I'd be in a few weeks.

A tall, dark figure suddenly appeared from behind the house. The man wiped a cloth along his hands as he ate up the distance with long strides. That fresh, crisp evening air betrayed me, lodging in my throat, and I halted. The man's head turned in my direction, and his eyes locked on me. Eyes that I knew were a cornflower blue.

My heart raced as my gaze dropped to his dusty work boots. They looked strong and sturdy, like the man himself. He was no longer the beanpole who'd shot up several inches before our last summer together. That gangly boy from my memories had filled out in ways I hadn't let myself imagine but couldn't ignore now with him standing right in front of me. He was all man now. Hell, he looked like all my cowboy fantasies rolled into one attractive and vaguely familiar specimen.

Jacob Davidson.

We'd spent almost every waking moment together during my visits to his family's farm. It had taken a while for him to warm up to me, but after it happened, we'd been practically inseparable.

I'd hoped he'd still be here, working the land just like we'd talked about as children. He belonged here. Once upon a time, I'd fantasized about belonging here, too. With him. But reality had a funny way of sucking the air out of dreams. And real-world responsibilities had come flooding back once my bags had been packed and I'd had to return to New York and my dad.

"Can I help you, miss?" His voice sounded thick and sweet like warm honey. I swooned. His question zapped my brain back into action, and my feet started moving again. I took several steps before stopping, keeping a few yards between myself and the porch steps where he stood. My gaze fixed on the way his muscles bunched in the long-sleeved shirt he wore. Although it had been years since I'd last seen him, I'd have known him anywhere.

He'd made sure I could never forget.

"Hi, Jake."

The soft-spoken and hardworking boy who'd stolen my heart all those years ago stood before me in all his glory. Tall and rugged.

Although I hadn't expected to run into him so soon, I was over the moon. He snatched the breath right out of my chest, just like when we were kids.

Fate seemed to have a plan of her own for this little reunion.

I sent a quick prayer up to the heavens for a heads-up next time. Surprises were becoming my least favorite thing nowadays.

Squaring my shoulders, I waited for Jake to say something. Anything to get this ball rolling. Because I missed my friend.

I missed him more than he'd ever know.

. . .

"Shay? You gotta be shittin' me." Shock stole all the good sense and manners my parents had instilled in me. Shayna Pruitt had come back.

The curvy woman jerked at the coarse words. I knew my greeting left a lot to be desired, but she'd thrown my world into a tailspin. She should be grateful I had any words at all.

Her reappearance was equal parts a fantasy come to life and a kick in the gut by a frightened mare. It knocked the wind out of me like a damn sucker punch.

My gaze zeroed in on the self-conscious way her hands slid down her sides. The move showed her nervousness. *Good.* She should be shaken to her core because I felt stripped bare and wound tight.

Shay had always carried a little extra weight when we were younger, but it had never detracted from her beauty. She'd been a looker even then. Now, her curves made for the best feminine packaging. Wide hips called for the tight, bruising grip of my calloused hands. Her dark brown skin begged to be licked, sucked, bitten. My brain conjured the memory of the hickeys we'd given each other that last summer.

I shook my head at the erotic images my mind summoned. I hadn't seen her since we were teens, but all those horny, adolescent fantasies starring her came roaring back to life after I'd buried them long ago.

The adult version of Shay was temptation incarnate. All womanly curves. I'd blow a gasket sooner rather than later if I didn't get her off my property in quick order. The end of the day already found me grumpy, and this unexpected visit from the girl I'd dreamed about all through my youth didn't bode well for either of us—if my filthy thoughts were anything to go by.

She looked different but the same. I cataloged the subtle changes as tense silence stretched between us. She no longer wore her hair in long braids or straight and silky like I remembered. Instead, Shay fashioned her locks into these puffy twists that fell to her shoulders. My two heads pictured in high definition how it would feel gripping her hair in a tight fist while pounding into her snug cunt.

Fuck, I needed to find out what she wanted, and then end this little reunion. I was cracking at the seams from her unexpected visit. That adolescent love had turned to something deeper and darker over the years. Holding back the yearning bursting from my chest seemed impossible now that I had her in my sights again.

She'd made a grave error coming here tonight and finding me.

"It's been a while." Shay spoke again. Her voice used to play in my head all the time. Now, it had a richer quality to it. Raspier. And my cock perked up hearing it.

"What are you doing here, Shay?" My question

came out gruff, croaky. My parents would've kicked my hind-end if they'd heard how I'd spoken to my old friend, but my control was about ready to snap.

I waited.

"I-I'm here visiting Sarah and Tony's place, and thought I'd stop by to say hello to your parents. And you." She tacked on the last bit. I found her story hard to believe since I hadn't seen or heard from her in over a decade. She'd left one summer with a promise to come back, after we'd become closer than we'd ever been. And then nothing.

"Is that right?" She'd left out how long this so-called visit would last, and I picked up on her oversight immediately.

"Of course. It's good to see you, Jake."

I smirked. That was rich coming from her. Then, I remembered this quirk she had. The way she'd look at me from under her long, curly eyelashes like she was doing now. I'd wondered about those looks as a boy. They'd confused and frustrated me to no end. And then, I'd turned fourteen and my eyes had completely opened. It hadn't been until the year after when I'd finally done something about it. Gotten the guts to see if my feelings were reciprocated. And they had been. Then the summer had ended, and my boyish dreams with it.

"Yeah, you too, Shay." The words felt dry on my tongue, mostly because I'd meant them in one way or another, even though they were nearly impossible to utter. I shoved the dirty cloth in my hand into a back pocket for something to do. "You want to come in? I just finished up the last of the chores."

I cursed the question as it came out. Inviting her inside was a colossal mistake, but it was one I couldn't stop. No matter how hard I tried. Like the last moments before a train wreck. All parties knew the likelihood of survival was slim to none, but the collision couldn't be stopped or wished away.

"Yeah, sure."

"Well, alright then." I slapped my palm against a jean-clad thigh and turned on my heels. "Follow me."

She trailed a few steps behind, and I wondered if she regretted this side trip to the farm. Regretted accepting my impromptu offer to come inside. I felt like the big bad wolf in a fairy tale, ready to ravish her if the opportunity presented itself.

God, I hope it does. I thought the boy in me had outgrown this crush long ago, but here it was just as strong. Burning bigger and brighter than before with just one look at Shay all grown up and more beautiful than she had any business being.

Dammit, I was in trouble.

I plodded up the steps onto the porch, stomping my feet on the mat at the front door. Crossing the threshold, I flipped the light switch and motioned for Shay to enter.

Once inside, her fingers immediately went to the large buttons of her red peacoat. Some things hadn't changed. I recalled red being her favorite color, and the crimson shade looked good against her dark chocolate complexion.

Shay looks good enough to eat, a voice growled in my head.

"I can take that," I offered, remembering my manners.

Shrugging off the light coat, she revealed a char-coal-gray, long-sleeved T-shirt, which she'd paired with dark wash jeans. My gaze dropped to her shapely, thick legs and the way those jeans hugged every curve. Her shirt looked fitted and well-worn, accentuating the lines of her bountiful breasts. I imagined them being more than a handful. A beastly groan formed deep in my chest, and I bit my tongue to keep myself at bay.

She should've left when she'd had the chance. Or never come back at all. Now, the lamb was in the lion's den. And I didn't plan on letting her leave without an explanation.

She owed me that and more. Much more.

"It looks exactly how I remember it." Her words broke through a sea of unresolved anger. She smiled, a wistfulness settling on her pretty face, and I forced myself to look away after a long beat passed.

Shay walked into the family room, her hands gliding over the crocheted blanket draped along the sofa's back. She sighed. A breath full of sound with too much emotion and not enough context for me to wade through.

We had been close once. Inseparable in the weeks

when she'd stayed a mile down the road. I'd pined for my friend after she'd left for her home in the big city, wishing she could stay with me. The dynamics of our relationship had changed that long-ago summer when I'd been fifteen and she'd just recently celebrated her fourteenth birthday.

"Jake?" Shay stared at me from across the room. Her gaze drilled into me like it used to when we were kids. I realized it wasn't the first time she'd tried to get my attention.

"Yeah," I grunted.

"Is everything alright?"

"Not really, no."

Shay nodded sharply before dropping her gaze to her feet. The hurt look from her pierced straight through my chest cavity. Those big, brown eyes of hers still did a number on me. I was being an absolute prick. A dose of shame rolled through me.

Before I found the words to apologize, she headed toward me and the door. "I should go."

The sound of her cracked whisper damn near broke my heart. I'd made a promise never to hurt Shay when we'd been younger, but that's exactly what my disgruntled behavior was doing now.

"I'm sorry I bothered you, Jake." Shay stopped in front of me, extending a hand across my shoulder to reach for the coat I'd hung up behind me.

I couldn't let her leave me again. Not like this. Not if I had anything to say about it.

"You're not going anywhere, Shay."

I turned into her, catching and steering her body until her back hit the front door with a soft thud. Right where I wanted her.

We had unfinished business.

Business I intended to resolve here and now, and not a moment later.

This reunion had been fourteen years in the making. And I'd be damned if I let this woman walk away from me ever again.

It was about time I showed Shay the man I'd become.

A man who never gave up without a fight.

And she sure brought the fighter out in me.

JAKE SEETHED. He towered over me by at least half a foot, all long lines and fiery temper. So much anger brimming behind his strong, handsome features. I hadn't been sure if he'd truly be open to what I had to say, but leaving again without sharing my reasons felt like failure. Like taking the coward's way out.

He deserved more than that.

I gulped. "Jake, what are you doing?" The intensity in his eyes could only be described as scorching hot. No one had ever looked at me that way. As if he wrestled between throwing my ass out and ravishing me. And I couldn't really say which of his reactions I preferred more.

With the light casting a glow over the entryway and family room, my gaze roamed over his chiseled face, trying to see the quiet boy behind the scalding heat in his blue eyes. My fingers itched to run through the short strands of his dark brown hair. From the first moment I'd laid eyes on him more than seventeen years ago, I'd been gone over the boy. And now, this man left me tongue-tied. Speechless.

"We're older, Shay. Wiser. I won't let you walk away so easily this time. I can't."

His jaw clenched. I watched the play of emotions dance across his tan face. The five o'clock shadow added a certain level of ruggedness to the man in front of me. He was familiar and not. Sure, my childhood best friend but also a stranger.

His eyes had shuttered while grunting those bold statements. A shiver racked my body, and I wasn't altogether sure it had anything to do with fear.

At the back of my mind, I'd foolishly hoped for evidence of a spark. A glimmer of my girlhood crush and the burgeoning attraction I'd felt from all those years ago.

Instead, I seemed to have stepped right into a five-alarm blaze.

All I asked was that neither of us perished in the flames by the end of this.

"I forgot to mention that my folks are out of town for the next few days. It's just you and me here. And we have some catching up to do."

This is insane. Tiny tremors skated up and down my body as Jake cornered me against the front door. Big biceps came into focus in my periphery. He stood too close. Imposing. Warm puffs of air caressed my scalp and forehead while tense silence descended around us.

We hadn't seen each other in years, but I knew he'd never hurt me. Not physically, anyway. Memories of him had never been far from my mind. Back then, he hadn't possessed a hurtful bone in his body.

"Jake…"

The muscles in his jaw ticked, his fiery gaze studying my face. *Can he hear the desire in my voice? See the heat in my eyes.*

Before uttering another word, he growled. A raw, animalistic sound that rumbled from deep within his chest. Since recognizing me, he'd been all grunts and sharp angles. Another shiver tore through me, and I swore his body rippled with tension. His reaction seemed beastly, otherworldly. I shook my head at the implications.

"Damn you, Shay." Jake swooped down and crash-landed into my lips. He made room for himself, muscling in and staking his territory while teasing my bruised lips with his tongue. He gentled the harsh treatment with several flicks, making me gasp. Calloused hands settled on my face. He brushed my twists behind my ears and brought his hands to my cheeks. His body held me in place, and I wasn't going anywhere.

"That's it. Open for me."

My limbs weakened at the huskier, edgier octave of his voice. My sex clenched at the sultry promises behind his words. His command. And I responded by parting my lips for him. I wanted him. Come what may afterwards, I'd dreamed of our reunion countless times over the years. Always hoping some level of attraction and mutual interest lingered between us. Never in my wildest dreams had I imagined this version—a rough and tumble cowboy crowding me against a door and plundering my mouth. But God, it sure felt heavenly. And dangerous. The man would soon find himself in a pool of my juices if he kept this up. My panties were nearly soaked.

"What are we doing?" I asked again as we broke apart to suck in air. This was beyond crazy.

"Something I've wanted for too damn long, Shay." The startling blue of his irises darkened.

Ragged breaths caught in my throat at the intensity of the moment. I couldn't break this spell. It almost sounded like he'd never stopped thinking of me either. God, how I wished for that to be true.

His hands coasted over every inch of me within his reach. My body shook from the sensory overload. When those same hands slid down my sides and wrapped around my thighs, my mind blanked. Then he hoisted me clear off the floor, and I yelped. "Jake, put me down. I'm too heavy," I yelled.

"Like hell you are."

He kept me captive against the door, my inner thighs cradling his trim waist. Gah, my mind was turning into mush. The evidence of his growing arousal poked my belly before he'd gone and lifted me up like my weight was inconsequential. It was hot as hell, even though I'd screeched at him.

Our gazes locked and held as my body froze, ending my wriggling. My breath caught, and the air froze around us at the intensity in his eyes. I couldn't rightly explain how we'd gone from zero to sixty, but I wouldn't regret it either.

"Please, Jake," I moaned, desperate for him to do something, anything. This wasn't what I'd expected coming to the farm tonight. Hell, I hadn't even been sure he'd be here. Or that he wouldn't have a wife and children running around the property. It's what I'd always envisioned for him over the years. Never mind that my fantasies occasionally thrust me in the role of wife and mother in that scenario.

"Please what?"

"Kiss me again."

"I thought you'd never ask." The floodgates opened again as he closed the distance and claimed my mouth. Opening for him came easier this time, and he groaned as my tongue tangled with his.

"Fuck, you taste how I remember. Only better."

My body tingled at his statement and the memory it brought to the surface. We'd made out only a few times that last summer we'd been together. He'd been my first kiss and I'd been his, our lips sealing every youthful promise too many years ago. Ones I'd neglected to keep.

My hips rolled of their own accord, generating inadequate friction on my aching sex. I wanted more, desperate for whatever Jake had in mind. I knew it wasn't smart to give myself so freely. I barely knew this hardened version of Jake, but my body couldn't lie. Not with him. Not now.

"I need you naked and begging." Oh, the things that came out of grown-up Jake's mouth soaked my panties even more.

"I'm yours." An emotion sparked in those blue eyes of his before they shuttered again. He plunged forward to punish my lips with another bruising kiss.

"That's right, Shay. For now."

Making this trip to Kansas had felt unavoidable. Long overdue. As if losing my job had been the exact catalyst I'd needed to get me back here. Back to Jake.

I just hoped I wouldn't fall on my face.

Fourteen years of silence and broken promises had obviously hurt the boy I'd once known, and I had to make amends. Let Jake know that this place had never been far from my mind. This town. His family farm. *Him.*

Not an hour ago, I'd breathed a sigh of relief reading the sign welcoming me to Pierceville. It was like I was coming home again.

Jake Davidson was my home.

It's about time he knows it.

MY HEART GALLOPED in my chest. The feral animal inside was unleashed, and there was zero hope to save either of us now.

I'm yours. Shay's whispered declaration played on repeat in my head. Finally, I spun away from our position against the front door. Her legs squeezed my waist as I walked us toward my childhood bedroom. I should take her to my house just over the hill, but that would be too much trouble. We were alone here anyway. My parents had begun traveling around the country in their RV since I'd assumed responsibility and expanded the farm a few years ago.

My childhood bedroom would do just fine. For now. Plus, the wild beast inside me couldn't wait. The urge to claim this woman drove my actions. I was lost to lust and anger-filled desperation. I wanted to love on Shay even as I took from her, stripped her of any thoughts about what happened next. She was all mine for the time being, and I battled an insatiable hunger.

"We should talk," I said, knowing talking was the furthest thing from my mind, "but that can fucking wait. We have unfinished business. You and I."

Every dormant fantasy starring Shay came flooding back, electric currents zinging through my body. I felt alive, ravenous. As if a flip switched in my head, and I was finally awake from a long and deep slumber. My anger and confusion lingered, but they didn't come close to the fire riding me, telling me to lay claim to this woman before she left again.

The air sparked and crackled around us. Tight fists clenched at my clothes as I marched to our destination. Shay hadn't been here more than fifteen minutes before I'd turned into a caveman. Although she hadn't complained, I wondered what was going through her head. *Why is she really here? Fourteen years later.* I thought she'd be living it up in the city or something. Too good for farm life. And me.

But here she is. Coming apart in my arms like a goddamn dream.

That fifteen-year-old boy was still pissed at her for cutting him off, not coming back. After all these years, my anger and disappointment had never abated. I couldn't help taking out any lingering resentment on her body. At least until these violent emotions seeped out of me, no longer heating my blood and driving these frenzied actions.

A kick at the bedroom door pushed it open, and I walked in, tossing Shay on the full-size bed. Her eyes widened while she bounced on the mattress. The jiggle of her large breasts caught my eyes. I could hardly wait for my first look at her voluptuous body. She was a wet dream. Hell, my ultimate dream.

A couple condoms were stashed in my wallet for times like these. It was more of a habit than anything else because nowadays I stayed busy. I pulled them out and tossed the foil packets on the sheet. They landed right beside Shay's head.

Her audible gulp made my dick twitch in my boxers. Her brown eyes locked onto mine while I stood over her.

I wanted answers. Obviously, she owed me more than a few. But I needed my dick inside her more than a trip down memory lane. Since it had taken years for her to come back, her explanation would hold. At least, until I got my fill of her. Or we used up both condoms. Whichever came first.

"Take off your clothes, Shay." My words sounded guttural, demanding. After a moment, she pushed up to her elbows and started with her shirt, showing off beautiful tits that damn near over-flowed from their lacy purple prison. My palms itched to touch her. Claim her as mine. If only for today.

My gaze tracked every inch of skin she revealed, and I took it all in. She'd been beautiful before, but Shay had blossomed. Curves upon curves. She was ample enough to take the hard fuck I had in mind. It was inevitable. And I knew I wouldn't break her by letting loose.

Her skinny jeans came next. Trembling fingers fumbled over the button and zipper. I watched, offering no assistance. She laid before me in just her bra and panties, her chest heaving. Shay couldn't mask the desire and slight worry in her gaze. She had every reason to be scared, unsure. I was not myself. Stripped raw from her unexpected arrival, I wanted to push her over the edge.

In one fluid movement, I reached down and flipped her over.

"On your knees," I growled, wrestling Shay's arms behind her back. She followed my hint and clasped her elbows. With her face and shoulders pressed into the mattress, this position gave me proper leverage to fuck her good and hard.

Tremors racked her body as she waited for my next move. The urge to smack her ass tickled my palm, a phantom sensation. So, I did.

The sharp clap rang through the room. A purple flush swept across her dark brown skin, a yelp hitting the air.

"You like that, don't you, Shay?" She kept her head down, one cheek pressed against the sheets.

My patience was non-existent. I unbuckled my belt, unzipped and pushed down my jeans. Then I grabbed a condom and freed my erection from its cage. Without preamble, I pressed into her tight cunt, growling as her wet heat engulfed me so damn good. Jesus Christ, I ached from the pleasure sweeping my body. I'd never be satisfied with one go with this woman. I'd known it before this thing had even started, as soon as I'd recognized who'd come knocking at my door, uninvited and as beautiful as ever.

Shay's whimpers and moans egged me on. Fully seated inside her, my brain short-circuited. I had to move.

Her ass jiggled with my harsh thrusts. The sounds of our mating filled my ears and my bruised heart.

When she moaned my name in a small, broken voice, it worked to obliterate any leftover bottled-up anger. Slowing my thrusts, I whipped my shirt off and leaned my bare chest against her back. I craved more contact. Skin to skin. Punishing her with my piss-poor attitude had to end. I remembered wanting nothing more than having Shay in my arms. And now, here she was. Ruining our time together wouldn't do me any favors, except get my rocks off. But I wanted everything from this woman. Her gasps and smiles. Her hands and eyes on me.

Decision made, I pulled out and flipped her around, needing to see her.

Witnessing her dazed look and the tear tracks streaming down her cheeks brought me to my knees. I was a right bastard for hurting her. No matter her reasons all those years ago, she didn't deserve this shitty treatment. Not from me. She deserved my care. My love.

"Fuck, I've missed you. Please forgive me." I pressed into her, our bodies now chest to chest. My gaze raked over her wet face. "I'm so damn sorry, Shay."

"Me, too. More than you know."

The rhythm of my thrusts changed, pushing her over the edge as I claimed her mouth. Just like I aimed to claim this woman. I never wanted this to end.

"Stay with me." I groaned the desperate plea into her neck as she quivered around me, finding her release.

"There's nowhere else I'd rather be, Jake."

Thank Christ for that.

We'd figure the rest out together.

EAST OF THE RIFT

January George

MADELINE PARKED the car and glanced up at the familiar farmhouse, her heart tightening. There were a lot of trucks parked on the edge of the driveway already, glints of battered metal reflecting the afternoon sunlight and clusters of men in their Sunday best and Stetsons. She glanced over at Jackson in the front seat, the foil-wrapped casserole dish on his lap. "Come on."

"Is Grandpa still dead?" Sarah asked from the backseat. "Can I touch him to see if he wakes up?"

"Don't be morbid," Maya chided.

"What's morbid?"

Next to her, Jackson sighed as he looked up at the porch. He looked older than his fourteen years, not just because he was now taller than she was, but it was the way he carried himself. "Pop was cremated."

"What's cremated?"

"It's when they burn you up," Maya said. "And all that's left is little chunks of bone."

"Maya, stop." Maddy let out a breath and hooked her hand through the door handle, finally pushing it open. "And I don't want to hear any more of this when we get inside."

Maddy straightened her simple back sheath dress as she herded the kids up the hardpacked dirt driveway. Jackson held the dish; Sarah had the card she'd made. The rough-hewn wire fence of the ranch's boundaries ran the length of the property to the right of them, stretching as far as she could see. A few locals and ranch hands tipped their hats to her, mumbling greetings as she passed.

The ranch had been Rafferty land for four generations. Luke had nearly doubled the acreage since he'd taken over for his father as Jack's health had declined the last few years. It was one of the things that had driven them apart. The hours he'd spent working had always left her feeling like she was trailing behind the kids and the cattle and the equipment and the weather reports, and whatever else Luke had on his mind that day. She imagined that Jackson would take over one day, maybe the girls, too. It almost made her smile to think of the three of them as adults, arguing over the price of grain the way they fought over the remote.

"I don't want to go," Sarah whined, stopping short in her black patent-leather shoes just steps from the porch. "I thought Pop would still be here. But dead."

Maddy didn't want to be there either. Her father-in-law had been one of the kindest men she'd ever known, and even after she and Luke had separated, he'd never stopped treating her like his daughter-in-law. She couldn't imagine the house without him.

Maya cut in, maybe sensing her mood. "Colton and Lacey will be here."

Sarah, hearing her cousins' names shot forward, practically running up the stairs. Maddy shot Maya a smile, *mostly* forgiving her for telling Sarah what cremation was.

Inside, Grace Rafferty stood in the foyer, greeting people as they came in. Maddy had known her long enough to see the heartbreak in her eyes, the puffiness in the crepe folds. Maddy embraced her for a long moment, and then Grace pulled back, pressing Madeline's hand between her soft, wrinkled ones. "He always loved you so much. I hope you know that."

Maddy nodded, struggling against the lump in her throat and the tears burning her eyes. "I'm going to miss him."

"Me too, honey," Grace smiled, giving her hand another squeeze, and then turned to the kids. "How are my loves?"

"I made you a picture of grandpa to remember him since he got burned up in a fire and all that's left of him is little chunks of bones," Sarah said loudly, holding out the piece of hot pink construction paper with a stick figure drawn on it.

"Oh, thank you," Grace said, without missing a beat. "It looks just like him."

"Can I see the chunks of bones?"

"Uh, no dear."

"Sarah," Maddy warned, taking the casserole dish from Jackson. "We brought chilaquiles. I'll just go put the dish in the fridge."

The kitchen counters were littered with pies and cakes. Maddy opened the fridge and frowned at the stacks of casseroles that filled it. She shoved her dish into the last available spot, and then headed back to the great room just as the kids streaked past her.

"Mom, we're going outside," Maya yelled. "I'll watch Sarah."

"Did you see your father?" she asked, but they had already run out the backdoor. She followed them onto the porch, watching the five shadows dancing as they crossed the lawn, backlit by the late afternoon sun. "Jackson, keep an eye on them. Don't let them play in the arroyo," she called, not really expecting a response.

Maddy went back inside, letting the screen door slap closed and reluctantly glanced around the room. She was dreading what to say, part of her wanting to get it over with, part of her hoping she would miss Luke entirely. She hated the feeling that she felt the loss of his father more than he did. When they'd first married, she'd thought his reserved nature and quiet stoicism hid a gentle vulnerability, that it was protective. But it wasn't. He was as unyielding and unfeeling as steel. The long hours and the hard work she could have looked past, but the way he'd just nodded when he'd seen her bags beside the door, and how after eighteen years he hadn't even looked at her… He'd just gone back to the office and shut the door. That had shattered her heart.

Dorothy Miller and Francine Abbott approached her with their plates of coffee cake and paper cups, asking how the kids were taking it. Maddy nodded and smiled, answered their questions, but her gaze kept roaming the room.

The coffee ran out. She heard the sputter of the last dregs into Doug Fink's cup, and it was a welcome excuse to escape Dorothy's detailed instructions on how Maddy could turn some of Jack's old shirts into teddy bears for the kids. She excused herself, taking the pot to the kitchen. She felt awkward in her grief, like the separation between her and Luke should have buffered the pain, and even though Jack had been sick a long time, she still wasn't prepared for his loss.

Maddy flipped open cabinets to take out the canister of coffee and the measuring spoons. It had been a while since she'd been in the kitchen, but she still knew where everything was. She plugged the machine in, filling the reservoir with a pitcher, and then rinsed her hands and dried them on a towel before turning to lean against the sink.

She started when she saw him at the table. He'd been so silent she hadn't even felt his presence. Her hand flew to her throat. "Oh God, Luke, you startled me."

His forearms were on the table, big hands clasped together on the smooth wood. There was nothing soft or pretty about Luke Rafferty. He fit into the rugged landscape, tall and broad and made up of sharp ledges and hard lines. Fine creases had formed around his eyes from squinting into the sun, and there were strands of grey mixed into the hair at his temples and the scruff across his cheeks, but he still took her breath away. And she hated herself for it.

He didn't say anything, but she was used to his silence. "I won't ask how you are," she said, turning around and wiping the droplets of water she'd spilled when refilling the reservoir. "And you know how much I cared for him, so you know how sorry I am."

He stayed quiet, and she set about wiping the sink faucet, talking to fill the silence. The only other sound was the low murmur of voices from the great room and the hiss of the coffee pot. "The kids are out back with Colton and Lacey. I told them to come see you, but as soon as they saw their cousins, they took off for that damned arroyo. I told Jackson to keep them out of it." She set the coffee canister back in the cabinet. "They're all handling it so differently. Sarah drew a picture of him for your mom. Maya is sad; she understands it more than Sarah does. Jackson is more like you, reserved. I know he misses him, but he doesn't want to talk about it. Not yet. Not like the girls." She started absently picking up mugs from the dish drainer, using the cloth to dry them and set them on a tray to go out when the coffee finished. "I hope that he will talk about it—"

"Stop."

The word was almost a growl, nearly unrecognizable as his voice. She set the mug down and turned, keeping the towel knotted against her waist.

He'd raised his hands to his forehead and his head was bowed, so she couldn't see his eyes. There was tension is his broad shoulders. Pain radiated from him, and her breath caught. "Stop what?"

He got up abruptly, the chair legs clattering against the floor, keeping his eyes downcast, and without answering, he pushed open the door to the small, walk-in pantry and slammed it behind him.

Maddy stared after him for a long moment. She glanced at the coffee pot. She should go back out into the living room. Go finish Dorothy's tutorial about memory bears. But something kept her frozen there.

"You're such an idiot," she muttered under her breath. She was still giving him emotions, making excuses for him. Wanting him to be *feeling* things that he wasn't.

But he was the father of her children, and he had just lost his own father, and in the twenty years she'd known him, this was the first time he'd hidden in a pantry. She set the rag down and went to the door, wrapping her hand around the old brass knob. This was stupid. He wanted to be alone, or he wouldn't have been sitting in the kitchen by himself, and he wouldn't have retreated from her. But she still couldn't shake the feeling he really didn't want to be alone. That he was hurting. That he needed her.

Stupid thoughts. Stupid thoughts that should make her let go of the doorknob and return to the living room to sit and listen to murmured condolences and stories of Jack Rafferty's life; she should go check on the kids.

But she didn't. Instead, she turned the knob quietly and slipped inside before she thought any more about it. She closed it behind her and leaned against the old wood before she lifted her eyes.

There was a small, high window in the back of the room, and it was the only source of light unless she pulled on the cord for the single bulb above her head. The afternoon sunlight filtered in dully through the leaves and branches of the juniper tree at the back of the house. It was dim, but dust particles danced in the streams of light that outlined Luke. He stood with his arms braced against his mom's canning table, head low. He filled the tiny room.

"Luke," she said softly, not knowing what to say but wanting to make her presence known.

"I'm sorry," he said it so softly she almost thought she'd imagined it.

She stilled. It had always been hard for him to say

it. He'd always been more about action than words. At first, it had bothered her that he rarely told her he loved her, but she'd grown to see that he always showed her. Little things…taking care of the cars and yard…the nights when the kids were small and he'd worked all day, backbreaking work, but still, he'd swoop the kids up to give her a break and rope them into making dinner for her. All of that had changed when he'd taken over for Jack on the day-to-day duties of the ranch.

"For what?" she asked, sagging against the door. She didn't want to talk about this; it was too painful.

"For this." He made a dismissive motion, but he still didn't turn to face her.

"It's in the past, Luke."

He finally turned, leaned back against the table, crossing his ankles and folding his arms over his chest. He wore jeans and an untucked button-down shirt that folded against the concave slope of his abdomen. The cords and ropes of muscles peeked out from below his rolled sleeves. He'd somehow managed to get more handsome as he'd gotten older. He never gained weight from the bowl of chocolate ice cream he ate every night after dinner. She'd gotten softer and rounder with every baby, and even though it had been nearly seven years since her last one, the extra weight had stubbornly held on.

"Before he died…" he cleared his throat, as if he was having a hard time speaking. "He said I was a fool. A stubborn fool."

She smiled, picturing Jack saying it. "You are."

"Because I shouldn't have ever let you go."

"Luke," she said softly. Her heart, already fragile and splintering, split wide open. It was what she had always wanted to hear, two years ago, eighteen months ago, a year ago. "Your dad just died. You're feeling a lot of things..."

"No, dammit." He lifted his hands to run through his hair. "I'm not saying it because of that."

God, she'd wanted to hear this for so long, and it hurt so deeply that it would come on the heels of Jack's death that she couldn't trust it, that it felt like misguided injury. "Please don't."

"I'm not good with words, you know that." He shoved off the table and brought himself up to his full height. "I don't know what I did to make you leave..."

"I never wanted to leave." Maddy blinked back the sudden blurriness in her eyes. "I just wanted you to care enough about me to try to keep me. I was bluffing, and you called it."

She could see that her admission stunned him. He just stared at her, his eyes aching and raw. "I thought..."

Maddy dashed at her eyes with the backs of her hands, blinking the tears away furiously. She had to go back out into the kitchen and bring out the coffee pot. She looked away, trying to compose herself. "It doesn't matter."

He closed the distance between them, towering

over her and absorbing every bit of oxygen in the small space. The scent of his shampoo, the laundry detergent on his clothes, the fragrance so uniquely him, overwhelmed her with the urge to bow into him and ball the fabric of his shirt in her fists.

"It matters." He didn't touch her, but he was so close only an inch of electrified air crackled between them. "I thought it was what you wanted. I thought you were unhappy."

A wave of white-hot rage filled her. "You *thought* I was unhappy? I *was* unhappy. I was unhappy because I had to raise three kids by myself, because every-thing else in the world was more important than me. I was unhappy because you didn't listen to anything I said when I told you that. I was unhappy because I didn't matter enough for you to try to make me happy." She shoved his chest with her palms. "You let me go. You didn't care enough. You didn't care enough about me…" She punctuated each word with a strike against his chest, hot tears spilling against her cheeks. He'd retreated back against the canning table, but she knew it wasn't her weak blows that had driven him back. "And now, you want to tell me you didn't know any of that?"

"Maddy," he said, softly catching her hands in his huge ones. They engulfed hers in their warmth. "Maddy."

"No," she tried to push him away, but he kept her hands trapped inside his. "I'm not doing this. I said I wasn't doing this right now. You're only saying this because you think you disappointed your father, or you feel something for the first time in your whole miserable unfeeling life." She yanked her hands free and turned to the door. Her hand was on the knob, turning it.

"Fuck." Luke lunged forward and flattened a hand against the door to keep it shut. "We need to finish this."

"In your parents' pantry? Really?"

He let go of the door long enough to grab her arms and spin her to face him. His eyes shone with hurt, a rare and disconcerting emotion. "Maddy, just listen. For one goddamn second."

She fought him, mindful of the narrow and cluttered shelves. She tried to jerk free from of him, and in the process, managed to erase the space between them. Her gaze raised to his, and she jutted her chin out defiantly.

But his eyes didn't reflect sadness or hurt.

Something in the air shifted. Her breath came fast and hot—too fast to fill her lungs. She hadn't felt it in such a long time it took a second to recognize the quicksilver flush of frantic, maddening desire, pulsating in her blood vessels. The heat spread through her; the ache deepened. Maddy yanked on her arms again, but the effort had shifted from freeing them to pulling him closer.

His breath sped up. He was staring down at her, eyes hooded, lips parted. And then his mouth was on her. It wasn't a kind kiss; it wasn't romantic. There was nothing sweet about the way his lips claimed hers. How he dropped her arms so he could tangle his fingers in her hair, angling her head back to give him a better angle to feast on her mouth. His tongue swirled against hers, deep strokes that ignited the smoldering ache into a full-fledged wildfire. He tasted so good, the familiarity of his kiss, of his fingers, of him. She clawed at his shirt then curled her arms around his neck. He lifted her easily, and she felt a flicker of self-consciousness, but it was erased when set her onto the small table and his free hand slid up her leg, under the hem of her dress. His movements were jerky with want, his fingers bold as they brushed against her. She leaned back, lifted herself long enough for him to work his hand up to the waistband of her pantyhose and yank them down. Every nerve in her body screamed. He was familiar and new, bold and comfortable. Even though it had been months, her body reacted to him with the intimacy and desire it always had. The stockings didn't get past her thighs, the tight control top cutting into her flesh. But she didn't care because he was pushing aside her panties, already damp, so he could touch her.

"Fucking Christ, Maddy," he murmured against her lips as his fingers slid against her, brushing against that tender bead and making her come off the table, chasing the motion.

His fingers pushed into her; his thumb flickered against the swollen bud. A wave of pleasure rolled over her, and she buried her face in his shoulder to muffle the sound of her moan. A single high heel dropped as her foot arched, and then the second. He moved his fingers. Her muscles flexed and tensed, building towards that delicious release. If she stopped to think about this, it was crazy, but she couldn't stop to think, because every time she did, Luke hooked his finger in a motion he knew nearly made her explode. She worked a free hand between them to roll the pantyhose down further, and he paused long enough to tug off her underwear, too.

Then his mouth closed on hers. One hand kneaded her breast through the top of her dress, the other pushed the fabric up, revealing the cup of her bra. Maddy leaned back, pushing against his other hand, the one inside her, but the movement offered her breast to him, and he tore his mouth away from hers to nuzzle it. She yanked him closer, feeling the hard length of his erection against his jeans, and she fumbled with the top of his pants to free it.

When her fingers stalled, Luke withdrew his hand, popped the button and pushed the jeans and his boxers down, allowing his cock to spring free.

There was no finesse as he pushed into her, sinking in and burying himself to the hilt. Maddy gasped at the intrusion, at the feel of him filling her. She clung to his shoulders as he began to rock against her, fast hard strokes that stretched her deliciously.

"Christ, Maddy, you feel so good," he whispered.

She clung to him as he drove into her, rattling the table. She was on the verge of coming, of screaming his name, but he pulled out and dropped to his knees in front of her. Before she even realized what he was doing, his mouth was on her, applying suction, lavishing her, kissing her as deeply as if it were her mouth. Waves of pleasure rolled over her at the slick wetness and heat of his tongue. Maddy grabbed the lip of the table, and her thighs closed around his head to hold it in place as she angled her hips to maximize every stroke of his tongue. Her orgasm tore through her, arching her back, curling her toes. Her head banged against the spice rack, and she bit down hard on the cry that was threatening. Luke didn't let up, even as her body jerked. He plunged his tongue into her, yanking her legs apart to give him better access. Her eyes were closed, her torso collapsed against the wall, but she felt his fingers, gliding smoothly in rhythm with his tongue. Her thighs tightened around his head again, her stomach tightened.

"Fuck me," she whispered, a moment before she climaxed again.

Luke rose to his feet and pushed into her for the second time, pulling her hips to meet his.

Her body was spent, but she came again, shuddering around him. He pumped into her, dragging her closer to kiss her, and she could taste herself on his lips, on his tongue, as he devoured her. Her arms came around him and tightened with more than desire, more than lust.

With love.

Luke collapsed, shuddering as he emptied into her. She didn't want to let go; she didn't want to ever let go.

Reality returned slowly and painfully. Luke pulled away, and then pulled up the boxers and jeans that had been on his thighs. Maddy climbed unsteadily from the table to pick up her pantyhose and underwear.

"Here." Luke pulled a bandana from his back pocket. Maddy snatched it from him and cleaned herself up, awkwardly bumping into a shelf as she pulled her underwear and pantyhose back on.

"Maddy," he said. He took the bandana back and folded it, stuffing it back into his pocket.

"We shouldn't have..." But she couldn't finish the sentence because she didn't really regret it. She just wished that it meant to him what it had to her.

Luke caught her hand, forcing her to look up at him. "Don't do that."

Tears blurred her eyes again. This time the tears spilled so fast they were hot darts on her cheeks. "I'm so stupid."

His hands came up to frame her face, tilting it upward. She closed her eyes because it was too painful to look at him. Everything she wanted was right here but still outside her grasp. He pressed his lips to her eyes, to the paths of her tears. "You are so many things, but stupid isn't one of them."

She blinked her eyes open, detangling from him.

"I have to get back out there; people are going to come looking for more coffee."

"Maddy, let me say what I need to."

She'd turned to the door, her hand on the knob, but she stopped.

His breath hitched. "I let you go because I thought that was what you wanted. I thought I was doing the right thing. I care. Fuck, I cared enough that I let you go even though it felt like it ripped my guts out. That night, when you left? It was all I could go to get to the office before I broken down. I lost my best friend, the only person who got me." He paused. "Maddy, I wake up missing you every day and go to bed every night missing you. I don't want anyone else. I love you."

The words were like a healing salve on a wound, and the relief she felt was palpable. The glint of hope became a bright light that showed her, for the first time, the darkness she'd dwelled inside. But she wasn't going to let him off that easy. She didn't turn, but she didn't open the door.

"And I will do whatever it takes to get you back."

She glanced down, straightening her dress, and then she turned back to face him as she opened the door. At the sight of him, his face so earnest and open, she couldn't stop the smile from spreading across the lips still burning from his kisses.

"I'm looking forward to it."

TYING THE KNOT

Jennie Kew

ALLY

Un-fucking-believable.

My first night in town and my BFF bails on me. Not that I can be mad at her for it. She's an ER nurse and volunteered to do a double shift to help out with the heavier-than-usual traffic coming through the hospital doors at this particular time of year.

The time being January, and the particularity being the Tamworth Country Music Festival, when the population of the town swells to five times its usual size or more, and the propensity for people to wind up in the ER is in direct correlation with how much they've had to drink and whatever stupid thing they did after yelling at their mate to "Hold my beer."

So, all of that just means I'm now sitting in a pub, drinking whiskey...*alone*.

And the sharks have started to circle.

And by sharks, I mean cowboy wannabes. These guys stick out like a sore thumb in their unscuffed boots and ostentatious belt buckles, jeans that are just a little too blue, and Akubra hats straight from the saddlery store, their pristine condition a dead giveaway their owners wouldn't know the arse end of a horse if it shit on their shoes.

Right now, there are two of these morons trying to draw me into conversation, full of looking-to-get-laid swagger and not taking no for an answer. I've tried all the usual tricks to dissuade them, all the things women say to politely decline the advances of some random twat who may or may not turn out to be a serial killer.

"No."

"No, thank you."

"No, I don't want you to buy me a drink."

"Sorry, but I'm waiting for my boyfriend."

"Yes, my boyfriend is real."

"No, I don't want to save a horse and ride a cowboy."

"No, I'm not a lesbian."

All the shit women say while actively looking for ways to hobble the arsehole so we can make a clean getaway. But after driving for seven and a half hours to get here, then being ditched by my bestie, then dealing with these idiots, I'm no longer feeling very polite.

I raise my voice. "What part of *no* do you fuck-knuckles not understand? How many times do I have to say it before you get the fucking hint and back the fuck off? Jesus *fucking* Christ!"

Moron One and Moron Two stare at me like I've just sprouted a second head, and maybe I have. The Anti-Ally. That part of me that explodes outwards when confronted with arseholes either too clueless to realise they're making women uncomfortable or too selfish to care.

Then, just because I'm me and it couldn't end there, Moron Three joins the party.

"Ah, excuse me," he says loud enough to be heard over the din of the pub.

But before he can get in another word, I go on the attack.

"Oh, for fuck's sake. All I want to do is listen to music, sip whiskey, and be left alone. Is that really so much to fucking ask?"

Morons One and Two exchange a sidelong glance, then slowly—*finally*—back away from the crazy lady. But Moron Three folds his thick arms across his sizeable chest, stares down at me, and grins. He fucking *grins* at me, and then an even weirder thing happens.

The anger burning in my chest stalls then arrows downwards, morphing into a different kind of heat low in my belly, lower even than that.

Maybe it's the warmth and humour shining in the depths of his dark brown eyes, or maybe it's the way

DELILAH DEVLIN

his sinful lips kick up in one corner that makes my mind nosedive into the gutter, imagining all the naughty things I want him to do to me with his mouth. Whatever it is, I don't expect what he says next.

"Trinity said you had a mouth on you." He chuckles. "I guess she wasn't kidding."

I narrow my eyes on the newcomer, my lust momentarily forgotten as all my senses go back on alert. "Who are you, and how do you know Trinity?"

His grin broadens, and he nods ever so slightly and pinches the brim of his hat. "I'm Kade, her cousin. She said she tried calling to let you know I was coming to your rescue. You might want to check your phone."

Keeping one eye on my best friend's not unattractive alleged cousin, I fish my phone out of my handbag and see I have four missed calls, two voice messages, and one text. Pressing the phone to my ear, I try to listen to the voice messages, but the noise in the pub is ceaseless and the most I can make out is Trinity's voice saying, "...Ally, I... my cousin... you. Don't... Kade's like... fuck... the morning."

Okay.... Obviously, I'm going to have to listen to that again later.

When I open the text message, a photo of Moron Three pops up, smouldering dark gaze, devilish grin and all, confirming he is who he says he is. Trinity's cousin.

Kade.

148

My rescuer, apparently.

Tucking my phone back in my bag, I let my gaze slide from the top of his worn but cared-for Akubra, down the front of his checkered cotton shirt, faded blue jeans, sensible belt buckle, and polished yet well-used work boots. Kade is definitely not a wannabe cowboy.

He's the real deal.

When I drag my gaze back to his, he has one brow cocked, and his grin has bloomed into a full-on panty-melting, making-me-weak-at-the-knees smile.

Holding his hands out to his sides, he says, "Do I pass muster, or would you like me to turn around so you can check out my arse?" Even through the noise in the increasingly crowded pub, Kade's deep voice carries. All the way to every single one of my sex receptors.

My nipples tighten. My clit pulses. My pussy grows wet, and my thighs clench around the empti-ness between them, hoping, wishing Kade will step up and fill the void.

Please God, yes.

I haven't had sex in a while. Not since my loser ex decided he needed to be a "lone wolf" and ended our relationship. Seeing as he started banging anyone with two legs and a vagina the day after he dumped me, I assumed lone wolf was code for "I want to fuck other women and not feel like a dick about it."

Douchebag.

But what pisses me off the most is how deeply he

made me doubt myself. I mean, I spent most of my twenties working to become the positive, confident woman I am today, so the fact one sorry excuse for a man could inflict such a massive dent in my self-esteem is *really* annoying. But maybe, just maybe, it's time to buff that dent out.

As I look my fill of the big man standing before me, I think I know exactly who to ask for a damn good buffing.

Mirroring Kade's grin, I ask, "Do you wanna get out of here?"

His eyes widen for just a moment, and I don't miss the way his gaze slides down my body and back again, checking me out the way I had him. By the time his eyes meet mine again, they're hooded, almost predatory, and he growls, "Abso-fucking-lutely."

Resting his hand on the small of my back, Kade guides me through the sea of bodies and back towards the entrance. The heat from his palm burns me through my T-shirt, and by the time we hit the street, I feel like I'm on fire. The air outside is muggy, like a storm's brewing, but it's cooler than the oppressive heat of the pub, and I take a much-needed breath.

What the hell am I doing?

"Did you drive in or walk?" Kade asks, steering me down the street, away from the pub and the crowd milling around outside.

"Walked." My voice is soft, subdued by the enormity of what I'm about to do. I don't usually jump into bed with strange men. That's just not who I am. As a sexual submissive, I need to know a man, know I can trust him before I let him anywhere near my body. But I'm sick of always being alone, and *who I am* is getting me nowhere right now.

So maybe it's time to be someone else.

"I'm staying at that boutique hotel just down the street," I add, not so subtly hinting at the close proximity of an available bed.

Kade smiles down at me, and my knees actually wobble, but just as he opens his mouth to reply, a swarm of loud drunken women wearing miniature pink cowboy hats and belting out Dolly Parton's "Jolene" bustles past us. They knock me sideways, and my knees give out completely. But before I get the chance to swear at them for being rude, a thick arm wraps around my waist, and suddenly, I'm nestled against a hard body and—*sweet Jesus!*—an even harder cock.

"Are you all right?" Kade's concern melts the last of my indignation.

I swallow hard. "Uh-huh."

"Good," he says, and I feel the press of his lips against my ear. "Now, the way I see it, sweetheart, we have three options."

"Oh?" I really want to wiggle my butt against his erection, but when he tightens his grip, I instinctively hold still and wait.

Apparently, my submissive side is eager to please him.

"One, I walk you back to your hotel room, and we say goodnight."

I shrug and play it cool, attempting to calm my raging heartbeat. "Meh. What else you got?"

"Two, we find someplace we can eat and talk for a few hours, and then I walk you back to your hotel room and we say goodnight."

"Hmm, not that I'm not tempted, but unless you booked a table two weeks ago, I doubt we're eating out tonight. Besides,"—I reach back and slide my hands up Kade's muscular thighs then turn my head to whisper over my shoulder—"it's not food I'm hungry for."

Kade's grin is wide and wicked. "That just leaves option three," he says, his voice a velvety purr.

"Oh? And what's option three?"

"I take you back to my place, tie you up, and fuck you so goddamn hard you forget your own name."

My entire body shivers with anticipation—a feeling completely at odds with the heated throbbing between my thighs—and I suck down an excited breath.

Kade chuckles. "Three it is, then."

Kade

When my cousin rang me in a panic and asked me to entertain her friend because she'd had to ditch her at the last minute for work, I'd grumbled at her about owing me one. Then I'd done what family does: changed into my nicer jeans and a clean shirt, grabbed my hat, and headed into town. Trinity had texted me the name of the pub, a photograph, and a brief description of her friend—tall, angry, swears like a soldier—so it wasn't difficult to find the woman.

The photo didn't do her justice, but the description was spot on.

Her anger was glorious, and the mouth on her... *fuck*. My cock has throbbed with need from the moment I heard her chewing out those fuckwit townies playing at dress-ups.

Wearing tight blue jeans and a pink T-shirt with "Spurs and Bling, It's a Cowgirl Thing" printed across her perfect tits in scrolling silver lettering, it was easy to see why she'd attracted the attention of said fuckwit townies. But I'm guessing that's all they saw, long legs and a nice rack. They weren't the sort to appreciate a strong woman like Ally, as they'd proven at the first hint of her temper when they'd tucked tail and run.

Me? I like strong. I like smart and confident and independent. I like a woman who knows what she wants and what she doesn't. And it was pretty damn obvious to me from the moment I saw her that what those idiots were offering was nothing she wanted.

Definitely nothing she needed.

And it hadn't taken me long to figure out what that was.

Ally revealed her hand when she let me lead her out of the pub, and again, when that hen party barged past us on the footpath, knocking her into me. Not once did she try to swat my hands away as I'd wrapped them around her body, or swear at me like she had with everyone else. It was almost like her submissive nature had sensed my dominant one, and Ally had settled against me like a contented cat, held still, and let me push my rock-hard erection against her soft arse as I kissed the shell of her ear and murmured my salacious suggestions.

She was eager for me, too. She wouldn't have volunteered the whereabouts of her accommodations so easily otherwise. Or touched my thighs, or blatantly told me she was hungry for something other than food.

Suddenly, I'm thinking it might be me owing Trinity a favour and not the other way around.

"So, where's this place of yours, then?" Ally asks as we climb into my car.

"I own a ten-acre stretch in the next town over. It's only a fifteen-minute drive." Which is fifteen minutes too many that I'm not inside this woman. Sure, I could've taken her back to her hotel and been balls deep already, but I have a hunch my Ally-Cat is a screamer, and I don't want anything inhibiting her tonight. Taking her to my place, where my nearest neighbour is almost a kilometre away, should allow her the freedom to be herself.

Me too.

After a quick stop to buy condoms, we fill the time with idle chit-chat, that sort of nervous talk two people engage in when they're counting down the minutes to showtime and, through no fault of their own, have to keep their hands to themselves. I tell her I breed horses; she informs me she owns a cat. I invite her to go riding while she's visiting; she admits she's never ridden a horse before.

Then, for some completely unfathomable reason, I tell her my cousin thinks I need a wife.

And just as I pull up in front of my house, Ally tells me she's *very* single.

I cut the engine, and we both sit there, silently staring out the windscreen, the air between us thick with expectation. Then the storm that's been threatening all afternoon cracks open the sky and fat droplets of rain start falling, hitting the car with a rhythmic *thud, thud, thud,* quickly increasing in speed and volume until it's almost deafening.

Ally flashes a grin and yells over the noise, "Race you!" Then she's out of the car and running towards the house, undaunted by the deluge of water soaking her to the bone.

It takes mere seconds for me to catch her on the stairs, wrap my arm around her waist, and lift her off her feet. I pin her to my front door, sopping wet and laughing, and kiss the ever-loving hell out of her.

When I take Ally's mouth, the taste of smooth whiskey explodes across my tongue, and suddenly, I'm dying of thirst. I can't get enough of her. But my girl starts to shiver as the cold and the wet overtake her lust, and I have to take care of her first.

"Let's get inside and get out of these clothes," I murmur against her lips.

She fists her hands in my shirtfront and offers me a coy little smile. "I thought you'd never ask."

As soon as the door is open, I toss Ally over my shoulder and head straight for the living room. "Strip," I command, putting the wriggling woman back on her feet. "I'll get a fire going."

Ally toes off her boots. "In the middle of summer?" Her sweet voice holds a teasing lilt, and I can't wait to hear it hitch with passion. Hear her moan.

Make her beg.

"That storm isn't going anywhere anytime soon, Ally-Cat. And your skin is like ice. A fire will take the chill off. Now, do as you're told and strip off those wet clothes."

She grins at me then peels her sodden T-shirt over her head, dropping it to the timber floor with a wet *slap*. "Yes, Sir."

Ignoring the rush of lust filling my veins at the sound of her calling me "Sir", I stare at the mess on my floor before raising my unimpressed gaze to her defiant one. "Hmm… maybe I should call you Ally-Brat."

My unrepentant girl laughs, but when I cock one brow and fold my arms across my chest, she bites her lip and drops her gaze, and my dick hammers at my zipper, demanding release from its denim prison.

But first we need to get warm—dry, at the very least—so I crouch down and make short work of lighting a fire in the hearth. By the time I'm done, Ally is down to her underwear and busying herself draping clothes over chairs. I take a moment to enjoy the view then hang my hat and toe off my boots, setting them near the fire. I strip my shirt off next and hand it to Ally to hang up while I fetch us some towels and the quilt off my bed.

When I return, I find Ally in front of the fire, wringing water from her long blonde hair, shivering as it trickles down her back. I cast aside the blanket, pull her into my arms, wrap a towel around her shoulders, and begin drying her.

"I must look like a drowned rat," she murmurs, her gaze diverted and her mouth pulling south at the corners. "Not exactly sexy."

Not exactly sexy? Fuck that.

I drop the towel and unfasten my jeans, releasing my cock—my very hard, very eager cock. "I beg to differ."

Ally drops her gaze then drops her jaw, and I'd be lying if I said I'm not preening just a little bit. Especially when she sinks her teeth into her bottom lip and whimpers.

I know I'm a big man. At six-feet-four, I'm taller

than the average bloke, a little broader in the shoulders and thicker through the middle. I have big hands, big feet and… Well, you know what they say about men with big feet. But with greying hair, mud brown eyes, and a nose I've broken more times than I can remember, I'm not winning any beauty contests either, so the last thing I want is Ally thinking she doesn't measure up.

Threading my fingers through her still damp hair, I push it away from her face, stare deep into her gorgeous blue eyes, and hide my smile. "You are the sexiest drowned rat I've ever seen." And when a burst of laughter escapes her, I let loose my grin then take her mouth in a slow and torturous kiss. "Beautiful."

"Kade," she moans, the sound hitting me right in my balls. I feel her hands on my hips, urging my jeans down over my arse and thighs, and I growl my approval.

Fuck, she tastes good, and I don't just mean the whiskey lingering on her tongue. Ally is heat and lust, sex and longing and need.

Hunger.

Or maybe that's me.

I don't remember the last time I was with any woman, let alone one as beautiful as Ally. Sure, she's tall and has nice tits, but *fuck*, there's something about her that makes me want to wrap her up and keep her. Something vulnerable in the depths of her eyes, something that begs me to keep her safe. It's the way she touches me, like she's exploring unchartered territory, learning every inch of my body the way I long to learn about hers.

Reaching behind her, I unclasp her bra then tug it free and cup her breasts. Her skin is pale and still slightly damp, but her nipples respond to my touch, hardening against my palms, two perfect pink peaks begging for attention. Breaking away from our kiss, I trail my lips along her jaw and down her throat, across her shoulder, along her collarbone, and down the centre of her chest.

But before I take one more liberty, I ask, "What's your safe word, Ally?" Because I know she has one.

Her eyes flutter open, she audibly swallows then confirms my suspicions. "Banana bread."

I can't disguise my grin. "Seriously?"

Ally shrugs. "What? I hate banana bread. It's not something I'm likely to blurt out for no reason."

"Good point. Banana bread, it is. Now, come here, little cat."

Her smile is blinding, and as I bend and take her breast in my mouth, her quick gasp and sultry moan are like music to my ears. And when I pinch her nipple between my teeth and gently tug on it, I feel her claws dig into my shoulders like she's hanging on for dear life, determined not to fall.

"That feels so fucking good." Her voice is barely a whisper, escaping her mouth on a shuddering breath. I continue sucking and biting her breasts, massaging and plumping them. Then I squeeze them, increasing the pressure until her mouth falls open, her eyes roll back, and her keening cry fills the room. "Kade!"

I press my lips to her ear and snarl, "Bend over the fucking couch."

I pull back to enjoy her whimper and revel in the unrestrained lust I see written across her face, in the blush of colour staining her cheeks and the slight parting of her lips as she whispers, "Yes, Sir."

ALLY

In-fucking-credible!

Thank you, Trinity, for working overtime.

Thank you, douchebag ex, for dumping my arse.

And thank you, powers that be, for sending Kade to my rescue tonight, because *damn*, if this man fucks as well as he kisses, then stick a fork in me because I am done.

Ruined for all other men.

Kade is sexy as fuck. A silver fox with rakish good looks, a rich, velvety voice, and a strong, thick body. And I can't wait to feel that monster he calls a cock deep inside me. Stretching me open.

I turn to face the couch and bend at the waist as instructed, bracing my hands on the seat cushions. "Like this?"

"Exactly like that. Good girl," Kade says, his praise sending warmth of another kind careening through me, making me happy.

I look over my shoulder in time to see him kick

off his jeans and realise he's not wearing any underwear. I'd missed that tiny detail when I was gawking at his enormous dick.

"Eyes front, sweetheart."

"Yes, Sir."

I don't know where this submissive side of me comes from—it's just always sort of been there—but I do know finding someone who understands, someone who gets it, and doesn't make fun or ridicule or take advantage, is as rare as fucking hen's teeth.

Kade gets it, he understands, and I trust he won't take advantage. I trust him because I trust Trinity, because she knows and accepts me for what I am—a kinky bitch who loves being tied up, spanked, fucked, and treated like a pet—and she would never hurt me.

Kade strokes his big hands over my arse, and I can't help but clench up. Not out of fear, mind you, but anticipation. Will he spank me? Won't he? Will he rip my panties off with his teeth? A girl can hope.

"You have the cutest bum. So round. So soft." *Slap.* My arse jiggles, and I hear Kade groan. "So pliant."

My breath saws in and out of my lungs in short excited bursts. The slap on my arse didn't hurt, but it wasn't tentative either. Kade is just warming up.

Slap. His hand lands on the other cheek.

Slap, slap. My arse is starting to burn.

Slap, slap, slap, slap. My skin is tight and hot, my body needy. I arch my back and cry out. "More! Please, more."

"Beautiful," he murmurs, stroking his hands over me again, gently raking his fingernails over my sensitive flesh before slipping one hand between my legs, shifting my lacy underwear aside, and spearing two fingers inside my cunt. My legs quiver, threatening to give out beneath me. Kade speaks again, his voice awed. "So pink. So pretty." One more *slap*. "So wet and so very fuckable."

Before I can respond, Kade hooks his fingers through my panties and slips them down my legs. Then I hear the crinkle of a condom wrapper, and suddenly, the blunt head of his cock is prodding between my thighs. I stay facing forward as commanded, but I can't help the eager little wiggle in my hips as he lines up our bodies and slams home.

"Ally." Kade's voice is pure pleasure, and for a moment he doesn't move. Then he rocks his hips and begins that erotic slide of flesh on flesh, of sex. *Fucking*. "Ally," he groans again. "This is going to be quick and dirty, sweetheart. I haven't had a woman in a very long time, and you're so fucking tight."

"Do it," I beg him. "Take me. Use me. I want this." I push back as he thrusts forwards. "I want you."

"My little Ally-Cat." He anchors himself to me with one hand tightening on my waist and the other fisting in my hair, pulling my head back like he's reining in a wilful horse. "I'm gunna make you scream."

Kade keeps his promise.

He fucks me hard and fast and hits every nerve

ending along the way. I'm so wet I feel it slipping down my thighs, so desperate to come my fingers are ready to tear the couch cushions apart. And when he bottoms out inside me, when he slams his hips against my arse and shouts my name to the heavens, I scream in ecstasy.

I scream so goddamn loud. More than I think I ever have. I feel no inhibition with this man, no reason not to yell and scream and beg for more. Besides, we're in the middle of bloody nowhere with a storm raging all around us. Who's going to hear me?

When Kade pulls out, I collapse on the couch. His warm chuckle follows me. "I hope I didn't wear you out."

"Not a chance."

"Good girl." He strokes my cheek. "Wait here."

Kade disappears for a few minutes then returns with a fresh erection and what looks like a length of satin rope. My interest piques.

"Stand up, little cat, and turn around."

I like Kade's pet name for me. Hell, I like a lot of things about this man. As I climb to my feet and face away from him again, I think about what he said earlier, how Trinity said he needs a wife.

And I told him I was available.

"Hands behind your back."

Kade's voice is rough and sexy, a deep masculine rumble I would happily listen to for as long as we both shall live. He sweeps my hair over my shoulder and out of his way then gathers my wrists in one large hand and wraps the satin cord around them, binding them securely.

"Our first time was over too fast for my liking, sweetheart." He presses a kiss to my shoulder, nuzzles against my neck. "This time will be slower. This time you don't come until I say so. Understand?"

"Yes, Sir."

"Good girl." With one last slap on my tender arse, he positions us so he's sitting on the couch and I'm straddling his lap. I watch him roll a fresh condom over his huge erection—*sexy as fuck*—then gasp as he lifts me up like I weigh nothing at all, notches his cock against my pussy, and slides home.

"Oh my God!" If I thought Kade was big before, it's nothing compared to what I think now. This new position, this new angle is... *everything*. I'm full to the point of pain, but it's a hurt I crave. Wetness gushes from my body, and we're not even moving. Then Kade cups my aching arse cheeks and slowly lifts me up and down and up and down, rolling his hips so the head of his cock strokes over my G-spot every fucking time. My head lolls back, and his name escapes me on a moan. "Kade."

"I've got you, little cat. I've got you."

Yes, you do.

I feel my orgasm building. I want to spill over the edge, but I also want Kade to control my pleasure. I want to hear his commanding voice giving me permission, want to feel his heated breath on my throat when he orders me to come.

I need a distraction. Something, anything to slow myself down. Like conversation. "Did Trinity really say...you need a wife?"

Kade chuckles, and our bodies bounce together, edging me even closer to orgasm. Staring up at me with his gorgeous chocolate-coloured eyes and broad grin, he says, "She did." He tilts his head to one side, his gaze growing shrewd. "You want the job?"

"Depends. What would the job...entail?" I'm struggling to breathe, every little thrust of his hips pushing the air from my lungs. "What do you want in a wife?"

Breaking neither pace nor eye contact, Kade says, "Well, I like smart women. Strong, too. Beautiful." He moans, and his eyelids shutter. "With blue eyes and long blond hair. And a temper...she has to have a temper." His grin broadens. "And say 'fuck' a lot."

Barely restraining my smile of glee, I ask, "Is that all?"

"Nope. I want a submissive woman...sexually speaking. One who loves...being spanked and tied up and fucked." Then he looks away, like he's thinking. "Hmm... Cooking skills are advantageous but not necessary, and the big one, obviously... Oh, God," he groans and bucks up into me, his breathing as staggered as my own. "She must love riding horses."

Now, I look away and pretend to think, a ruse that would've been more effective had my hands not been tied behind my back. Tapping my finger against my chin really would've sold it. "What if she just loves riding a man,"—I gasp—"who's hung like a horse?"

Kade chuckles again, and the rich sound vibrates down through his body then up through mine. "Where the fuck have you been all my life?"

I shrug. "Queensland."

Kade picks up his pace, and I cry out, the delicious sensations he's wringing from my body making me hungry for more.

Our slow fuck full of tenderness turns brutal. Kade's fingers dig into my hips as he works my body faster and slams us together harder. Our conversation dissolves into grunts and gasping, and what was languid and controlled is now a frenzy of need and wanting.

My head falls back, and my body shakes. I'm so close. So *fucking* close. But I can't come yet. Not until Kade says so.

"Look at me, Ally." Kade's voice is barely a growl. So guttural and demanding. "Don't you dare look away."

I nod my compliance as I return his molten gaze. My body is hot, my skin beaded with sweat. Lightning crashes outside, but it's the storm in my mind and in my heart that's charging the air with electricity.

"Please, Sir. Please, I need to come."

Kade's eyes soften, and he cups my cheek. "Little

cat, you beg so beautifully." He wraps that hand around my throat, restricts my breathing to the bare minimum needed to survive, then grits his teeth and snarls at me. "Come for me, Ally. Come now."

Tears stream down my cheeks as I scream my release. More intense than the last, it takes hold of me entirely and doesn't let go. Shakes me to my core.

Beneath me, Kade still bucks and writhes, thrusting up into me like a man possessed until his own roar of completion threatens to drown out the storm.

He lets go of my throat, and I fall forwards on his chest, both of us sucking down much-needed air. Then I feel the quilt being dragged over the top of us and Kade's hands stroking my body, petting me and offering comfort.

When he finally speaks, his voice is warm but unsure, cautious. "Did I hurt you, little cat? Did I push you too hard?"

I shake my head and snuggle closer, burrowing against his chest. "I liked it."

His chest bounces with a chuckle, and he plants a kiss on top of my head. "In that case, wanna do it again?"

I lift my gaze to his, let him see my smile, my eagerness. My submission. "Abso-fucking-lutely."

SECOND CHANCES

Megan Ryder

How long would she have to suffer alone before she'd paid her debt?

Considering the person to whom she owed the debt was dead, it would probably be until the end of time, and that was a long time to go without a man-given orgasm. Her fingers and toys could only do so much, but they would have to suffice because the only man she wanted in her bed was the one man she could never have.

"Jessie? Hey, are you asleep on your feet? Because I sure as hell wouldn't blame you after three days of branding and castrating the spring calves."

A man's voice penetrated her daydream, and she

blinked to see the object of her fantasies standing in front of her. The dirt, blood, and other assorted detritus of the day, did nothing to detract from the sheer beauty of Slade Donovan. He wasn't beautiful like an Adonis or Michelangelo's David. No, Slade was more of a working man's rugged handsome, with a face and body carved from the granite that the town was named for, eyes like bitter dark chocolate, and dark wavy hair that her fingers itched to run through, especially during passion.

But he was the one man she couldn't have—her best friend, her husband's best friend, and her neighbor.

Instead, she pasted on a smile and ran a hand through her long hair, feeling the sweat and dirt that was caked on her. "Not asleep, not yet. You staying for the dinner after? Earl is catering."

His eyes softened, and he reached out a finger, gently swiping her cheek. "Aw, Jessie, girl. You need to rest. This is getting to be too much for you."

She backed up, pulling away from him, and glared. "I've been handling the ranch just fine. I've got this."

He dropped his hand, his gaze growing distant and formal, the same way they'd been for the past two years since her husband's funeral. "I know that, Jessie. But Mark wouldn't have wanted this for you. Working yourself to death for a ranch on the verge of bankruptcy... You can't save it."

"I have to," she whispered, then turned and

walked away without a backwards glance for fear her heart would betray her.

A COUPLE DAYS LATER, Slade Donovan cursed the Montana spring. Yeah, Spring, his ass—though it wasn't atypical of Montana to have snow into June, and this was only April. However, he was over the cold winter feedings, the worrying about the herd, and the stress over his neighbor, Jessie McAdams, and how she was faring over the long and brutal months. The previous couple of days had only confirmed his fears. Her herd was smaller than before, and she was struggling to hang on to the ranch since her husband's death. Slade had headed out to check for stragglers from his own herd and couldn't help but drift over onto her land, since they shared a boundary, to make sure they hadn't missed any cows or calves on her side. Unfortunately, the storm had come up quick, and he needed to seek shelter until it passed.

Damn, Mark McAdams, his best friend and neighbor. He'd always had the devil's own luck while they'd been growing up, first as a top athlete and popular guy at school, and then meeting and marrying Jessie while away at college. For the five years of his friend's marriage, Slade had kept quiet about his feelings for Jessie. Then Mark rode out one spring day and got caught in a freak spring storm, similar to this one, and his luck ran out.

Mark's good luck hadn't held true with the ranch either; he'd been letting some things slide, including the line cabins built along their property lines, which hadn't been as well-maintained as Slade kept them now. Slade had found him a week after he'd disappeared and had been the one to deliver the news to Jessie. It had been the worst day of Slade's life, edging out Mark and Jessie's wedding day. Since then, he'd tried to help her, tried to be there for her, but the slippery slope Mark had been on with the ranch had only grown steeper, and no matter how hard she worked, Jessie wasn't keeping it together.

He'd tried to make her see reason, to see the reality of her situation, offering assistance where he could. But Jessie had always been stubborn and was determined to keep the ranch going on her own. She'd placed him firmly in the friend zone, relegating him to the role of spectator in the ranch's demise, and the specter of Mark stood between them.

Slade stoked the fire in the stove in the center of the line cabin, grateful they'd stocked them all the previous week with wood and canned goods. Snow swirled the air outside, the flakes growing fatter with every minute. It wouldn't be long before he'd be blind to everything and would have to wait it out.

A noise and a faint movement in the distance caught his eye, and he strained to make out if it was friend or foe. Predator or something else. Slowly, the shape took form and revealed itself to be a horse with a tiny figure huddled on its back.

Shit. He grabbed his fleece jacket. He'd recognize that deep bay gelding anywhere. That was Starry Night, Jessie's horse. What the hell was she doing out in this weather, alone?

DAMMIT, she knew she'd rounded up the herd too early for branding. She'd had to if she'd wanted the help of her fellow ranchers, most of whom thought it was ridiculous she was trying to keep the ranch going on her own since her husband's death. But she'd promised Mark, and honestly, she had nowhere else to go. Deep inside, she also knew if she left, she'd be leaving Slade Donovan behind, and she couldn't bear not seeing him, even if she couldn't have him. Maybe if there came a day that he found his special woman and settled down, the pain would take over and she'd finally have the guts to walk away. She'd need to. Though, the bank might take the ranch long before that happened, forcing her into a new reality.

But that wasn't her problem today. No, right now, she was out looking for calves born after the round-up, in particular one stubborn pregnant cow that had evaded her hands and whose absence hadn't been noticed until after the round-up. Now, Jessie was hunting her down while the hands were taking the rest of the herd to the spring pastures.

She shivered in her fleece coat and eyed the threatening clouds. Dammit. It better not be anything more than a spring squall. She didn't want to be stuck out here if the squall turned into something worse. She should probably turn back now. A smart woman would do that, but that damned cow was the first one she'd seen born when Mark had brought her here as a bride, and she wasn't going to give up looking up unless she had to.

A few flakes started swirling in the air around her, and she sighed. Of course, that was her luck. The smart thing to do would be to head for home. She reined the horse around but scanned the valley one last time and spied movement in a cluster of brush, a brown flash and a low sound, not too far down the valley floor. She had come too far to ignore it. She kneed the horse and headed down the hill to the calf, ignoring the snow coming down heavier with every hoofbeat.

By the time she reached the calf and the dead momma cow, the snow was coming down fast and furious, and it wouldn't be long before everything was covered. Sight would be limited soon; hell, it already was, and she needed to get her ass somewhere safe and warm, not to mention the calf and her horse. She racked her brain trying to think of where she could go for safety. She was too far from the ranch house or outbuildings and too damn far from Slade's property, too. Her best chance to get through the storm safely was to make for the line cabins in the valley. Hopefully, her foreman had made sure they were stocked and maintained, as she had requested before he'd bailed on her. A cabin would give her some shelter, if nothing else.

She threw the weak calf onto the horse, mounted behind it, and steered her horse toward the cabins, praying she'd make it there in time.

SLADE BOLTED OUT of the cabin and grabbed the horse's bridle. "Jessie! What in the hell are you doing out in this weather?"

"I could say the same to you, Slade. Why are you here?" Her teeth were chattering hard, and her lips were blue. She was hunched over a brown shape on the saddle in front of her.

"What do you have there? A calf?"

"His mother was killed by a wolf, I think. Or maybe she died and scavengers got to it. But they didn't get the baby. Take him inside, quickly. I'll get my horse stabled." Her tone was surprisingly strong, but he already knew he was going to ignore her.

He grabbed the calf, which kicked weakly but subsided quickly. Damn, he hoped this baby made it, or Jessie would be all torn up inside. She'd always had a soft spot for these little ones. He rushed the calf inside and laid it out on a blanket by the iron stove then headed back outside to find Jessie already leading her horse toward the shelter where his horse was stabled. He brushed her hand aside.

"Go inside. You're too cold for this. Check on the baby, and I'll take care of your horse. I brought some milk replacement in case I found calves. It's in my bags next to the door."

She must have been colder than he'd thought because she only nodded and headed inside. After taking care of the horses and making sure they were settled with hay and water, he went inside. Jessie was settled on the floor on top of a blanket, with another two blankets wrapped around the calf and herself. She looked up at him with her large dark eyes that always seemed to peer into his soul.

"I found your milk replacement. It's lucky you brought it. Why did you have it with you?"

He stripped off his coat and gloves, avoiding her gaze. "I was out looking for orphaned calves, like you, I assume. I didn't know if some of them might need to be fed, but I carry replacement with me in case of emergencies."

She cursed under her breath. "I should've thought of that."

He squatted next to her, knowing he was tempting fate, but he figured he'd be tempting far worse over the next day or so while they were stuck in this cabin. "Don't beat yourself up. Most ranchers or cowboys don't carry it. I only started doing that last season when I lost a calf because I didn't have any with me. I can't really stock our line cabins with it, so I carry it instead."

She avoided his gaze, instead focusing on the calf who was busily nursing, which was a good sign. "Well, he's certainly glad for it. He's a strong little guy, thank goodness. You still didn't answer me about why you're here."

"I drifted over onto your property while checking for my own cows. Wanted to see if any calves went missing during your roundup."

Her gaze drifted up to his, guilt written on her face, then she glanced away. "Our herd has gotten smaller. I had to sell off more cows than I would've liked last season to keep up with the bills."

He let out a breath. "Why didn't you come to me?"

She jerked hard and glared at him. "For what? What could you have done? What could anyone do? Tell me to sell? Believe me, I've heard that from just about everyone. The bank, the other ranchers… Everyone wants a piece of the ranch. But I promised Mark."

"He wouldn't want you to kill yourself over this ranch, Jessie. No one would. Ranching is a tough business for anyone."

"But especially for a woman, right? I never thought you'd be sexist," she said, her voice bitter and biting.

He nudged her chin up with two fingers, ignoring the zing of awareness that darted through him at the connection. "For *anyone*, Jessie. And if Mark demanded that you do this, he was wrong. He was barely keeping it afloat. You deserve more."

"What else can I do?" Her voice was barely a whisper, and his heart clenched at the thought of her leaving Granite Junction and finding someone else, somewhere else, far from him.

He swallowed hard, vowing to put his own feelings aside for her. "You could do anything you want. You're smart, a hard worker, and beautiful. You deserve the best of everything. Not a failing ranch and sixteen-hour days with all that worry and stress."

The calf finished his bottle and started rubbing all over her, drenching her with his milk-soaked face.

Slade quickly grabbed the little guy and headed for the door. "Get the door, quick."

Jessie scrambled to her feet and opened the door, still looking a bit shocked. "You can't put him outside. He'll freeze."

"He'll be fine with the horses. Get changed. You'll find some clothes in my saddlebag. Be right back."

And he made his escape, praying the calf wouldn't have any accidents before he got him to the fenced-in barn area.

How could today have gone so wrong? Or maybe it had gone right? It was closing in on the anniversary of Mark's death two years ago, and she was already thinking of cheating on him with his best friend. But was it really cheating if she was a widow and the object of her desire was also single? Hell, she deserved a man-given orgasm, considering all the shit she'd put up with over the past few years, literally and figuratively. She would never have considered straying from their vows under any circumstance, but now, she was lonely. She couldn't mourn her husband forever. Her friends were right about that. Plus, Mark wouldn't want her to be alone forever. He'd want her to move on.

What would he say if he knew she wanted Slade with every fiber of her being? That she fantasized about him every night, the images so real that she could almost feel him in her bed, feel the heat of his bronzed skin and powerful, corded muscles under her fingertips, and the power of his thrusts as he drove deep inside her. Hell, she could come from her dreams alone. She didn't need her vibrators or her trusty rabbit, which was good because she'd long ago run out of batteries and hadn't had a chance to replace them in weeks. Her memory and fantasies were enough to get her off these days, with a little help from her fingers.

Now, she was stuck at this cabin in a snowstorm with the object of her fantasies, and she couldn't help but think it was fate, or maybe Mark, telling her it was time to move on, before she had to sell and leave Granite Junction forever. But before she left, she could have a memory to treasure for all time. If she had the guts to reach out and take it.

Slowly, she unbuttoned her milk-soaked shirt and tossed it on the cot, her decision made.

. . .

GOD, he hated bottle-feeding calves. Sure, they were adorable in an awkward, teenager, klutzy endearing way, but they were so demanding, looking for more milk and seeking it everywhere. They were the messiest critters. Once Slade made his escape and got the calf settled, he stood outside the pen to ensure the little guy snuggled into the hay bed Slade had made for him. He was a like a puppy, all milk-drunk and cuddly. The horses were less than impressed but were used to calves. They would tolerate him.

Convinced all was well, Slade knew he had to go back inside, to the one woman he so desperately wanted to spend time with, yet knew he shouldn't. Jessie, his best friend's wife. God, he'd stroked himself off to her more times than he could count, more in the past two years since he'd spent so much time with her, helping her around the ranch, just the two of them since Mark's passing, and his dreams had become more vivid of late. His buddies at the bar couldn't understand why he wouldn't make a move. Two years was more than enough time, and she had been seen having dinner with Jerry from the feed store, on what was clearly a date, so she was ready to move on. Why not with him?

Because it felt like a betrayal of his friendship, and he couldn't do that to Mark even though he wanted Jessie and knew he could make her happy. However, she deserved a better life than that of a rancher's wife. She'd had that and was probably sick of dealing with ranching. She should free herself from those chains. He was never leaving. It was in his blood, a part of his heritage. She had too much to live for to be tied down to a ranch or this small town.

He opened the door to the cabin, praying that she had fallen asleep while he was out with the calf.

Jessie turned from the iron stove, draped in a blanket. Then she dropped it, leaving her in nothing but her sun-kissed skin.

THE COLD WIND and snow swirled around Slade, making Jessie's skin prickle and her nipples pucker. She shivered but refused to grab the blanket and cover up, especially not when she saw his hot gaze take her in greedily, like a thirsty man who hadn't had anything to drink in days. Unfortunately, he was standing in the doorway, letting in the freezing air, and she might freeze to death before he got his ass in gear, completely ruining her seduction efforts.

"Could you close the door before I become a block of ice?"

He cleared his throat and pulled the door shut, never taking his eyes off her, still looking a bit like he'd swallowed his tongue. It was a heady feeling to see the desire written on Slade's face, the pure want in his expression. It was the biggest turn on she'd ever felt in her life, barring the actual touch of a man.

Slade finally looked away, deliberately taking off his jacket and hanging it on the hook by the door. He then laid his gloves on the small table there and paused, taking a deep breath. Finally, he slowly pivoted and faced her, his gaze never leaving her face.

"Jessie, what are you doing?"

She gathered her courage, which was failing every second he remained by the door and refused to truly look at her. She lifted her chin. "I'm doing what I should've done a long time ago."

He shook his head, but she noted the tension in his body, the fists clenched by his sides, the shoulders rigid and high, and the way his jaw tightened. "We can't do this. No matter how…"

"No matter what, Slade?" She stepped closer to him, forcing him to look down at her as she left the blanket on the floor behind her, her security, even as every ounce of her pride screamed at her to grab the blanket and give up. "Mark is gone, and I need to move on. I'll never forget him, but it's time. And I think you know that. I think you want me, or have I misread the situation?"

Doubt crept into her voice, and her fingers trembled against her sides, so she clenched her fists, her nails digging gouges into her palms as she waited with bated breath for his answer.

His dark eyes studied her, as if searching for an answer to a question he refused to put into words. After several long minutes passed, she couldn't take it any longer. Her head dipped, and tears stung her eyes.

She stepped backwards and blindly reached for

the blanket on the ground, squatting and feeling for it, praying he couldn't see the wetness already streaking down her cheeks. "Never mind, Slade. I was wrong. I won't make this mistake again."

His feet scraped on the plank floor, and he groaned and grabbed her arms, gently lifting her and pulling her into his embrace. He tilted her chin, forcing her to look at him. "I have to know you're sure, sweetheart. Because if we do this, I'm never letting you go. I won't let you go. I'm not strong enough."

She sucked in a breath at the longing in his voice and nodded. He stared at her for a long moment, as if giving her one last chance to change her mind, and then nodded. He crushed his lips to hers, and the kiss was everything she'd ever thought it would be, and like nothing she'd expected.

SLADE COULDN'T BELIEVE he finally had Jessie where he'd always wanted her—in his arms. Her naked body pressed against his and her mouth opened beneath his, her tongue sweeping into his mouth to tangle with his. She clutched the front of his shirt, tugging at the buttons, trying to open it. Finally, the material separated as buttons flew, and his skin was exposed to her gaze and fingers. She pressed a hot kiss to his chest, and he groaned, almost unable to believe this was really happening, that this wasn't a dream, and he wouldn't wake up to find his release staining his sheets again.

She spread her hands under his shirt, but he grabbed them. "Hang on a minute."

Her head lifted, surprise widening her eyes, and he grinned. "I can't afford for you to ruin any more of my clothes, darlin'."

He quickly took off his shirt and stripped off his jeans until he stood naked in front of her, his erection bobbing. She licked her lips as her gaze trailed down his body. Then she reached for him, but he took her hands and led her to the cot, laying her down on her back and coming over her.

"Not this time. It would be over almost before we started, and I've been dreaming of this for two years."

She pouted for a moment. "I'm the one who started this."

"And I'll finish it. On my terms, baby."

He lowered his head and took her lips in a deep, passionate kiss that had her arching into his body within seconds, her heart pounding against his chest. He swept his hand down her side, and she giggled into his mouth.

"Ticklish, Jessie? Maybe a little pain is more your style."

He tweaked her nipple, and she gasped, twisting into his hold.

Slade kissed his way down to her breasts. So many times, when they'd been working, he'd imagined what they'd look like under those flannel shirts and T-shirts she wore while working the herd. He paused above them, staring at the creamy flesh topped with rosy-pink nipples, jutting proudly at him.

"Jessie, baby, you're so goddamned beautiful," he breathed.

Bending down, he sucked one into his mouth, laving it with his tongue until she writhed under him. Jessie's legs twined around him, and she arched her hips against him. He lowered his hips onto hers to hold her in place. His cock nestled in the warm place between her thighs, but he wasn't ready for the final act, not just yet. He switched to the other side and loved on the tip, tormenting it, the sound of her moans providing encouragement. With her head thrown back, she gasped and pleaded for him to take her. She buried her fingers in his hair, and her nails lightly scored his scalp.

He let go of her nipple with a light pop and grinned up at her. "Still with me, Jessie?"

She stared down at him, her gaze heavy-lidded and dazed with passion.

Yeah, this is what he'd been fantasizing about for years. He kissed his way down her body until he reached her mound.

Her eyes widened. "Slade, what are you...?"

"Shh, Jessie."

He placed a kiss at the top of her slit, and then slid his tongue through her folds. Her head thumped down on the pillow. Her eyes rolled back in her head, and she moaned. He spread her with his thumbs and traced the tip of his tongue all over her. She tasted creamy and rich, and he couldn't get enough. She twisted and rolled inside his hold, and he gripped her tight so she couldn't squirm away from him. He licked her clitoris and inserted one finger, noting how tight she was. Then he gave her a second digit, curving both upward to find her spot. Her back arched up, and she came with a cry, her channel spasming around him.

He continued to lightly lick and stroke her through her climax until she slowly came back down. Scooting upward, he settled next to her until she opened her eyes, her expression languid and loose.

She gave him a smile. "Wow, that was better than I dreamed it would be. But we're not done, are we?" She frowned at him.

"For now, we are. I may have been prepared for orphaned calves, but I sure as hell wasn't prepared for you, Jessie." He groaned as she shifted against him, her leg brushing his iron-hard cock.

She reached down and gripped his cock in her soft hand, giving him a smooth stroke. "I'm protected, and I trust you, Slade. Please."

That was all she had to say. He wasn't going to question her, not when he'd been living like a goddamn monk for the past two years—hell, longer really, not that he cared to admit it. But he needed to tell her; she needed to know he would take care of her. He peered into her eyes, willing her to believe him. "There's been no one else, Jessie. Not for years."

Her eyes widened in surprise, and her mouth opened to ask him a question he wasn't ready to answer. So, he swooped in, kissing her hard and settling over her, his cock at her entrance staving off her words.

He notched himself at her opening and, mindful of her recent orgasm and tightness, slowly pushed inside, letting her adjust to his size. She lifted her hips, begging him to move faster and deeper, then wrapping her legs around his hips to pull him closer. He lifted his head and stared down as he drove all the way inside with one final thrust. She arched her neck and let out a soft cry. He stilled, holding himself deep, waiting for her to adjust. After a few moments, she moved her hips, her hands gripping his arms, and he began to move, both of them falling into a rhythm that seemed as if they'd practiced it forever. As he drove deeper, faster, he kept his gaze on her, staring deep into her eyes, trying to reach for that deep connection he'd never felt with another person.

Suddenly, her eyes closed, and she clenched around him, coming with a loud cry, and he followed her over the precipice, gripping her to him as he emptied himself inside her, the sensation over-whelming him. He sagged against her, his face buried in her neck, while her hands gently stroked his back.

. . .

JESSIE STARED down at the bank papers delivered earlier that day and sipped a glass of whiskey, the last bit that remained of Mark's favorite brand. It seemed fitting to finish off that bottle just as she was about to begin the process of looking for a buyer for Mark's family's ranch. It was time for her to let go of the past. She'd started the process with Slade, and this was the last tie to cut. Now to figure out her next steps. She wasn't close to her own family, so she didn't need to move nearer to them in Washington State. She'd never used her degree before coming to Granite Junction, since she'd only completed a pre-veterinary program. She had always planned on either going to veterinary school or at least getting her technician's license, but she'd married Mark and gotten sucked into being a rancher's wife. It was all she knew. Now, she could figure out what she wanted to do with the rest of her life.

Maybe she would do what she'd been toying with for the past year. Fulfilling her dream of becoming a veterinarian. Mark had laughed when she'd suggested it, asking how could she ever do that, especially once they started having children? Of course, they'd never had those mythical kids, and then Mark had died, leaving her with the ranch and no money or time for vet school. But she'd found she liked working with animals and would miss that when she left the ranch. Selling the ranch would give her the money to pursue that dream.

If only she didn't have to leave everyone else

behind since Montana didn't have a veterinarian program. But what was keeping her here anyway? She'd had her night with Slade, and it had been a memorable one. The next day, they'd gone their separate ways to deal with their herds, and she hadn't seen him since. It had been two weeks. Of course, he'd been busy with his own roundup and branding during that time, so she hadn't expected to see him. She'd used the excuse of her foreman quitting to send a couple of hands while she'd stayed home. He'd sent a thank you message back with the hands, but nothing else.

So, that was it then. She was done. It was time to move on. She had said her goodbyes to Mark, to the ranch, and now to Slade.

She downed the last bit of whiskey and slammed the glass down on the table, the fire of the alcohol burning a path down her throat to her stomach, almost burning away the sting of the tears that threatened. She picked up the pen, and through the tears in her eyes, she focused on where she had to sign.

A slam of a truck door out front made her pause.

"Jessie Marie Haymond McAdams. Get your goddamn ass out here now."

Well fuck, if that didn't sound like Slade. What was he doing here?

She stood, swaying slightly. Maybe she'd had more whiskey than she'd thought. She opened the kitchen door and blinked at the bright sunlight and at Slade standing at the bottom of her porch, his hands on his hips, glaring up at her. What the hell did he have to be angry about? She was the one leaving everything. She was the one he'd ignored for two weeks after the best sex she'd ever had. What the hell was his problem?

"What's my problem?" he bellowed. "Are you fucking kidding me?"

Huh, so she must have said that out loud. Yeah, no maybes about it—she'd had a little too much whiskey. Especially now that she was seeing more than one Slade, and she didn't think he had a twin brother. But if he did, that would make for some interesting fantasies.

"I do not have a twin, and what the hell have you been drinking? Never mind, I can smell it from here. Some of that goddamn whiskey Mark loved." He strode up the steps and gripped her arms, steering her towards the porch swing where he sat her down a little harder than she thought necessary, though she could've done that herself.

"What are you doing here, Slade? I don't think we have anything to talk about." Hurt laced her tone, and she regretted letting him know how she felt.

He pulled her close, his arm draping around her shoulders. "Sweetheart, I just heard you're selling the ranch. Why didn't you tell me?"

"It's not your business." She sighed. "Fine. I can't keep it going anymore. After I started the process, they were supposed to go to you and give you first

189

rights. It's what Mark would've wanted. I'm leaving Granite Junction."

"And what are you going to do? Where are you going?" His tone was neutral, but his body was stiff, his fingers digging into her arm, the only outward sign of his tension.

"I might go back to veterinary school in Oregon or somewhere. There's no option here in Montana, and nothing's keeping me here."

"Nothing?"

She looked up at him, something in his tone giving her hope, but she didn't dare to dream. "What are you saying, Slade?"

"This is your home. You don't have to leave."

"I can't stay here. I have nowhere to live, and I can't go to school here."

He stared out over the fields, his jaw clenching then relaxing. "I talked to Doc Sorenson. Montana State is starting a new program for veterinary medicine with Washington State. You might be able to get in. You might have to live in Bozeman for a while, but you could get your degree that way—if you wanted to stay in Montana."

She held her breath, her heart freezing in her chest. "Do I have a reason to stay?"

He turned his dark eyes on her. "I love you, Jessie. I've always loved you. I'll wait for you forever, if that's what it takes. We'll find a way for you to go to school if you want. But please marry me. Be my wife."

Wetness dropped on her hand, and he used his

thumbs to swipe at her cheeks, tenderness in his expression. "Please tell me you're happy and not sad, sweetheart."

"I love you so much, Slade. I never thought you'd ask. Never thought we'd have our time."

He pulled her close and kissed her. "We'll figure it out together, Jessie. Always."

THE PATIENCE OF UNANSWERED PRAYER

Michal Scott

ELEANOR TAYLOR LAY on her side, kinks knotting her back, cramps burning her thighs. Her muscles strained with each attempt to ease her discomfort. Instead of relief, the movement tightened the rope pinning her arms to her body. The blanket beneath which Sheriff Radcliffe concealed her smelled of horse sweat. Its scratchy wool surface set her cheeks afire.

Dirt coated the cloth he'd stuffed into her mouth. She moaned, unable to avoid swallowing the grit now smeared across her teeth and tongue. Afraid she'd wretch, she raised her head, an action that forced the grimy gag further down her throat.

"Keep still, you uppity mulatto bitch."

She shuddered at the menace in Radcliffe's tone. The same menace glinted in his icy blue eyes when he'd entered her cell and tried to violate her. He'd covered her mouth, but she'd sunk her teeth into his hand, eliciting a satisfying pain-drenched yowl from the bastard. A well-placed kick to the balls had laid him low. His groan had flooded her huntress spirit with joy.

If his deputy hadn't rushed in, she'd have gotten away.

The coppery tang from Radcliffe's blood renewed her desire to be the hunter, not the hunted. Tapping carefully into that desire had enabled her to thwart the hostilities all independent Black business owners faced in this post-Reconstruction era. Acting on that desire now, however, could lead to her death. She had to find another avenue of escape before that desire resurfaced and revealed what no one should know about her.

"Seems your fears about the jail being overrun by her foes was misplaced, Sheriff."

Radcliffe snorted. "Better safe than sorry, Jim. Something could've happened before we got her on the stage in the morning."

The sounds of horse hooves clopping, drunken laughter, and saloon music had faded long ago. Only chirruping crickets, croaking bullfrogs, and Sheriff Radcliffe's lies penetrated Eleanor's covering. Where were they taking her?

The wagon wheels creaked with every rut they

hit. Eleanor wheezed, desperate for fresh air. Nausea roiled at the base of her throat. Would she die choking on her own vomit? Fear squeezed her chest as *yes* flitted through her mind like a lightning bug.

The wagon lurched to the right. Her nausea intensified.

"Mind how you go there, boy. We don't want to be accused of mistreating the prisoner."

Being arrested on false charges didn't count as mistreatment? How about being abducted by ones sworn to uphold the law? Eleanor's agony mirrored that of Christ's on the cross.

My God, My God, why hast thou forsaken me?

She moaned, her spirit smothered by despair. The pressure at the small of her back eased only to be followed by a sharp jab to her spine.

"Shut up, damn you," Radcliffe snapped. "Your days of troubling me will soon be over."

"What was that you said, Sheriff?"

"Thank God this trouble'll soon be over. We'll have delivered her safe and sound to the county seat tomorrow."

"Safe and sound," Deputy Jim Flyte said. "Thank the good Lord."

His tone, full of innocence and ignorance, penetrated Eleanor's cloth prison and killed all hope that he'd be of any help. She stifled a groan lest her tormentor kicked her again. Flyte was too young to know that safe and sound to Sheriff Hobart Radcliffe meant only one thing: Eleanor's death.

. . .

SOMETHING SINISTER WAFTED in the still night air from the edge of Franklin Adams's property. The low growl from the wolf by his side signaled the animal had detected it, too.

"Too quiet, eh, Zeb?"

The wolf tensed as if in agreement.

Franklin sucked in a lungful of warm Oklahoma summer air and scanned the sky. Too quiet like that night a week ago when eight sheet-shrouded night riders thought they'd scare him off his land. No jigaboo had money for a spread like this, they'd shouted. None should be allowed to have one outside of the Black townships anyway. Calls to tar and feather and ride his nappy-headed ass out on a rail followed.

Steel from Franklin's Winchester and the attack of Zeb's wolf pack had put the fear of God into those shivering cowards. All fled screaming into the night, bruised, bloodied, and bullet-ridden. Surely, they hadn't come back for a second try? Although many a drunk might grow brave and stupid and forgetful, if they let enough time pass and consumed enough whiskey.

A breeze troubled the leaves of the oak in the front yard. Birdwings fluttered anxious sounds into the air.

Yep. Someone was out there.

Three someones.

From their scent, two were male and the third female.

Franklin frowned. What kind of clown would bring their woman on a night ride? What kind of a woman would go? Foolish question. Gender hadn't prevented his former master's wife from being as malicious as her husband.

Franklin sucked his teeth. He'd long given up on finding a love he'd give his all to protect. If he'd ever found her, he'd never expose her to possible danger.

"Guess I'd best check things out, Zeb."

Zeb's ears pricked up. He tensed his limbs, ready to go.

"No. You stay here in case their presence is some sort of diversion."

Zeb sat but remained alert, eyes scanning the rolling yard before them. Zeb and the rest of the pack could handle anyone foolhardy, drunk, or just plain stupid enough to attack the house.

Franklin knelt beside the wolf that had adopted him into his pack five years ago. Zeb had been stalking some cattle in Franklin's pasture. He'd caught the wolf in his rifle sight. The animal bared his teeth and faced him down. Their gazes locked. A rush of recognition passed between the animal before him and the animal within him. He'd lowered his rifle and let the wolf retreat.

Like had called to like.

More accurately like had called to almost-like.

Franklin stripped off his clothes, stretched his

arms, then crouched on all fours until hands yielded to paws, nails became claws, smooth ebony muscle transformed into black fur. Fully transformed, he sniffed what his human intuition had sensed.

With a final shake, he loped into the night toward the creek and the three people who'd soon learn how Franklin dealt with trespassers.

THE SCRATCHY BLANKET LIFTED. Cool air swirled over Eleanor's heated flesh. Alarm squeezed her gut and summoned the bitter tang of bile up her throat.

Rough hands pulled her across a coarse wooden surface. Splinters pricked through her petticoats and stockings. Her boots connected with the ground, but her knees buckled. She fell, turning her head in time to avoid a face full of grass. She looked up at Radcliffe glaring down on her.

"I've got to relieve myself, Jim. Take her over to the creek and let her get a drink. We've a ways to go yet."

He strode away while Flyte gentled Eleanor to her feet.

She prayed Flyte would ungag her quickly, prayed her gut was right that he wasn't party to whatever Radcliffe had planned.

Flyte pulled down the gag. "He's going to kill me," she rasped, her mouth free of the loathsome muzzle. "You have to stop him."

"Kill you?" Flyte blenched. "He's done this for your safety."

"Taking me the long way round to Darlington City in the dead of night is for my safety?"

"A mob was waiting to lynch you."

"You know that's not true. Radcliffe trumped up these charges against me to put me at his mercy."

"Gordon Daniels brought the charges against you."

"At Radcliffe's urging. Daniels is ex-Confederate and can't cotton any Black—man or woman—doing better than Whites."

"Why would the sheriff do that? He's an ex-Yankee who hates confederates like Daniels."

"Radcliffe hates me more. He wants revenge on me for rebuffing his attentions."

"I can't believe—" Flyte paused, then looked thoughtful. A frown filled his face. "Yet…"

His hesitation gave her hope. Her gut tensed, and her heart beat until her chest hurt.

"You know full well taking me from jail is either foolishness or mischief."

The cock of a gun hammer turned them both in the same direction. Radcliffe aimed at her and fired. The shot burned its way into her shoulder, knocking her to the ground onto her back.

A second shot shattered the night silence. Through pain-drenched tears, she saw Flyte whirl, stumble backwards, and collapse with a splash into the creek.

Eleanor lay spent, her shoulder warmed by her blood, her chest no longer tight with fear. Above, the moon shone through a black canopy of leaves. The smell of creek water, crisp and clean, filled her lungs. She'd never imagined where she would die, but a place of beauty like this was as good as any.

Radcliffe's grin loomed over her.

She stared into the barrel of his gun then closed her eyes as surrender seeped through her.

Father into thy hands I commit my spirit.

A peace descended upon her mind, the peace that passeth all understanding spoken of in the Bible. Although feeling peaceful at this moment made no sense.

Neither did the screaming, cursing and snarling that rent the air.

FRANKLIN CROUCHED HIDDEN in the tall grass. The smells of oil and sulfur assaulted his nostrils. Echoes of the two explosions that ripped the night apart still played in his ears. The first body thudded against the ground. The second splashed into the creek. Moonlight glinted off the shooter's gun and chest. Franklin recognized the metal of a sheriff's badge.

The sheriff stalked over to the body sprawled beside the creek bank.

A Black woman's body.

The cur gloated and pointed his gun barrel at her unmoving form.

Franklin's upper lip lifted over his incisors. He growled and leapt straight for the sheriff's throat. The man's horrified cry yielded to stuttered curses as he writhed in the grip of Franklin's jaws. Warmth from the man's blood fueled Franklin's indignation. Flesh and bone yielded to canines and incisors. The crunch of cartilage sounded lovely in Franklin's ears.

Lithe and lean in his wolf form, he still carried the heft of his human two-hundred-and-fifty pounds. The sheriff convulsed beneath Franklin, slumped, then stilled. Life flowed in the villain's veins but wouldn't for long. The merciful thing to do would be to finish him off before some other predators made a meal of him.

Franklin felt nothing akin to mercy.

He shifted to human form then turned his attention to the woman.

He froze with recognition.

Eleanor Taylor.

She ran the dry goods store that gave lousy Reb Daniels's overpriced mercantile a run for his money.

Blood drenched the right side of her blouse. A murmur disturbed her lips. He cupped the back of her head and leaned closer to hear her whisper.

"Father, into thy hands I commit my spirit."

Franklin clenched his teeth. He'd never read much of the Bible, but he recognized those words from the New Testament.

And when Jesus had cried with a loud voice, he said,

Father, into thy hands I commit my spirit: and having said thus, he gave up the ghost.

Anger, bile-bitter, roiled in Franklin's throat. He took Eleanor into his arms then stood. She weighed nothing at all. Her battered bosom heaved up and down on wheezy breaths, the biblical plea still on her lips. Life flowed strong in her veins.

Through his rage, Franklin gazed at her.

"You may have given God your spirit," he growled, "but I'm damned if you're giving up the ghost."

He cradled her with the warmth of his naked body and stalked back to his homestead.

Zeb and others from the pack greeted his return with joyous howls, approving sniffs, and a circling welcome-home dance. Each time Franklin returned from the trail smelling of sweat and cows and humans, their wolf-like ritual filled him with the sense of family, which slavery had stolen.

Cubs rolling in the grass and nipping at one another stilled their play at his approach. Their mothers lay relaxed but alert not far away. Franklin strode past them, without a nod or even a sniff of acknowledgment. He had only one thing on his mind.

Saving the woman he carried.

Zeb trotted down the porch steps and studied the prize in Franklin's arms.

Franklin nodded behind him. "There's something for you by the creek if you've a mind for a snack."

Zeb and the rest of the pack ran off in that direction.

Franklin carried Eleanor into the house and laid her on the bed. He peeled away her blood-soaked blouse and chemise to examine her wound. A through and through.

Thank you, Jesus, for small mercies.

Franklin gathered a basin, hot water, soap, and towels and set to ministering to her.

"Father, into thy hands I commit my spirit," she continued to whisper.

He finished dressing her wound then gazed upon her. It never ceased to amaze him how many colored folk—especially women—put their faith in this supposedly all-knowing, ever-present being. Franklin had little time for church or the White man's God, but he did honor the power of ancestral spirits.

"How come Your loving God always does so poorly by His children?"

He shook his head and picked up the basin and bloody towels.

Well, what else could be expected from a parent who'd let his own child be crucified?

So, this was how one got to heaven in the arms of a beautiful Black angel. Eleanor had made a game of memorizing images of blackness from the Bible. A description from the Book of Revelation surged to the fore.

His head and his hairs were white like wool, as white as snow; and his eyes were as a flame of fire.

This had to be heaven. Where else but heaven would she find a fine Black angel with hair like wool —not white, but black with threads of gray—and with wonderfully hairy arms to escort her into the next life?

No. This had to be heaven. She'd never experienced this kind of ecstasy burning between her thighs on earth.

A different kind of fire burned along her shoulder. She hissed against the pain. Pain in heaven? Perhaps the transition from the earthly to the heavenly came with pain at first. Like having a tooth pulled. Ache and pang overwhelmed until a peace settled.

Like the peace of surrendering to the patience of unanswered prayer.

Her angel sat and studied her. The words of Jesus often intoned at funerals came to her.

In my father's house there are many mansions: if it were not so, I would have told you. I go to prepare a place for you.

Was this angel sizing her up for the mansion Jesus had prepared for her?

His gaze illuminated the places in her soul where loneliness hid. The light from his eyes dispersed her feelings of unworthiness. A feeling of blessedness filled the void loneliness and unworthiness had left behind.

Another flash of pain streaked across her shoulder, but this time, a flash of pleasure shot to her groin as well.

Bane and blessing, pain and pleasure, by the cross are sanctified;

Peace is there that knows no measure, joys that through all time abide.

How could the writer of that hymn have known so exactly the experience of heaven without having died? Women knew the joy of death when their sex button was pushed just right. Eleanor's was being pushed right now.

Pushed just right by the gaze of a Black angel.

No more sighing, no more sorrow, no more seeing through a glass darkly. She was face to face with the splendor of heaven in this fine example of Black angelic presence. Truly no eye had seen nor ear heard nor mind conceived what God had in store for those who loved Him. Heaven was more heavenly than she'd ever imagined.

She reached up and touched the face of her angel. A soft fuzz coated his jaw. Her fingers played across his broad full lips.

"Greet me with a holy kiss, angel."

FRANKLIN FLINCHED. Her fingers on his face stirred a longing in his heart. A longing he experienced whenever he observed the pack with their mates. A longing that could be satisfied only by a human she-wolf, thus a longing he'd carry to the grave since he lived among humans or full wolves.

Her slender hands held his cheeks possessively, drew him to her, and pulled his mouth onto hers.

He moaned against the captivity of her lips. She'd mistaken him for an angel but bestowed a kiss that had nothing to do with holiness.

Her tongue lined the seam of his lips, insisting on admittance, which he willingly granted. The sweet taste of vanilla contrasted strangely with grit as her tongue swept the confines of his mouth. He angled his head left, and she tilted hers right as their mouths struggled for dominance. When he went right, she countered left. Their fit was perfect.

He took her in his arms, surrendering to her while seeking to conquer her.

She smoothed her fingertips up his arms, down his chest, across his belly, along his inner thighs. His naked flesh quivered beneath her touch. His cock pulsed as she captured his penis and deftly stroked him to hardness.

"Angel," she whispered against his mouth. "Dear angel. Share with me all the joy of heaven."

Franklin gritted his teeth and stilled her hand. A cold sweat broke out across his temple. With strength he hadn't known he had, he rose from the bed, gave her hand a gentle pat, then covered her with the blanket.

"You need to rest now."

"No, angel. No." She pulled him back to her side. "Satisfy me as only heaven can."

She placed his hand between her legs then coaxed his fingers into the fragrant wet warmth there.

Franklin's heartbeat stuttered.

"Please, angel," she whispered. "Please." Delusion laced each breathy syllable she spoke.

Franklin's chest throbbed once more with the pangs of mate craving. He'd never expected to experience a desire this strong. This was as close to mating as he'd ever get. He exhaled a long hard breath.

Slowly and steadily, he thrust then withdrew his fingers then thrust them again into her welcoming sex. Her honey-scented arousal, surprisingly like that of the she-wolves in heat, filled his lungs. Her vagina gripped his fingers with amazing force.

Franklin closed his eyes and imagined those muscles around his cock, imagined her core surrounding him with her warmth. He groaned, his groin painfully tight. He crooked his fingers inside her harder and faster and prayed she'd come quickly.

"Yes, angel. Oh yes. Thank you, thank you, thank you."

Her chest heaved in time to her rapid pleading. Her voice hitched higher and higher until her gratitude rang through the air in cries of delight that wrung similar ecstasy from him.

She collapsed against the bedding, her smile serene.

"Thank you, angel."

She gathered his fingers in both her hands and kissed each one.

Franklin gulped air through his mouth. The smell of her arousal invited him to go against his human nature, goaded him to succumb to his animal instincts and take her.

He shuddered, stood, then staggered away from this woman and the heated craving she incited.

He entered the barn and flung himself into an empty stall, buried his nose into the smell of horse and cow and hay and manure, and gave himself to the cold comfort of his own hand.

Relieved but far from satisfied, he lay on his back and engaged in a fantasy that had sustained him on every dusty mile he'd ridden driving cattle to Cheyenne or Abilene, the fantasy that layered soul-mate significance upon the smiles and teasing Eleanor Taylor exchanged with him each time he'd come into her store.

The fantasy of him and Eleanor mated for life.

A beautiful dilemma occupied his bed. He wanted her more than he'd ever wanted anyone, longed for her to want him, too.

But why would she once she learned what he was?

. . .

ELEANOR BLINKED against the sunlight poking at her eyelids. The throb at her shoulder brought back last night's events in a rush.

Most of last night's events anyway.

She struggled to a sitting position and gazed around her. Where was she? How had she gotten here? She pressed a hand to her temple, but clarity evaded her.

Radcliffe had shot her and killed Jim Flyte. Why hadn't he killed her, too? Why was there a sweet soreness between her thighs?

She closed her eyes, repulsed by an unwelcome possibility. No. Her body wouldn't throb with this kind of yearning if Radcliffe had raped her. She pressed a hand between her legs.

No, God. Please don't let that be what happened.

The cabin's front door swung open.

She clutched the blankets to her throat and stared horrified at what might come into the room in answer to her prayer. She trembled, mesmerized at the man standing before her with his arms full of wood.

"Are you back on earth or do you still insist you're in heaven?" he asked.

Heaven. Recollection flooded her senses. Her thighs tensed. Her sex trembled with ecstatic glee.

Oh yes, angel. Thank you, thank you, thank you.

Her Black angel—not Radcliffe—had made love to her.

"I—I know you. You're Adams. Franklin Adams."

He nodded. "And you're generous Eleanor Taylor, who always sets aside supplies for me each time I've returned from a round up. Many thanks for choosing to supply me over a chance to make a quick profit."

He strode to the fireplace and laid the wood in a box. He clapped the dirt from his hands then faced her. "Need some water?"

He went to the table at the side of the bed then pointed to a pitcher and a glass.

She shook her head. "How did I get here?"

"That, Miss Taylor is my question. How did you come to be on my property last night?"

Eleanor pressed herself against the bed's brass headboard. "Sheriff Radcliffe kidnapped me."

"Why?"

"He's in cahoots with Gordon Daniels to take my store. They charged me with theft, but my lawyer has every confidence I'll be proven innocent once we go to court."

"What happens if you don't appear in court?"

Eleanor cringed. The image of poor Jim Flyte falling into the water flashed before her. "They planned that I wouldn't."

The unlatched door slid open, and a wolf trotted in. Eleanor frowned at his studied perusal of her. He let off a low growl, turning Adams in his direction.

Adams's handsome features darkened. He strode to a corner and returned with a revolver.

"You know how to use one of these?"

She shook her head. He cursed, left the room then

returned with two knives. One was the biggest carving knife she'd ever seen in her life.

"Here." He handed her the smaller knife. "Throwing this first may give you a chance to lunge with the other." He placed the carver on her lap. "Don't think when you use it. Go for the stomach. Plunge until it's buried up to the hilt."

He strode toward the door, the wolf at his side.

Dread slithered up Eleanor's throat. "Where are you going?"

"To check on some unfinished business."

Eleanor latched the door behind him then clambered back onto the bed. She hid the knives beneath the pillow then squeezed herself into a corner formed by the bed and the window. She clutched the blanket to her chest, chilled but not, because she was clothed only in a chemise and drawers.

Adams had taken any sense of warmth and security with him.

FRANKLIN SURVEYED the site of last night's attack with dismay. Radcliffe's body was gone. So was the horse and wagon.

Damn it.

Zeb and the males of the pack had come into the barn last night. Franklin had been so focused on getting himself off, he'd paid no attention to the signs and signals they'd been giving him.

He kicked the matted grass where Radcliffe had fallen.

"Should have finished him off. Should have come back here and made sure I'd finished him off."

Now the bastard was gone. If he'd survived the wounds Franklin had inflicted, he'd have headed back to town. The bull he'd planned to spread when questioned about Eleanor's disappearance would fire up every able-bodied bigot who'd listen.

And they'd listen.

Franklin spat.

Of course, they would. That was the way of it when White sparred against Black or man against woman.

Franklin stripped out of his clothes, lowered to hands and knees, then shifted. As a wolf he'd be better able to nose which way Radcliffe had gone.

He gave Zeb a head nod, and together they settled on a scent to follow.

THE LOGS in the fireplace still glowed red, but heat waned as the room cooled with the setting sun. Eleanor crawled from the bed and added two more logs to the fire. She poked and stirred the ashes beneath them. Flame licked wood. The crackle of heated embers accompanied the room's rise in temperature.

She sat on the floor and stared into the fire,

conjuring the warmth of Adams's arms around her, the tenderness of his fingers inside her.

Last night wasn't the first time she'd imagined coupling with the handsome cowboy. Setting supplies aside for him wasn't as selfless an act as he might have supposed. How else could she have seen him otherwise?

She'd counted the days until his return from his cattle drives, imagined him coming one day to her store not for supplies but for her.

Imagined her coming for him like she must have last night.

She'd never experienced the sweet soreness lingering between her legs now whenever she'd self-pleasured herself.

Greet me with a holy kiss, angel.

She'd been delirious, but the angelic encounter had been real. She'd spoken it into existence.

Satisfy me as only heaven can.

And her Black angel had obliged.

But out of mutual desire or one-sided pity?

She looked at her hand and remembered the proof of Adams's yearning beneath her palm, remembered it growing harder as she'd stroked him.

But he'd stopped her.

Perhaps for the best. Resignation weighed on her spirit like a wet wool blanket. Bringing him off wouldn't have satisfied her for long. She needed him buried deep inside her, wanted him deep enough to free the huntress she suppressed. Once set free, how would he have reacted when she orgasmed and—

An explosion shattered the air.

Eleanor screamed and fell to the floor. The poker rolled from her hand. A second explosion wrenched the door from its hinges. Wood splinters showered down on her.

"Thought you'd gotten away, eh, bitch?"

She gawked in horror at Sheriff Radcliffe silhouetted in the doorway. Fading sunlight filtered in behind him. A once-white neckerchief now soaked in blood encircled his throat.

He thrust his shotgun away and withdrew a revolver from his belt.

"Here's as good a place as any to finally put an end to you."

Eleanor clutched her throat. Time slowed. Once more she saw death beckoning for her. Once more the desire to hunt rather than be hunted called to her.

Once more snarls and growls tore through the air.

Radcliffe screamed, yanked to the side by Adams's wolf, its jaws clamped on Radcliffe's wrist. Man and animal rolled away from the gun that had clattered to the floor.

Radcliffe pulled a knife and raised it.

Gunfire pinged in the air. The weapon flew from Radcliffe's hand.

Adams stood in the door, barefoot and clad only in trousers. He pointed Radcliffe's gun in the villain's direction.

"Zeb," Adams called.

The wolf released Radcliffe and backed away; its upper lip curled in a snarl over teeth coated with the sheriff's blood.

The smell of blood called Eleanor's huntress spirit to surface. She gnawed her lip to keep it at bay.

Radcliffe cradled his injured wrist against his chest. "You've got no business interfering here." He pointed with his good hand at Eleanor. "She's a prisoner who shot my deputy then, thanks to your wolf, escaped me."

Adams raised an eyebrow. "Is that right?"

"I'm duty-bound to take her into custody. If you aid and abet her, you're going against the law."

"Do tell? And what if another account contradicts yours?"

"Hers?" A smirk rippled across Radcliffe's face. "Who'd believe her?"

Eleanor's heartbeat pounded in her ears. The answer to his question was all too painfully clear.

No one.

Adams snorted. "I'm not talking about her."

"Who else?" Radcliffe laughed. "You?"

"No, me."

Jim Flyte, arm in a sling, appeared next to Adams. Behind him, four other men glared at the sheriff. One of them in handcuffs.

Gordan Daniels.

"I just wanted her shop," he exclaimed. "I didn't know nothin' 'bout killin' her."

Radcliffe's face took on a ghostly pallor. Flyte stepped aside and let the men behind him take the sheriff out, cursing a blue streak.

Flyte looked at the door's remnants. "Do you need help fixing this?"

Franklin shook his head. "My pack provides more protection than any door ever could."

Zeb growled in confirmation.

Flyte extended his hand. "Thank you for finding me." He looked to Eleanor. "Forgive me for not believing you."

"I'm just glad we both survived him."

Survived. The word ricocheted through her body like a gunshot.

Adams joined her on the floor. She crumbled in a mass of tears and clung to him.

"I don't understand." She hiccupped a sob. "I thought Radcliffe had killed him."

"Flyte had been hit, but like you, not mortally. He floated downriver and sought shelter in my hayfield. Zeb and I found him this morning, got him back to town, got the truth out of Daniels, and hightailed it back here when we couldn't find Radcliffe." Adams's embrace tightened. "All I could think of was you having to fend him off with only knives."

She sank into the hug. Could she trust the concern she heard in his voice? "I might have been able to fight him off, just not with knives."

"How?"

Eleanor pulled back, clasped her hands against

the *no* knotting her stomach, prayed she could trust the *yes* pounding in her heart.

"I—I'm a huntress."

She watched shock brighten his face.

"You're a wolf shifter?"

He knew the coded term. Was that good or bad?

"I might have been able to shift in time to protect myself."

His ensuing silence filled her with anxiety. "How do you know what a huntress is?"

"I get around." He angled his head. "You've known me for years. Why are you sharing your secret with me now?"

How could she not when a chance at the love she'd prayed years for might be hers for the asking? She pried her tongue from the roof of her mouth. "I've longed for us to be together…" She cast her gaze to the floor. Even now the familiar scent of her she-wolf arousal graced the air. "I hadn't the nerve to approach you, didn't dare believe if you knew my secret you would want me."

"No?" he asked.

His chuckle drew her attention to him. She shook her head. "I know the patience of unanswered prayer."

"Do you now?"

Eleanor frowned, confused by the grin on his face and the heated glint in his eyes.

Adams unbuttoned his trousers, kicked them off, then got on all fours.

Eleanor gawked then gazed in wonder as lamp-light played across her black angel turned wolf.

He trotted over to her, nuzzled her hand with his muzzle, then shifted back to human form. He captured her mouth in a searing kiss, then carried her and laid her upon the bed.

"There's no such thing as unanswered prayer," he said in a tone half-laugh, half-growl. "All prayer is answered when the time is right."

Eleanor's heart beat wildly; fear and hope warred in her spirit.

He climbed onto the bed and straddled her. "Is the time right, my huntress?"

"Yes, my Black angel. Yes, the time is right."

She removed her undergarments, lay back, then spread her arms and legs in welcome, grateful the patience of unanswered prayer had finally paid off.

SOMETHING TO TALK ABOUT

Izzy Archer

THE JOB AD WAS UNUSUAL, to say the least. "More than just a nanny..." posted on the grad student bulletin board outside the Psych Department. But at fifty dollars an hour, including room and board, Kristi was more than happy to cook "healthy dinners" and shuttle two little kids back and forth from school in between giving speech therapy to the youngest. This would be the start of making a dent in her student loan payments. Besides, she'd grown tired of the beach scene at UC Santa Barbara. Not that she had time to date while working on her thesis. Hook-ups with aimless surfers, fellow grad students, or often a combination of the two categories, didn't fuel her fire anymore. She had goals and had to ignore her need for companionship and any hopes of hot sex in the near future.

Kristi drove the beautiful San Marcos pass, cutting through the mountains overlooking the Santa Ynez Valley. Hills sprinkled with cows, horses, and the occasional row of grapevines rolled on and on. She came to a tall iron gate, big enough for the entering Ford F-450 with its double-wide horse trailer, and waited as instructed in front of a large sign with gold lettering: *Sunny Creek Ranch*.

Mr. Richards, Senior, was tall, bent over and wiry, with a crinkle of mischief in his pale blue eyes. He met Kristi at the gatehouse, and with gnarled hands gave a firm but warm shake and then a frisky and not-so-subtle look at her backside. The old man hired her on the spot.

"I'm not yer boss though, young lady. I'll bring you down to the office so he can give ya the onceover."

Kristi chuckled. "Does he think he's buying a horse?"

"No, no, sweetheart. He's a good boy. Just a warnin'. He don't talk much, my son. You know, ever since..."

She nodded and smiled, pretending to understand. She was a little nervous, but this old coot made corny grandad jokes the entire way to the stone structure that turned out to be part office and part stable.

"This ain't the main stable. It's just for looks or visiting horses."

"Horses visit?" she asked, giving him a wink.

He held the door open for her and chuckled. "Oh, you'll do fine here, sweetheart."

As Kristi turned to enter the office, a force stepped forward, blocking her path. A tall man with wavy dark hair, who stood at least a full foot taller than Kristi without the giant white straw hat he wore, was clean-shaven and sported a dress shirt tucked into crisp dark jeans. Her gaze dove to his waist, punctuated by a large gold belt buckle, the kind that looked more like an award than a functional clothing accessory.

"Excuse *me*," she said, looking up at the broad V of his chest and straight into his piercing aqua eyes.

He stepped away, allowing the two to pass through the door, and then tipping his hat, he continued in the opposite direction.

"You don't want to meet her?" the elderly man called out.

Without looking back, the cowboy raised a thumbs up in the air as he climbed into a black Tesla and headed towards the ranch exit.

"He's flying down to the Fairgrounds today, I think. Del Mar. Quarter horses. I can never keep up if we have one in a race, or he may be just buying. I mainly help with my grandkids these days."

She nodded, looking around the office. A stereotype of Western decor: signature antlered head of some poor hoofed beast, hide-covered floors, a leather loveseat, a wide, wooden desk with rope-carved legs. And picture frames filled with laughing children and a straight-faced, but patient-looking young father.

She lifted a trophy off a dusty shelf, dated ten years earlier, *Cutting Champion, Houston, Texas.* Her new boss was as tough as he was quiet, handsome as he was mysterious.

"When do I start?" she asked.

A MONTH INTO THE JOB, Kristi was ready to pull out her hair. It wasn't because of the kids. They were adorable, delightful, funny, and well-mannered. But they were also sad and missing their father, who traveled often. It pissed Kristi off that a man with such blessings of wealth and healthy children could avoid them as he did. Cayden, who had hated school when she arrived, now was in the top reading group of his third-grade class. And Emma, well, Emma was only in preschool. Kristi's job involved giving her attention, which was difficult to capture. It wasn't that Emma couldn't speak, but more like she wouldn't. She had an agenda of her own, perhaps. Kristi thought, *Like father, like daughter.* Mr. Deacon Richards had not given her the time of day to talk about his own kids.

After another week of leaving voice messages for the children's father, Kristi reached out to him by email. A very long email, detailing not only her work with the kids, but their blow-by-blow schedule, their progresses and setbacks. Because, dammit, shouldn't he know? And then she couldn't stop herself. In between citing research in child and family psychology, and work from her own master's degree thesis about the study of trauma on speech and communication, she shamed Mr. Richards into joining them all for dinner. The timing was perfect because she'd made an exciting discovery regarding Emma.

"Daddy's here!" shouted Cayden, jumping into the bronze arms of his father as he cautiously entered the kitchen.

Deacon Richards kissed and ruffled the top of the boy's head.

Kristi almost dumped the bowl of pasta onto the table. She'd only seen the elusive man as he came and went in his dressy business-cowboy attire. Today, he wore faded jeans and a T-shirt stretched across defined pectorals and taut biceps. Kristi's mouth watered with hunger, but she shook it off aware it was not for her homemade tomato sauce.

He nodded at Kristi as he sat at the table. He gave Emma's hand a pat, and she nuzzled his powerful forearm, but they spoke no words to each other.

"I have to tell you something, Mr. Richards," Kristi began.

He cleared his throat. "Uh, Deacon... is okay."

"Great. Well, Deacon, I have something to show you actually. Don't panic now."

Kristi picked up the heavy metal serving spoon and dropped it on the floor with a loud clang.

Deacon and Cayden jumped in their chairs, but Emma looked unfazed. Then, Kristi said in a low voice, "Emma, do you want ice cream now?"

Emma again stared at her plate, waiting for her serving of pasta. Kristi snapped her fingers in front of Emma's face. "Emma, look at me, sweetie." Their eyes connected. "Ice cream?"

Emma grinned and clapped, bouncing in her chair.

Deacon withdrew his hands from the table and sat back. "So?" he said in a challenging tone.

"Mr. Richards–Deacon–Emma can't hear properly. She's been reading our lips."

That night, Kristi couldn't sleep thinking over events at dinner. She was incredibly satisfied with herself. Deacon, although not saying much, consistently smiled at her in between hugging and roughhousing with the kids. Emma would get the help she needed, and then Kristi could begin proper speech therapy with her. Around one AM, still tossing and turning, Kristi heard a noise in the hall. She pushed back the covers and crept to the door to peek into the hallway.

"Oh, it's you," she said to Deacon, who was turning out the hall lights she must have forgotten to check. "Can't sleep?"

He shook his head. Deacon took a few steps out of the shadows toward Kristi and paused. The moon would be full in the next night or so but already illuminated the dark house, streaming through its tall windows. A shine swept across Deacon's naked upper torso. A light speckling of hair across his chest taunted Kristi. Her nipples rubbed against her T-shirt and goose bumps tickled her thighs and buttocks.

Deacon walked up to her and touched her cheek with his steady thumb. "Thank you," he whispered close to her ear and continued down the hall.

"You're welcome," she said, but he was already gone. She quietly closed her door. Out of instinct and sheer physical need, she placed her palm to her mound and pressed, feeling the pulses. When she climbed into bed, she knew she needed a release in order to sleep. She sucked on her two fingers and collected the moisture she'd need to pleasure herself, all the while picturing Deacon's thumb, Deacon's tongue, rolling over her clit, and pushing into her body. She fingered herself and used her thumb to come to climax, bearing down hard into her hand, turning her face into her pillow to muffle her cry of pleasure. Was he thinking of her tonight? Was he thinking and doing the same thing?

Dinners became lively and happy at the Richards' ranch house. Emma sported a flesh-pink hearing aid and couldn't stop chatting, singing, and being silly as a four-year-old should. She became the evening entertainment they all looked forward to, constantly cracking up her big brother, her father, and Grandpa when he visited.

"I knew you were the one," the senior Mr. Richards said, patting Kristi's shoulder.

"I'm not sure what you mean, but okay," Kristi said, avoiding his focused gaze. He was up to trouble; she could sense it.

"Why don't you take a night off? Let me watch scary movies with my grandkids."

Deacon shook his head. An emphatic, *No.*

"All right then, let me have some time with them. We'll play Candyland or some such bullshit–oops–I mean game. Really. I'll behave. You're both too young to sit around like you're retired old fogies. Go to a bar. Go dancing."

Deacon rolled his eyes like he was a teenager embarrassed by his parent, causing Kristi to laugh out loud. A deep blush spread beneath the five o'clock shadow of scruff he'd been allowing himself to grow these days. It was sexy as hell, and she longed to rub her hands or any other open space of her skin against it. He cocked his head at her stare, so she glanced away.

"Mr. Richards, if you're willing to put the kids to bed tonight, I'll take you up on it. I could use some extra time on my thesis paper."

Deacon shrugged his shoulders and crossed his arms, as if saying, if she won't go then fine by me.

"Junior! You take this lady out for a night on the town, or so help me, you are not the man I raised you to be."

Deacon, the accomplished entrepreneur, rancher and rugged cowboy, jumped a little at the change of tone in his father's voice. "Yes'r," he said, while dropping his head, blushing again. He moistened his lips with his tongue and chewed on his lower lip. Then, he nodded at Kristi, holding her gaze. If she could read his body language correctly, he'd just accepted the challenge of taking her on what seemed to be an actual date.

THE BOOTHS LINING the perimeter of a local honky-tonk bar were a tight space to share. Their knees brushed every time one of them shifted. Deacon mumbled what she thought was maybe a *pardon* or *sorry* for every time his foot bumped hers under the table, but other than that, he wasn't talking. Big shock.

"And two shots of Don Julio—blanco," Kristi said to the server who finally showed up with the beers.

Deacon raised his brows but nodded in agreement.

"Maybe that will get you to talk to me," she said, arching an eyebrow.

He sighed. "Sorry." He fingered the moisture on her mug of beer, the closest he'd intentionally come to touching her since the night they'd met in the hall. The night she'd fantasized about every inch of him touching every inch of her.

"I know about your past, Deacon. I can't imagine the loss. I'm truly sorry."

He nodded without taking his gaze off her beer. She put her hands over his and he didn't pull away.

"That feels like a long time ago now," he said. "Time to move on, maybe. For the kids."

Kristi sat back. He seemed ready to talk to her. "Your kids are fine, Deacon. But what about you? Sure, they miss their mom. They'll always love their mother. But they were so little when she passed. It's you they miss when you're not around."

She regretted it immediately. He pulled his hands away, folding his arms across his chest. Kristi started to back pedal to save the moment. "Look, I care about...your kids. I care about your family." Staring into his liquid aqua eyes was like bathing in the Caribbean Sea...warm, salty, inviting. "I have some experience with loss. I mean, not just from my studies." She shook her head, glancing away. Her story was for another time. She wanted to reach Deacon, even if only as a friend, if being more was a far-reaching fantasy. "I apologize if I've overstepped. I just want...you...should know..." Her eyes welled with tears.

Before she could look back, Deacon leaned across the table, gently pulling her chin to his face, and placed his lips on hers. One kiss was all the communication she needed from him at this moment. It was chaste and pure, but not enough. He hovered an inch from her, gauging her reaction. Kristi tilted her head and caught his lip playfully between her teeth, ending in a kiss that was the opposite of what he'd given her.

She softly brushed her tongue over his bottom lip and devoured him with soft kisses until they both needed a breath.

"We can't do this now," Deacon said as he slid back into his seat.

"Then, I quit," she said, assuming he was going to use their professional relationship as an excuse to not get close. "Because I need to do this now."

He laughed out loud, a full belly laugh she'd only heard when he wrestled with the kids. "I mean...here. In the bar. Small town, you know? You're no one's business but mine. And I don't accept your resignation. We'll work something out."

"You don't want people to know about us?" She hadn't pegged him for someone sneaky. Her spirits and desire were deflating.

Deacon stood and held his hand out to her. "I mean, what I want to do to you should not be for public eyes, is all."

As she stood, he pulled her to his chest, squeezed her bottom and nibbled teasingly into the side of her neck. "Things like that, darlin'. Things I've wanted to do with you, to you, since the day you walked onto my ranch."

Kristi shivered with longing. He was right. With the sparks flying between them, they'd be lucky to make it fully clothed to his truck in the parking lot. As he opened the door on the passenger side of the truck, he pinned her against the side, pressing his erection against her stomach.

"Easy there, cowboy," she said, breathing against his chest.

"Sorry, I may have forgotten my manners. It's been so long."

"I'm right there with you. It's just, where can we go? The kids, and your dad, are home."

"Hop in," he said, patting the truck seat, and leaning in for another sensuous kiss before darting around to the driver's side.

The ranch was only a few miles from town, but Deacon drove slowly and fell quiet again.

"What are you thinking, cowboy?" she asked.

"I might be nervous. A little."

Kristi smiled, knowing he couldn't see her goofy grin in the dark. She wasn't as nervous as she was excited, like one of his quarter horses at the starting gate. Inching over to his side, Kristi kissed his neck while moving her hand over the bulge in his jeans. It was easy, and necessary, to unbutton and release his cock. Her fingers brushed over the tip and felt the sticky pre-cum.

Deacon sighed deep in his throat, like a feral dog more than the sweet man she'd been witnessing of late. She stroked him, as best as she could reach in the confines of his pants, and then, leaning down, covered the head of his prick with her mouth.

"*Ohhh*, God, yes," he moaned.

Kristi sucked and tongued the head of his cock until gravel rumbled under the vehicle's tires and they came to a stop.

"You have to give me a moment," he said.

She pulled away, but he caught her before she could get too far. "You are amazing," he said, and planted a kiss full on her mouth. "I'm about to show you what I'd like to say..." The words caught, and he sighed, leaning his head against the seat rest.

"Then show me, Deacon," she said. "I'll hear you. I promise."

Kristi, linked by his hand, trailed Deacon in the moon's light into the same office and stables where she'd first laid eyes on him. He knew his place well, yet with the lights off, they stumbled a little into the room, landing against his sturdy desk. Kristi could feel the rise of his pulse, the beating in his chest as her hands roamed under his shirt.

"Take it off," she said, as she kissed his stomach, near his navel and up and up. "Your hands are shaking." She grabbed them and placed them on her breasts. "I want you, Deacon. Tell me what you want."

She meant, *show me*, because action was his language, so he proceeded to do just that, weaving his hands through her hair, kissing her mouth, and sucking her lips. He tugged at her sweater, bringing it up over her head. No bra. She'd been hanging out around the house, not expecting to go out. But the effect was all the better. Deacon dove at her breast, taking a nipple into his mouth, rolling it with his tongue and gently nipping. Kristi ground her pelvis into his thigh, letting her head fall back.

Then Deacon slowly unbuttoned and pulled off

her jeans. He French-kissed her stomach, cupping her bottom, squeezing until she cried out. With his teeth, he cleverly pulled down her thong, but she was impatient and wriggled out of it, hoping he would place his tongue to her clit, just like in her fantasy.

"I imagined this, you know," she said. "Often."

He didn't need the encouragement. Deacon parted her labia with his long, strong fingers and rubbed his nose against her, kissing and inhaling her scent.

"Delicious," he murmured.

He lapped at her clitoris and sunk his tongue into her slit again and again. Kristi hitched her hips higher, pressing into his mouth as he swirled his tongue stronger in just the right consistent circles to make her come.

"Oh, yes," she cried, gripping his dark, wavy hair at the scalp. When her stomach finally finished with its last spasm, she felt Deacon swallow the juices she made for him.

"That was amazing," she said.

"Not done, beautiful. Not yet."

He handed her a tissue, making her giggle. He laughed too, as he knocked around the office looking for something.

"Shit," he said.

"Condom?" Kristi was on the pill, but a STD was a sure-fire relationship killer, especially at the start. "I know I don't have any. I wasn't expecting... it's been a while."

"Well, it's been a while for me, too. I'm healthy, if that counts."

Kristi hesitated. Damn. As a responsible adult, she'd never caved before. But this felt different. Deacon was different than any man she'd ever been with. "How do you know?"

He chuckled, but grew serious, taking her face in his hands. "I never lie. And I will never hurt you. I may not say much, but I am a man of my words. When I use them." He smiled and kissed her on the forehead. "Let's go. Change of venue."

Deacon led Kristi to a horse stall with an open barred window, allowing the moonlight to streak the ground. It was picturesque and smelled of fresh-shaved pine. "It's clean, promise," he said, laying out a thick wool blanket he took from his office couch. "I'd like to do more with you, but I'm happy to lay here for a while before we go back to the house. I can dig around there for some condoms." He took her by the hand and brought her to the blanket.

"There's always tomorrow," she said.

He wrapped her in his arms as they lay side by side, looking at the swaying branches of an olive tree against the moon. "Wish that were true," he said.

Kristi knew he meant about his wife, taken way too young from this world.

"Deacon," Kristi said, nuzzling into his face and then neck. "Make love to me. I want you so badly. This is right. I feel it."

Deacon turned on his side, pressing a new erection into her hip.

"I feel that, too," she said, referring to his pulsing cock, making them both laugh.

"I'm in love with you, Kristi."

With that, maybe another man would have gone in to all the reasons. Talk, talk, talk. But she knew her worth to him. She felt it. She knew her value to his family. She loved the children, his quirky father, and the ranch, the horses, the life in the valley. All of them.

"Show me, cowboy," she said.

Deacon chuckled in her ear before running his tongue from earlobe to neck, and back to the front of her chest. With her on her back, Deacon pressed up onto his brawny arms, holding himself above her, looking deep into her eyes. Kristi arched her back and circled her legs around his waist, feeling the length of his cock, then wiggling until the tip was at the entrance to what now felt was like her soul.

Deacon slowly pushed himself into her then began pumping at a fast pace. Kristi moved her hips to his rhythm, bucking. But he was used to this. He was a cowboy. A champion. Their mouths locked, melted together, and merged. They tasted each other's tongues and shared each other's breath. When Deacon suddenly stopped moving, Kristi held his face.

"What's wrong? Deacon?"

He brought his forehead to hers. "Nothing. I'm

not used to feeling right."

She withdrew from his body to make sure he was okay. A phantom pulse continued in her cunt. "I love you. I love you too, Deacon. Don't stop now."

He took her quickly by the hips and turned her, rubbing her buttocks around and around with the heat of his calloused palms. She backed in to him slowly, inch by inch, lowering herself onto his throbbing cock, teasing him, until he pulled her down. She lifted slightly and pushed down on him again, feeling the length of his cock filling and targeting just the right spot. She did it again, and he held her to him. "Wait," he said, but she couldn't be still with him inside of her.

"Don't stop, please," Kristi said through her panting, grinding into him again. His stomach clenched, and he released inside her, making waves of pleasure she felt like aftershocks.

They fell together onto the blanket, Deacon staying inside until he was once again soft, all the while massaging her breasts, her back, and kissing her neck.

"You let me come inside you," he said.

"Hope you wanted more kids," Kristi said with a laugh, then added, "I'm kidding. We're good. No worries."

Deacon twisted her around to face him, nose to nose. He kissed her long and deep. He didn't have to respond in words. She heard him. He wasn't worried at all.

THE SCOUNDREL

Natasha Moore

I WIPE the sweat from my brow and pace the uneven wooden floor. I hate waiting.

It's another hot summer day but autumn's just around the corner. I can hear him singing outside, strumming his guitar, crooning a tragic western love song. It fits my mood perfectly, not that he's singing to me. He might as well be. Tonight will be the last time I'll see Will Bennett. The last time I'll hear the voice that sends erotic shivers up my spine.

No more admiring his broad shoulders and those dark eyes with the crinkles at the corners that always have a wink for me. My fingers itch to touch his skin, tanned from days, weeks, years working under the beating sun. But I never have.

I can see him through the window. His Stetson sits low over his wavy, salt and pepper hair. His leather boots are as well-worn as the jeans that cup his very nice ass. I can't help noticing everything about him. How the ends of his hair brush the collar of his chambray shirt. How he rolls the sleeves up to the elbow and reveals his muscular forearms. So many nights, I've dreamed of feeling those arms around me.

Yeah, I know he's a scoundrel, a hopeless flirt. I'm old enough to know better, but somehow, I fell for the whole package. A foolish widow more afraid of rejection than a life of never knowing his taste, his touch. Never knowing the pleasure of his hard body pressing into mine.

He's only here for the summer. Why would I want to get involved with someone who's not sticking around, regardless of the attraction that vibrates in the air between us? I thought I was saving myself from heartache, but it couldn't have been any worse than this bone-aching yearning.

My heart thumps as I wait, knowing what will happen and not knowing how to stop it. The clock on the wall ticks away, counting down the seconds, the minutes, the rest of my life. Even if I speak up this late in the game, would it make a difference? Hell, *he* hasn't spoken up either. He winks at all the women. Calls them darlin' and favors them with his crooked grins.

Who knows what else he gives them?

I'm not one of the saloon girls in their fancy dresses, the ones who press up against him and offer what I've never dared. In the three months since he came to town, I've only watched him from behind the scenes. I was brought up to be quiet, to mind my business, mind my tongue. Look where that's gotten me.

When I hear the shouts, I rush from the school-house, my fingers clenching the skirts of my plain, calico dress. The showdown has already begun on the dusty road that runs through the center of town. Four men face each other. White hats. Black hats. The sheriff and his deputy against the robbers clenching their bags of loot. Someone shouts out that the bad guys killed everyone in the bank. A gasp runs through the crowd. The men stare each other down, guns still in their holsters, but their fingers are twitching at their hips. So many people are standing around, doing nothing but watching. Waiting.

Am I any better than them?

The steady thud of boots rings out, and I turn to eagerly feast my eyes on the approaching man with his brown hat and intense gaze. He doesn't wear a star on his leather vest, never did, never would. He doesn't even have a stake in this fight, except for doing what's right. Only minutes ago, he'd strolled these boards with his guitar, serenading anyone who wanted to listen to his smooth voice and expert fingers plucking music from wood and steel. Everyone is focused on him now, and he hasn't said a word yet. He has that kind of presence. What would he possibly want with a meek and mild woman like me, anyway?

Will's gaze darts away from the stand-off and locks with mine. My mouth dries, my body heats, throbs. Tears prickle my eyes. This is it. I've waited too long. I'm going to lose him. He gives me a nod and turns his focus to the stupid men bent on killing each other.

He doesn't reach for his gun. Instead, he hands his guitar to the nearest bystander. "There's been enough killing today, fellas," he says in that deep, lazy voice I hear in my dreams. The seductive voice that's kept me wet between my thighs for the past three months.

"Stay out of this," one of the black hats calls out. He's called Mean Mick. "This doesn't concern you."

Will slowly shakes his head, his hands loose at his side. "You killed townsfolk. That makes it my business."

Mick never takes his gaze off the lawmen. "You ain't the sheriff. You ain't the mayor. Leave it alone."

"Can't do that." Will takes a step forward.

It happens so fast I can barely grasp it, even though I've been watching for it. Mick whirls as he reaches for his gun. He pulls the trigger, and it's loud enough to make me jump. Will crumbles, a gush of red staining the front of his shirt.

I scream, "No!" and dash to him, almost tripping over the damned skirt. I drop to my knees beside him. I don't even think as I yank the gun from his holster and point it at Mean Mick. I don't hesitate as I pull the trigger, slow and smooth, the way my daddy taught me when I was a kid. Mick shouts in surprise and falls, a plume of dust rising around him. Right through the heart. With a ragged cry, I toss away the weapon and throw myself over Will's body. I hear another shot, and the other robber falls, too.

Applause rings out around us, but I can't make myself move from Will's warm body. My heart still races. The scents of leather and manly musk wrap around me, as they have twice a day, six days a week, for the past three months. But Old West Village is closing for the season, and this was the last performance of the year.

I don't want to let him go, but he's stirring beneath me. I raise my head. He opens his eyes, and there's that wink. I don't want to see it. Not now.

"You can let me up now, darlin'."

I push to my knees and snap, "My name is Iris."

He frowns and sits up. "I know your name."

"Maybe you should use it then." I know how I sound. Just as foolish as I feel.

His expression softens. "Iris," he murmurs and brushes his fingers against mine.

"Don't." I glance around, but no one's paying any attention to us. The rest of the players have gone to change. Most of the visitors have scattered to the shops and stables and parking lots.

I struggle to my feet, the long skirts and leather boots hampering me. "I don't know how anyone wore these stupid things. Just another way to shackle women."

"Don't take your anger out on the poor dress." Will stands and takes my hands. It's the first time we've touched outside of the performances. His hands are so big and warm. He'd been a real cowboy most of his life. The friction from his rough palms shoots tingles through my needy body. "Go ahead. Take it out on me."

I look anywhere but in his eyes. "What makes you think I care one way or the other?" Still, I don't pull my hands away.

His low chuckle pisses me off. Or is it the itch of arousal that irritates every inch of my body? "Iris, look at me."

I'm breathing hard, and I don't know why. That's a lie. I know why. I tug my hands from his and pluck at the ugly dress. "I have to change."

He whispers my name again and leans in to brush his lips against mine. Nothing but a tease. Then he pulls back and studies me, as if he doesn't know how I'm going to react. Yeah, I don't know either.

My tongue darts out to sample the hint of his taste, smoky and sweet—he must have had barbeque for dinner. A sample? That's all I get after all this time? The anger's back. "Now?" I ground out. "Now, you kiss me?"

That rule I was taught…to mind my tongue? Yeah, I'm throwing that one out the window.

His intense gaze heats me, excites me. "I couldn't wait any longer," he admits. "I had to steal just one."

"Why did you wait?" Why did he think he had to steal it to begin with? I would've given my kisses freely if he'd only asked.

"We were working together. If you hadn't appreciated my advances, it would've made for a long, awkward summer. But we're done now."

Will grabs my hand and pulls me through the swinging door of the make-believe saloon. There wasn't much to the interior. A few old tables and chairs and a long bar, its surface empty. There'd been some talk about turning it into a functioning saloon, but since the Old West Village catered to families, it never happened. No one's in here now.

I let him tug me behind the bar and through a small door that opens to one of the dressing rooms. The players have left. Costumes and props hang from hooks or are scattered in piles on the floor, dresses and boots and make-believe pistols. Someone will collect them to clean and pack away for next summer.

He pulls me into the dark office in the back and gracefully...forcefully...whirls me around, slamming the door closed with my body. He doesn't even bother flipping the light switch, but I hear the click of the lock. I lick my lips as anticipation makes my body sing.

I'm done waiting. I lean forward and take his mouth, if not gracefully, then certainly forcefully. No more samples. I'm not sneaking a taste; I'm capturing the full kiss. I won't be a meek and mild widow again. Will cups my face in his hands and moves his mouth over mine. We're both hungry. Thirsty. Needy.

I knock his hat off as I drive my fingers into his hair, tangling them in his soft curls. I hold his head in place as if I'm afraid he'll move away.

I *am* afraid, afraid this moment is only a sweet dream, one I'll wake from, still longing for more. I groan into his mouth. I know he's leaving. So what? I'd rather enjoy this time with him than push him away before we can work off this tension humming through me. I should've made a move months ago.

The door knob digs into my hip, but I can't move. His erection presses into me, making my breasts swell and my panties even wetter. I pull him closer still, not wanting the kiss to ever end.

Of course, it ends. Nothing lasts forever.

"Come home with me tonight?" Will's voice is breathless in the darkness that surrounds us. "I want to bury myself so deep inside you that I'll never get out."

My head buzzes from the heat and from the arousal running rampant through my body. His words break the dam of need that's been building for weeks. For months. I press my hip into the bulge of his arousal. From now on, I'm asking for what I want. "Do it now."

"I don't want to rush this." He sweeps his fingers

lightly across my cheek. "I want to take my time with you."

"Later. Take time later." We might not even get later. I want now.

I pull him in for a quick hard kiss. Who knows what might happen once we leave this room? What if this is our only chance? "I want to feel you inside me now. Right now."

"Iris." His surprise is clear in his voice. These are the most words we've ever said to each other. We've had meals with the other players almost every day. Conversations flowed around the table but never strictly between the two of us. Our gazes would catch often, but I never got more than a wink. He never got more than a smile.

Yeah, I haven't been exactly assertive before now. "Does it bother you that I'm asking for what I want?"

His hands settle on my hips. "Bother me? Darlin', I'm thrilled." He reaches for the long line of tiny buttons that run down the bodice of the cotton dress.

"No time." The sudden urge to hurry sends my heart racing. "Sandy or Jim might need the office." But that's not the only reason I want to rush. Why I *need* to rush. I've never experienced such an overwhelming craving in all my forty-nine years.

I hike up the stupid long skirt and shimmy out of my soaked panties before I can have second thoughts. I won't worry about the future, won't think about him moving far away. *Live in the moment.* That's my new motto.

"Let me get the light." The blinds are down on the one window in the room. We're not much more than shadowy figures writhing around each other. I think I like it that way.

"I don't need the light. I just need you. Now." I surprise myself by reaching out and tracing the thick bulge in the front of his jeans. I smile at the moan that bursts out of the darkness. I unfasten his belt buckle and pull down the zipper.

"Hold on. Hold on," he mumbles. I hear him fumble with his pants. When I catch the rustle of a wrapper, I realize he's pulled a condom out of his wallet. "Got it."

He leans in and captures my lips again. But before I can help him push down his jeans, he drops to his knees. He disappears beneath the calico fabric. His hands slide up my legs. His breath is warm on my upper thighs as he pushes them apart.

His tongue is hot and wet on my slick flesh. I moan and rock my hips, pressing into him. Leaning back into the door. Searching for more...more. It's been so long.

I fly over the edge so quickly I almost don't believe it. But there I am, wriggling against his face, my hand over my mouth so my screeches don't reach the outside world. I feel more than hear his chuckles. The scoundrel sounds pretty proud of himself. I can't seem to mind.

He fights his way out from beneath my skirts and rises to his feet. I help him push down his jeans, breathing as heavily as he is. When our fingers meet, tangle, I take the condom out of his hand. My fingers tremble as I roll it over his hot, hard flesh. He moans into my mouth, and I taste myself on his lips. He cups my breast through the dress, but as much as I'd love him to play with it, the urgency is building in me again. I press my hip into him. My sex is throbbing again. That's never happened to me before.

Hurry. Hurry.

Will slides his hand beneath my skirt again, finds my thigh and hikes up my leg until I can wrap it around his hip. The rounded tip of his cock presses into me, rubbing up and down along my slick flesh, tickling that sensitive bud that throbs with need all over again.

Hurry. Hurry.

He grasps my hips and lifts me so he can plunge into me in one long, hard thrust that pushes my back into the door. The loud thud makes us both laugh out loud. I hope no one's in the changing room.

I wrap my arms around his neck and try to open wider for him. He stretches me in all the right places, touching me where no one else could. "Harder," I whimper.

He thrusts over and over again, faster, harder, just like I've ached for him to do. "You feel so good," he says on a moan. "So right."

I rock my hips, working to relieve some of the pressure building inside me. "More, Will, more."

He kisses me hard enough to take my breath

away, and then slips one hand between our bodies to finger me. "Come for me again, darlin'. I'm not going to last much longer." His cock drags along my sensitive core, and he slows his thrusts while he continues to rub my clit.

The orgasm surges through my body. This time, I bite my lip to stop from crying out. I wish we'd had the chance to do this somewhere I wouldn't have to worry about being quiet. Will crushes my mouth with his, swallowing my cries as I drink his in. His thrusts come faster, then harder, pounding me into the door, and I wonder why we even bother to quiet our cries. Will's shudders of completion follow shortly after my own.

We sink against the door, breathing heavily, laughing softly.

After a few sweet moments, Will shifts, lifting his weight off me. I moan my disappointment when he slides out of me. I drop my shaky leg to the floor. The skirts cover my nakedness. I wonder where my panties ended up.

He rests his forehead against mine, and we stand there a moment, neither one of us speaking. Then he says, "That was a long time coming."

I nod. Three months too long.

He reaches around me to hit the switch, and I blink at the sudden light. Will stands in front of me, his denims still around his ankles, his hair mussed by my fingers. He removes the condom and tosses it in the trash can in the corner.

The red stain stands out on his shirt. I tug on his shirttail. "You need to get this off." A slow smile spreads across his face before he strips off the shirt and fake-blood bag, and then tugs his pants back up where they belong.

He's kept himself in shape, as if I couldn't tell from draping myself over his body all those times. Still, it's very nice to see what's underneath the shirt.

Where do we go now? I like this man so much and wish we had longer together. But I'm not going to cling. I'm not going to beg. I tell myself to be glad I have this wonderful memory to keep me warm during the lonely nights to come.

I hold out my hand. It feels foolish after what we've just done, but I want to part on my terms. I gave my body willingly, but I won't give a scoundrel my heart. "Well, it was great working with you."

He frowns, looks at my outstretched hand. "What is this?"

Isn't it obvious? Or does he think we can screw around a few more times before he leaves. That's not going to happen. The shield around my heart would never hold. "This is goodbye, Will. Have a safe trip back to Wyoming."

"Who told you I was going back to Wyoming?"

"Sandy." His daughter and her husband own the tourist attraction. "She told me she talked you into helping out for the summer, but you'd be out of here as soon as we closed."

He smooths his hand over my hair. Most of it has

fallen out of the neat bun I wore earlier. I lean into his caress before I can stop myself.

"You haven't talked to her lately, have you?"

And damn him, he strokes my hair again, and I nearly purr. My face heats. "Not about you."

"I've decided to stay. Sandy and Jim have plans to expand the business to appeal to locals as well as the tourists. They have some good ideas to make this a year-round resort. They'll need help."

The old me, the meek, mild, mind-my-business-and-mind-my-tongue me, would have waited to hear what else he had to say. But not anymore. "Is that the only reason you're staying?" I demand.

His lips quirk. "Darlin', that's not even the most important reason."

Somehow, Will calling me darlin' now makes me feel all soft and warm instead of prickly. "And what's the most important reason?"

He slides his arm around my waist and tugs me against him. My body responds immediately, ready for more of that sexy action. Still, my heart doesn't dare hope, until... "You, of course. I think we might have something good...hell, something great together, if we give it a chance to grow."

My eyes prickle, and my voice breaks. "I thought I was never going to see you again."

He shakes his head as if I'd been crazy to ever worry about it. "I asked you a question a while ago, but I never heard the answer."

So much has happened, I can't remember

anything but his taste on my tongue and the sensation of his body in mine. "What question?"

"Iris, will you come home with me tonight?" He even throws in the wink and the crooked smile.

That scoundrel.

I'm done waiting. This time, I'm jumping in with both feet—even if they're stuck in old leather boots. "Hell, yeah."

SOLAR FLARE

Ava Cuvay

Planet Crysceous, Iona Quadrant

"Dad, the Coronal Mass Ejection will reach us tomorrow. Have you hired the replacements to herd —" Solarne Vacca jerked to a halt halfway into her father's office, her attention snagged by the three strangers standing there. Specifically, the tall drink of aqua at the front, one hip cocked and his arms crossed at his chest, far enough from the blaster strapped to his thigh to appear non-threatening.

One glance at his sharpshooter's face was enough to know his relaxed manner was an act.

Her heart hammered in her throat. She'd seen this

man on the "Wanted" holo-vids posted around this system, sporting a list of violent offenses. He was even more striking in person, lounging with all the self-assurance of a king. Nearly two meters tall, with a head of bedroom-mussed hair as dark as a starless night, eyes the color of a cloudy day, and a body built for sin. She wouldn't be a woman if the view didn't steal her breath and shoot heat straight to her core with laser-point accuracy. But she was also CEO in charge of her family's sprawling *crehdisth* worm ranch. This was *her* kingdom. And this man's visit was a threat.

He was not here for a casual social call. He was a hired gun.

Her knees quaked with fear and outrage, but she tamped it down and forced a calm demeanor. She'd wrangled interstellar worm herds since she could walk, and they were far more massive and unpredictable than this one man, no matter the stories which preceded him.

She whirled on her father. "Do you have any idea who *he* is?"

"Yes, I do." Amstar Vacca lumbered to a stand, his left side having been crushed and atrophied from a ranching accident years before, and yet he remained an imposing figure. "Solarne, this is Carrington Grote and his officers, Reber and Hinode. His crew have agreed to assist with the upcoming roundup."

"Oh, I'm sure they'll *assist*." She glared at Carrington. "Assist us out of everything we own."

"I assure you my crew will take only the agreed-upon payment." The corner of his mouth lifted in amusement, but his eyes turned stormy. "There's no cause to act as if we've pillaged and plundered your ranch, Miss Vacca."

"*Miss* Vacca?" Her face contorted like she'd licked the slimy underside of a *slehgah*. The title brought forth a lifetime of being underestimated by the staff. A lifetime of being *Young Miss* and told she was too small or too pretty to labor on the ranch, followed by being patted on the head like a tolerated pet when she ignored their patronizing words and worked to prove her worth anyway. Solarne planted her hands on her hips and straightened to her full height, still having to crane her neck to look Carrington in the eye. "I am a grown woman, Mr. Grote. Not a twelve-year-old."

His gaze raked over her, his deep-set eyes no doubt noting her shock of red hair cut severely at her jawline, slender curves many mistook for those of a budding adolescent, and worn and dirty work boots. His eyes flashed like a sun's rays between clouds, and the smile which lifted his lips promised a thousand carnal delights she dared not accept.

"Indeed, Ms. Vacca. You are very much a grown woman." He purred as if she was already roped and ready for his brand.

Need flooded her at the thought, but she shoved it back. He was just passing through, and she wasn't livestock. "Mr. Grote, whatever arrangement you've made with my father, consider it void."

Amstar lifted a hand to placate her objections. "Solarne, no one else has answered the job post—"

She turned to her father. "Then I'll drive the herd by myself. Better that than let a bunch of trigger-happy blaster-boys loose on our livelihood. Find another crew."

She whirled and exited the office to punctuate her order. Dad had transferred full responsibility of ranch operations to her several moonphases ago. She was now in charge of the sprawling metropolis here on Crysceous, the paddocks around the three adjacent moons, fifty-thousand head of space worms, and the support staff—although, many of the staff had quit because they disliked being under new management. She would not risk everything her family had built by employing men whose only work experience included killing and various illegal side jobs.

Carrington followed her down the hall, his sheer presence commanding attention more than the sound of his footsteps. She pointedly ignored him and quickened her pace.

"Ms. Vacca, my men are quick learners, disciplined, and well-trained." Anyone else would have sounded like a sniveling kiss-ass. Carrington Grote sounded like he was doing her a favor.

Without looking back, she bit out, "Mr. Grote, your reputation precedes you, as do the holo-vids.

You're wanted men. You have the death sentence on twelve systems."

"Mr. Grote is my father. I answer to Captain or Carrington. Or Carr, if we've fucked. The death sentences were only in three systems, and those were clerical errors that have been corrected by now."

"Corrected? Meaning you bought your innocence with either money or violence."

His longs legs brought him to her right side, so she pivoted away and marched through a long, open sitting area.

He followed her, snarling under his breath. "My men are unparalleled marksmen, but we're also skilled at handling delicate cargo and volatile situations. Your stock is safe in our care."

"Our herds aren't skittish masses you can threaten with a blaster or fragile trinkets that break when handled indelicately, Mr. Gro—er, Carrington. These are living creatures the size of warships with minds of their own. They don't always act as expected, and a thoughtless reaction on a wrangler's part can be fatal."

He stepped to her side again, but she turned left down a bisecting hall with a frustrated huff. He continued to argue his side. "Ms. Vacca, you can trust the skills of my crew. I've trusted them with my life countless times and have never had cause to doubt them."

"You ask me to trust them with more than just my life." She spoke through clenched teeth. "This ranch has been in my family for five generations. It's my birthright, and it's my responsibility to ensure its continued success and to keep it safe from harm. As a roaming mercenary, you can't possibly understand what it's like to have such deep roots."

He growled. Had she angered him? Why the urge to retract her words?

Once more, he stepped to her right, and she countered by turning down yet another hall, away from him, even though he refused to take the hint and cease following her. "So, why are you really here, Carrington?"

"Legitimate jobs are scarce for *roaming mercenaries* like us." He placed a derisive emphasis on her own words, and she felt them like a smack to her cheek. "I need to feed my crew, and you need ranch hands until you can hire replacements for all the staff who have quit these last few months."

Another smack, even if he hadn't intended it as such. "And you just happened to be in the area? Rumors have you entrenched in the Segota quadrant. You must've burned out your warp core getting here so quickly."

"Keeping tabs on me, eh?" His breath heated the back of her neck, and his voice rumbled in her ear like a lover's whisper. On a squeak, she lurched to a stop and spun to face him, expecting him to topple into her. Instead, he was an arm's length away, his hands raised as if in surrender and a knowing grin on his face.

"Yes, my crew has a reputation for danger. Your father believes showing you can successfully manage a group of vicious hired guns like us will prove your abilities to those who might still question them."

Solarne grunted from the blow of that gut punch. Even though her father had transferred full management of the family ranch to her, he didn't believe she could earn the respect that position warranted without his intervention.

She turned to head down yet another hall, away from Carrington and the anguish his admission caused. Before she took two steps, he blocked her path with a deft move. She spun back the way they came, but he sidestepped her again. She faced him, her fists clenched at her sides, chest heaving with outrage at her father's betrayal. Afraid to know the truth and hating that she needed it, she asked, "Do you agree with him?"

All lingering hints of seduction and humor melted from his expression, leaving only stark sincerity. His mouth tugged into a grim line. "Giving orders to mercenaries accustomed to following whoever is paying them? That won't mean shit to those who can't handle taking orders from the woman you are. Because, in their eyes, you'll only ever be a little girl running barefoot with wildflowers in her hair."

Her breath rushed out. Had he known that was exactly what she needed to hear?

Carrington stepped toward her, and she retreated a step. He was too close. His midnight storm aroma and the heat rolling off of him over-whelmed her senses and stole the breath from her lungs. He might be a man with elastic morals, but he was sexy as hell. Those womanly needs she usually kept corralled escaped and stampeded her self-control.

Bracing his arms against the doorframe on either side of her, he halted his advance. Her limbs quivered and need raged in her body. How she wanted to grasp his broad shoulders, wrap her legs around his hips, and ride him like she was taming a wild beast. She wanted to pull his lips to hers and drown in his potent kisses. She needed to slake this desire somehow before she burst into flames.

But this was a hallway, not a bedroom. And he was a hired hand, not a suitor.

She swallowed, forcing her eyes upward to meet his searching gaze.

"If any of them bothered to really look at you—at the fire in your eyes—they'd see just how passionate you are," he said, his voice softening to a lover's murmur. "About your ranch. Your legacy. You burn hotter than the surface of the sun. The man who can ignite that blaze would be a lucky bastard."

A soft cough at her back shocked Solarne out of the sensual haze his words crafted. She turned to see her father, still with Carrington's officers, waiting where she'd left them mere minutes ago. Her lips parted on a shocked gasp, and she looked at Carrington as he stepped to her side, one shoulder propped on the doorframe and a triumphant glint in his eyes.

How was it possible? How had she not recognized his maneuvers?

He'd herded her. With agility and subtlety that should only come from years of experience. He'd herded her right back to her father's office.

"So, Ms. Vacca," Carrington drawled with a smirk, "my crew'll start at dawn."

"THE WORMS CONSUME sunlight through their wings for energy." Solarne checked the readings on her single-flyer cowpony rocket as she condensed twenty-six years of ranch knowledge into the few minutes it took to reach the herd circling the second moon. "But they also need plasma ejecta from solar flares for a balanced diet."

Snickers and chortles from Carrington's crew of a dozen men rang out through the headset of her helmet.

"Cut the chatter." Carrington's voice was all-business. "We're grown men here."

"Yeah, grown men who are helping space worms eat star spunk," someone responded, followed by more snickers and chortles. Solarne bit back her own giggle. She'd used the ranching terminology all her life and had never considered it from an outsider's perspective. Turns out, it was funny.

"Last warning, Hinode." Carrington growled his

rebuke. "We're all greenhorns here, 'cept Ms. Vacca. Take her seriously."

Solarne's mouth dropped open. In three words, Carrington had issued more respect for her than anyone had her entire life. She hadn't earned it or fought for it. He'd just... *given* it, no questions asked. As his crew roger'd their assent and silence rang through her headset, her brain stumbled to catch up. For all her bluster about how seriously she took her family's livelihood, most ranch hands liked to cut-up on a drive. If Carrington's crew joked a little, she wouldn't mind. But neither would she contradict his orders.

Instead, she cleared her throat and continued. "I'll lead the herd to the grazing location. Station around the perimeter and let them flow. If they get jumpy, ease your distance, and they'll calm down."

"Hinode, Reber, Hodgson, you take our six." Carrington issued his directive with the calm confidence of a man accustomed to giving orders. "The rest, flank the herd."

"Roger that," Reber confirmed. "Sounds easy enough. Boss, is this why you said you could make the drive alone?"

Although Carrington was their Captain, his crew had taken to calling her "Boss." As the trail boss for this drive, the moniker fit. The men addressed her without a hint of spite, sarcasm, or side-eye—unlike so many of the ranch's long-time employees, now that she was their boss. How unexpected that a band of hired guns, loyal only to themselves, accepted her authority without question. The same band of hired guns she'd thought so poorly of just yesterday. Perhaps she'd been wrong about them.

"Boss?" Reber pulled her back to the present.

"Yes, sorry. To answer your question simply, if we're lucky, the drive will be hours of tedium. If not, there will be moments of sheer terror. The bulls can be unpredictable, which makes them dangerous."

"It's always the guys who fuck things up." Another voice in her headset, the joking tone inciting a growl from Carrington.

Solarne's chuckle drowned him out. "It's true. Ever heard the phrase *like a crehdisth worm to a solar flare*? That refers to the bulls. They're naturally aggressive, and solar ejecta can send them into a feeding frenzy. By their sheer size, they can cause a lot of damage."

"What should we do if a bull raises hell?" Carrington's level tone made her smile. She liked his voice. She shouldn't, but she did. Her nipples pearled at its deep rumble and rubbed deliciously against her sturdy solarsuit. She'd acquiesced to hiring him after his impromptu herding demonstration yesterday, and her body took that as permission to lust unfettered. She snuck a gloved hand to her chest, scratching the sensitive nub and swallowing her moan as sparks shot straight to her core, where she already seeped.

"Not to sound flippant, but you should fly away

and let me handle it," she answered on a cough, her face aflame with embarrassment that she'd fondled herself. Fortunately, the cowpony canopy had a one-way view, allowing her to see out while blocking harmful UV rays, gamma radiation, and the view of unwitting spectators. "Bulls require a subtle touch when riled."

She expected someone to make a lewd comment about the kind of touch one gives a bull—someone usually did during a drive—but no one took the bait.

They approached the moon, encircled by a herd so dense with translucent bodies it looked like a bubbling, gelatinous ring. When she deactivated a section of the energy field which served as a pasture fence, gasps of shock and wonder echoed in her ear as the first worms peeled from the herd and drifted out.

She hadn't exaggerated when she'd told Carrington they were as big as warships. The calves, which were barely older than her tenure as CEO, were already twice the size of the cowpony rockets. The cows were as large as an interplanetary shuttle that sat fifty. And the bulls were so large they had their own gravitational pull, albeit slight, and could swallow a cowpony whole.

Few people ever got this close, while Solarne had grown indifferent to the view she'd seen her entire life. The crew's reactions emphasized how much she'd taken her livelihood for granted. Had she similarly taken her father's employees for granted? She swept her gaze over Carrington's crew, hovering in their cowponies, and vowed to not to make the same mistake again.

"Don't crowd the gate, or they'll turn away," she advised. The crew had already proven capable, but she was responsible for them and didn't want anyone hurt just because she'd become jaded.

"Roger that. Retreating proximity," someone answered dutifully, and the two cowponies closest to the gate withdrew to a safer distance. The military vocabulary his crew used sounded odd, but their unquestioning immediacy of action was admirable. Carrington hadn't lied: they were well-trained, which bespoke his abilities as a commander.

Could she entice them to consider permanent employment at the ranch?

Could she keep her hands off Carrington if they accepted?

Turning her cowpony, she blew the horn, resonating a deep radio wave the herd understand meant food. The gentle giants followed her in a slow, surging wave. Their translucent wings, like triangular sails attached from head to tail, drifted up and down, their long, slender bodies undulating with each slow-motion beat.

"Holy shit, that thing's huge!" someone exclaimed. Solarne glanced behind her, where a few of the bulls had joined the herd, impressive in their size and power.

"Yeah, that's what *she* said," someone else quipped.

The crew snickered again even as Carrington growled his disapproval.

She bit her lip but not in time to hold back her own chuckle, and then couldn't help her response. "Where worms are concerned, gentlemen, it *is* all about size."

"No one better joke about the size of the *worm* between their own legs." Carrington warned, which only caused an uproar of laughter. Even Solarne joined in. Dare she tell them the bull penis could reach four meters in length?

The laughter dissolved any latent nerves the crew had. They settled into positions around the edges of the herd as if assigned to them, and drove to the grazing site without chatter or incident. The crew worked the flowing, swelling, gliding mass as if born to the job. Truth be told, they worked better together than any roundup crew she'd experienced before. Usually, someone's ego got bent, or something went wrong and fingers got pointed and excuses were thrown around.

Her father had always claimed a crew was only as good as its leader. Unfortunately, the former trail boss had been with her family forever, and as much as her father had complained about his faults, Amstar had never corrected or reprimanded the man's performance. Maybe his resignation, outraged at the thought of being managed by "a little welp who don't know shit about handlin' real men" was a blessing in disguise. Maybe she could find a new trail boss who could do the job with competence *and* respect.

Images of Carrington popped into her brain at the thought. Technically, he'd been on her mind since their meeting yesterday. He was certainly a real man, but thoughts of handling him always turned to images of him naked and in her bed.

The herd reached the grazing site just as the ejecta began to flow past on a solar wind. More gasps and exclamations of wonder transmitted as the worms opened their toothless mouths. Like ancient trolling boats with nets cast wide to catch food, the giant beasts tumbled and looped along the flow of the wind, swallowing plasma and particles from the star's corona.

With each pass along the ejecta, visible only to the worms and on the specialized instrument panel of the cowpony, bright blue lines unfurled like lightning along their luminescent bodies. The churning, heaving mass of glowing beasts, flashes of blue, and their wings fanning like a lazy summer day, enthralled Solarne. She'd forgotten what a majestic sight it was. And how lucky she was to have had a lifetime to enjoy it.

The flash of an enormous bull caught her attention. "Carrington, coming at you!"

Her heart lurched as the aggressive bull erupted through a cluster of cows, racing toward the sun. Carrington's pony rocket was in its line of trajectory, and Solarne would never make it in time to steer the bull away from him. He'd be smashed for sure, possibly swallowed, definitely injured, and his solar-suit wouldn't last until she reached him.

These were the moments of sheer terror she'd mentioned.

Hitting the pony's throttle to race just fast enough she didn't incite a stampede, she pointed her pony in his direction.

Her panic proved unnecessary. Carrington looped his cowpony in a tight circle to pull the bull's attention away from its destination, then flew along its flank, just close enough to make it uncomfortable. The bull eased away, and Carrington continued the gentle pressure, turning the bull in an expansive arc away from the ejecta and its feeding influence, before slipping the beast back into the herd as easy as laying a sleeping baby into its crib.

The man was a natural. Solarne's jaw dropped at how perfectly he'd handled the—

"Boss, beneath you!"

She yelped as a worm swooshed past and caught her pony with a wing. A beginner's mistake—she'd watched Carrington instead of her surroundings. The impact crushed her side gimbals and cracked the canopy, spinning her away from the herd. Queasy from the twirling scenery outside her cockpit, she unbuckled, held a deep breath, and shoved the damaged canopy off. Closing her eyes against the terror crawling up her esophagus, she jumped clear. Hopefully, someone would reach her before she ran out of oxygen or the suit's integrity gave way to the deadly vacuum of space.

Just as her lungs screamed for air, Carrington's soft murmur rang loudly in her headset. "I got ya, darlin'."

Strong arms banded her, pulling her against a powerful chest and into the cozy cockpit of a pony. She didn't open her eyes or breathe until he snapped the canopy shut and strapped her in, his own body her seat cushion. There wasn't much room with the two of them in a rocket built for one rider, but they fit. And she was alive.

Gulping oxygen into her lungs and tears burning her eyes, she trembled from the adrenaline that pumped through her system. If not for Carrington's swift rescue, she would have died. He must think she was a careless fool. An idiot. Certainly not someone capable of heading the family ranch.

Fortunately, she faced away from him. Any of her former herdsmen would have looked at her with annoyance or disdain, maybe even pity, and she couldn't stand the thought of seeing those emotions mirrored in Carrington's face.

Breaths hitching, she struggled to find her voice around the lump in her throat. "Th-thank you."

He clasped her upper arms and squeezed gently, his thumbs rubbing as if to reassure her. "I'm grateful you're safe, Solarne." His voice carried none of those emotions she'd dreaded. In fact, his voice matched the sincerity of his words. Then his low chuckle rolled over her fraught nerves like a balm. "But if you'd wanted in my arms, you could've just said so."

Laughter erupted through the headset. "Glad you're safe, Boss." Reber's voice rang out over the laughter. "When do we get those hours of tedium you promised?"

Solarne attempted a casual laugh, but it came out breathy and unnaturally shrill. She cleared her throat, this time sounding more like her normal self. "Hopefully, starting now."

"Reber, take point. We'll hang at the rear for a while." Carrington took charge, and she was happy to let him, still reeling from her near-death.

Carrington worked the pony controls, only needing a few suggestions or corrections. And he seemed content to let her use his body as a cushion. Soon, the initial surge of the herd's chaotic grazing relaxed from the churning storm of gluttony into gentle rolling waves of steady intake.

The view would have been relaxing, hypnotic even, if not for Carrington's hands. When not working the controls, he chuffed her arms slowly, warming her and calming the last remnants of distress away. Then he worked the muscles of her shoulders and neck until her tension from the last several moonphases evaporated, and she relaxed against his chest on a contented sigh.

As easily as he'd subdued and redirected the agitated bull, Carrington's touch melted her worries and threw plasma fuel on her desire. He couldn't know how quickly he fanned the smoldering embers of her need to a roaring blaze. And she couldn't tell him—hell, she couldn't even moan her encouragement—because their helmets transmitted continuous communications to all the others.

A safety precaution she'd never regretted until now.

Solarne bit back a gasp when he palmed the small mounds of her breasts through her suit and raked his thumbs across her sensitized nipples. He plumped and teased her breasts, and her fingers dug into his thigh muscles, anchoring her in the storm of his caresses. She held her breath and arched, her buttocks rocking against his erection. He inhaled on a hiss then cleared his throat to cover it. He dropped a hand and cupped her between her thighs. She coughed to hide her gasp.

Her heart raced from his touches and the monumental effort not to moan. His fingers traced the juncture of her thighs, somehow knowing exactly where to press to shoot bolts of electric heat through her. His other hand eased past the closure of her suit to grasp her bare breast, and she jumped at the intimate contact, her helmet clashing loudly against his.

"Ah! Sorry." Was her voice as breathless as is sounded?

Carrington chuckled and ground his cock against her ass. "Don't be."

"Boss, you good?" a voice inquired over the headset.

"Cramped quarters is all." She yipped as Carrington pinched her throbbing clit through the suit material.

"She's fine." He answered as well, somehow making it sound like sexual appreciation.

She turned as best as she could with his hands still gripping her breast and crotch and shook her head. This wouldn't work. If they continued, there was no way to be quiet, and his entire crew would get an auditory show. Then any respect they might have for her would give way to knowing leers.

Carrington removed his helmet, letting it drift away in the cramped space of their zero-gravity cockpit. His pupils were shot wide with arousal, his tongue swiping his lips as if he was starving and she was a feast. He removed her helmet, letting it drift away as well, then cupped her face, his thumb tracing the plump fullness of her bottom lip, his dark eyes searching hers for... what? Permission? Proof she was equally as aroused? That she wanted him more than she wanted her next breath?

He bent her over his arm and claimed her lips in a searing kiss that pulled the oxygen from her lungs and burned trails of lightning out her limbs to her fingertips and toes. His lips ravaged hers, his tongue sliding between her teeth to twine around hers. Flames like a solar flare shot through her, leaving her quaking, starving for more, feverish and desperate to strip away the chafing solarsuit.

On a choked groan, Carrington worked the

closure of her suit, peeling it over her shoulders and down her arms. Solarne pulled away to take over the hasty task, tugging and yanking her suit off while he did the same with his own. She swallowed a moan as he disrobed, revealing parsecs of muscles covered in a dusting of dark curls. When he shoved the material past his waist, she gasped at the cock rising at attention between his legs.

His throaty chuckle pulled her attention to his face, the uptick of an eyebrow and one lifted side of his mouth confirmed he'd heard the admiration in her gasp. Matching his arrogant expression, she clasped him around the thick base and stroked to the bulbous head.

Carrington inhaled with a hiss, and his eyelids fluttered closed.

Solarne shoved down her suit and toed off her boots in a few dexterous moves, and Carrington followed as best he could while she stroked his cock. He tucked each suit into a helmet so the fabric would mute the sounds they transmitted. She would still have to watch her volume, but at least she could breathe.

When she leaned forward to secure the helmets in an alcove, he palmed her ass and shoved her into the forward curve of the canopy. Before she could protest the awkward position, his hot mouth was on her, licking and sucking at the folds already slick with arousal. He spread her thighs wide, exposing her completely to his mercy. And he had none, working her with his lips and tongue and teeth until she panted, begging for release with each keening whine she exhaled. He moaned against her clitoris and flicked it until her legs quivered. As her orgasm struck, she clamped a hand over her mouth to stifle the scream, shuddering and bucking against his face.

She floated in a euphoric nebula as he gripped her hips and turned her. The cockpit was cramped, but the lack of gravity aided him in maneuvering her body. When she straddled him, he paused, eyebrows raised in question. A sweet but unnecessary gesture. At her nod, he pulled her down on his thick cock. She buried her face in his neck to drown out her long moan as he pushed deep inside her, filling and stretching her.

"Damn, you're as hot as a solar flare," he murmured in her ear, groaning as he lifted and tugged her along his shaft, setting a rhythm that quickly ignited her into an inferno once more.

"And you're a huge fucking bull," she panted. Big enough he had his own gravitational pull. Every time she slipped to the end of his cock, she came crashing back to the base, devouring him like gulping mouthfuls of ejecta.

They floated in the cramped space, rocking against each other, arms clutching and mouths exploring. Heaving and undulating, she rubbed her aching nipples against his chest, bucked against his muscular thigh, and clawed at his shoulders and back. When his mouth left hers to trail kisses down her neck, she gulped for air, desperate to have his lips on hers again even if it meant she suffocated.

She was a *crehdisth* worm to a solar flare. *Damn*, maybe this was what the phrase meant.

When her climax hit, it burst like a shockwave of charged particles through her body, radiating to her extremities, an aurora of light dancing in her vision. The struggle to remain quiet through her release amplified its intensity. She trembled, helpless against the storm of her orgasm, crying out her pleasure against Carrington's mouth, just as he groaned his own release.

Her thoughts drifted like her body, unfettered yet still intertwined with his. Their heaving breaths slowed to normal, and his cock softened and eased out of her. A wobbly bubble of white goo drifted past her half-closed eyes, and she swallowed her giggle. *Space spunk.* If they had time for another round, she might get to swallow some.

Carrington made no move to release her from his warm embrace. She glanced at the herd, which was nearly finished grazing. Soon, they'd have to return them to the pen. She and Carrington would have to dress and focus on the business at hand. Meaning, they'd have to act like this hadn't just happened.

"I get to call you Carr now, right?" She murmured against his shoulder. "Since we fucked."

Dare she hope she could be more than another notch on his bedpost?

"I, uh, lied about that. No one's ever called me

that." He exhaled as he pulled back to gaze into her eyes, his own as deep and fathomless as the cosmos. "But I like the way it sounds on your lips."

She smiled at the hesitant admission.

What would happen now? Knowing looks from his men and callous disregard by him. They'd move on to the next job, and she'd be left with only a memory to warm her. Perhaps, she could entice them to stay. Carrington seemed content in her arms. Could he be content on the ranch?

She cleared her throat and murmured, "If you and you crew are interested, I have several open positions at the ranch which need qualified individuals."

His arms tightened around her. "Hmm. Are you saying we're qualified individuals?"

"Very." The word emerged from her mouth like sexual appreciation, and her gaze dipped to his lips.

"Honestly, we're all looking for a place to set down some roots." He caressed her back and squeezed her ass. "If I can take my pick, I'm interested in the position where you're naked and I'm making you scream."

Her heart took flight as if released from its pen. "Naked and screaming, huh?" Her smile blossomed, and she lowered her lips to his. "I have the perfect opening for you to fill."

HUNK OF BURNING LOVE

Delilah Devlin

THE SECOND THE lovely Kelly Lehman left the fire-house after delivering her latest batch of imaginatively decorated cookies, Benny Smith slid his cookie, decorated with orange and yellow flickers of fire, into the trashcan. He let out a sigh as he did it because he really did love her sugar cookies.

"Why don't you just tell her that you're off sweets?" the fire chief, Blake Thacker, asked as he plucked a cookie from Kelly's pretty blue Kelly's Sweets cookie box.

"I don't want to hurt her feelings." Benny felt the tips of his ears get hot and knew his face was likely bright red.

"Are you sweet on the sweet shop lady?" Blake asked, a teasing glint in his eyes.

Benny cleared his throat and glanced around the firehouse, looking for any excuse not to have to answer that question. He spotted the firetruck and straightened his spine. Maybe Blake would let an abrupt change of subject slide. "So, am I back on the truck next shift?"

Blake nodded, his gaze narrowing on Benny's face. Then he slowly smiled. "Doc gave you the all clear. I'll be glad to have you back drivin'. Maybe you should spend the rest of this shift cleanin' out the cab. Capehart likes to sit in the cab when he's talkin' to his wife. He's probably left a ton of sunflower shells scattered all over the seat and floor."

Benny made a face, glad Blake was going easy on him and letting the subject of the pretty sweet shop lady drop. "I'll get right on it, Chief."

For the rest of his shift, Benny steered clear of the chief. Soon, it was nighttime, and as he lay on his narrow bunk, he thought about Kelly and why he hadn't yet worked up the guts to ask her out. Blake seemed to think she brought the cookies to the firehouse to get his attention, a concept that blew Benny's mind.

Blake had never had the problems getting girls to notice him that Benny had. Benny had always felt shy around women, even a little scared about the thoughts of getting naked with one. He'd been a big boy since he'd grown out of diapers, something he'd always thought was simply his lot in life. The extra pounds hadn't mattered all that much and had actually helped him from time to time. He'd played defense on the football team in high school, and his larger stature hid muscle that had gotten him through his rigorous training as a firefighter. Bulk and strength counted for more than a trim waist, or at least that's what he'd told himself. It wasn't until he'd been injured on the job, falling through the roof of a warehouse and breaking his tibia and hip, that he'd packed on enough weight that even he'd found it concerning.

The morning he hadn't been able to pull up his zipper and button his firefighter's trousers had been the day he'd finally had his "Come to Jesus" moment. "Food is not my friend—it's fuel!" became his mantra. Blake had supported him as his workout buddy at the firehouse and during long jogs on park trails, while he'd maintained his own large frame to keep his wife, the mayor, happy.

Benny had been on desk duty for fifteen months, and he was anxious to get back into the truck. The thing he'd missed most during his long rehabilitation had been firefighting—driving that great big rig, rushing into burning houses, saving those kittens stuck high in a tree. Really, everything about the job.

And now, he was back and in better shape than he'd ever been in his life, and suddenly, he'd begun casting a wider eye toward the world outside the firehouse. He'd started to think that he was ready for more of what his friends had—the love of a good woman, children, and the house with the white picket fence...

He was thirty-three and not getting any younger. As he drove home for the start of his two-day rotation off duty, he thought maybe he should stop by Kelly's Sweets and buy some donuts—not that he'd eat them, but just so he could see her smile over the counter and turn that pretty shade of pink that never failed to make him hot.

KELLY PACKAGED a dozen glazed donuts and handed them to the girl working the drive-thru window. The morning rush was in full swing, but she had everything under control. No one had called in sick. Everyone was at their station, and because she paid better than the going rate around town, all of her employees had been there a while and were well-trained and competent. If she wanted, she could take a day off now and then and the place wouldn't fall into ruin.

The bell over the door tinkled, and she glanced toward the sound, a smile already on her face to greet her next customer.

Firefighter Benny Smith walked through the door, dressed in his firehouse uniform of black trousers and T-shirt that conformed to the lovely muscles of his chest and arms. "Well, good morning,

Mr. Smith," she said after ungluing her tongue from the roof of her suddenly dry mouth. "What can I do for you?" *Give you a massage? A hand job? Make you breakfast after we have sex?*

Her cheeks heated as her mind went places that would've shocked the shy, handsome firefighter.

In turn, his gaze held hers for a second while he looked like he wanted to ask her to do one of those naughty things, but then he looked away and pointed at the glass cabinet. "Can I have some kolaches?"

Stifling her disappointment, she smiled. "How many would you like?"

He cleared his throat. "How many would you like?"

Kelly blinked, thinking maybe he'd misspoken.

He cleared his throat again then tugged at the neckline of his tee like it was choking him. "What I mean is, would you like to take a break? Sit with me?"

She watched him speak the words, but they seemed to come from far away, distorted by time and space, because she thought he'd actually asked her to take her break with him, and further, she thought he'd added, "Sit on me?" But that had to be wrong, right? Maybe he was like her and had been thinking the phrase but it had just exploded outward like air from a burst balloon.

Well, she'd never know for sure if she didn't ask. "Did you just ask me to sit on you?" she said, lowering her voice.

His eyes widened, and he leaned closer. "Only if you'd like that."

She couldn't help grinning. He looked so gob smacked, she knew those words hadn't come from him on purpose and might even have been borne from her overheated imagination, but she was also thrilled he didn't seem to mind the idea all that much.

Without looking away, because she was afraid he'd change his mind and disappear, she pointed a finger over her shoulder. "Let's get out of here. I'll just grab my purse and make sure the ladies know I'll be gone a while…"

He nodded and stood still as a statue in front of her counter as she stepped backward then turned on her heel and ran to the back. "Ella!" she called out. Her assistant glanced up from the oven where she was pulling out a fresh batch of kolaches. "I need four of those, and I'll be gone for a while."

Ella's eyes rounded. "This have anything to do with that firefighter you've been drooling over?"

Kelly grinned. "Be quick. I'm getting my purse." She ducked into her office, grabbed her purse from behind her desk, then checked her appearance in the small mirror beside the door. Lord, her cheeks were flushed, and any makeup she'd worn that morning was long gone, but she didn't dare give Benny time to change his mind, so she pushed through her office door and jogged to the door of the store before slowing her pace and walking through it with smile —not too big, not too small. No way did she want him to know that she'd been waiting for this chance forever.

AFTER HELPING her up into the cab of his older F-150 truck, Benny kept his eyes on the road. He worried that if he glanced her way, his gaze would stay there and he'd kill them both. The fact that Kelly sat in the truck next to him had him so hard his dick felt like it was strangling in his pants. At the same time, he felt truly terrified that he might just get the chance to use it.

"How's work been?" she asked.

"I'll be back on the rig next shift."

"The doctor cleared you?"

"Yeah."

"I'm happy for you."

"Thanks." When she went silent, he figured he ought to be polite and ask her about her work. "Been busy at the shop?"

"I have. I thought when that donut chain opened a store in town that I'd be out of business in a week."

"That'll never happen. Your donuts are better."

"I'm thinking about adding sandwiches to the menu and staying open through the afternoon."

The way her fingers plucked at her purse in her lap, he figured she might be as nervous as he was. That thought took a little bit of pressure off him. "I'd buy a sandwich from you every day."

"Would you?" she asked, her voice sounding a little breathless.

"I'd eat whatever you're serving." As soon as those words blurted from his mouth, he inwardly winced, thinking about how they might seem like a sexual innuendo. He didn't want Kelly to think he was crude and didn't see her as the lady she was. "I mean, I'm sure your sandwiches will be delicious."

"And there I was thinking you were still thinking about me sitting on you," she said, her voice a little muffled.

He glanced her way, just in time to see her chest shaking. She held up her hand. "I'm not laughing at you, promise. I'm laughing at me."

Benny arched an eyebrow, finally figuring out that she was as horny as he was, and that their inability to communicate was due to them both feeling a bit shy about revealing that fact. "Kelly, I planned on taking you for a picnic up on the canyon rim, but would you rather have dinner with me tonight? I think...maybe...we should take our time. Get to know each other—"

"Can I make you dinner tonight—at my place?"

She'd said it so eagerly, how could he refuse? "Well, let's have a kolache at the park. That way I'm not keeping you from anything, and I can go home and get a few hours of sleep. I wouldn't want to fall asleep on you." He gulped, because he pictured himself falling asleep mid-stroke.

"Benny, you do what you have to do. Whenever

you want, come on over to my place. I'll make you a nice homecooked meal…and then we'll see about you falling asleep on me."

THE BARBEQUE RIBS she'd put into the oven before her shower filled the air with their aromatic scent. When she finished rolling her hair in large rollers to make her straight blond hair look fluffy rather than flat, she'd place the potatoes in the oven to let them bake. She'd already finished chopping coleslaw and had set it in the fridge to chill. The table was set. Music was preprogrammed, old Motown hits, because she hoped he'd like to dance to "My Girl"—she'd always wanted a handsome man to dance with her in her living room.

Kelly wrapped one last lock of hair onto a large pink roller and stood back. Her makeup was subtle, her lipstick the same soft pink color as the panties and bra she stood in. She hoped he'd get a chance to see how much effort she'd taken to make the night perfect.

Benny Smith was one hunk of a man. She'd thought so before he'd injured himself and hadn't minded at all the love handles or the extra weight that had filled out his torso. She'd always thought of him as a big cuddly bear. Now, his face and waistline were trim. She'd thought that, after his transformation from cuddle-bear to muscled sex god, she wouldn't stand a chance of getting him to take notice of her.

Now, she was the one with a few extra pounds. She pinched her side then palmed her rounded belly. Lord, maybe the pretty underwear had been a waste of money because no way would she let him see her with the lights on.

A shrill beeping sounded from the kitchen, and she cursed. She hoped like hell she hadn't burned dinner. She picked up a magazine to wave at the smoke detector and hurried to the kitchen.

When she arrived, she saw a blaze burning inside her gas oven and panicked.

"Oh Lord! Jesus. Fuck. What do I do now?"

She had a fire extinguisher under the kitchen sink, so she ran to take it out, threw open the oven door, but then hesitated, because in her panic, she wondered if she'd make it worse. Should she use a fire extinguisher on a rack of ribs? Or was it never use one with oil on a pan? She tossed the fire extinguisher away and reached for the salt shaker, but other than dusting the flame, it didn't snuff the blaze. In fact, now, the flames licked at the end of the dish towel hanging over the edge of the counter top and traveled upward to light the paper towel dispenser next to the stove. Then it spread across the counter top she'd liberally doused with lemon oil to make it shine to the frilly curtains decorating her kitchen window.

In horror, she stepped back as her kitchen filled with smoke.

The phone! She dashed through the living room to find her cellphone resting on its charger and dialed 911.

BENNY WAS ALREADY on his way to Kelly's when he heard the call come over his radio. He had to ask dispatch to repeat the address to know it was Kelly's place. He stomped the gas pedal and drove as fast as he could safely, his heart in his throat.

When he reached her place, he could see flames through the living room window coming from somewhere beyond the room, and then a pink streak of woman as she dashed past the window.

Kelly! He parked in front of the neighbor's house, not wanting to be in the way of the firetruck when it came and ran to her door. When he twisted the doorknob, he found it locked. He heard a scream inside and decided pounding on her door would take too much time, so he lifted his leg and kicked near the handle, splintering the doorframe. The door fell with a thud to the floor inside.

Not that the owner of the house noticed, she was too busy flapping a rug at the flames, fanning them higher.

Benny ran to her, wrapped his arms around her, and lifted her off her feet. She struggled against him, nearly wriggling free.

"My ribs!"

He dropped his arms fearing he'd hurt her ribs. "Kelly, we have to get out of here," he shouted then drew a lungful of toxic smoke and coughed.

Kelly coughed as well, but shook her head. "My ribs!" she wailed before hacking again.

The woman was panicked, not listening to reason. He had to get her out of the fire so the men who were now pulling up in front of her house could do their job and save her house. He bent, pushed his shoulder against her soft belly, then rose with her in a fireman's carry and strode with purpose toward the front door.

Kelly still fought him. "My ass!" she shouted.

"Thought it was your ribs," he muttered, striding out onto the porch as men rushed inside in their bunker gear and carrying a large hose.

"You're showing my ass to the fucking world!"

Benny realized she was concerned about the fact she was in her underwear, but his first priority was delivering her to safety. He continued on, carrying her to his truck. Once there, he set her on her feet next to the passenger door then began unbuttoning his white dress shirt. He shrugged out of it then handed to her.

She ripped it from his hands and quickly drew it on, the hem reaching to mid-thigh and covering all her amazing girly parts.

When her gaze darted up to him, he averted his gaze. "Are you hurt? You mentioned your ribs."

"The ribs were your dinner," she bit out.

"You aren't burned?"

"No, just embarrassed."

Relief had him smiling.

She slapped his arm. "It's not funny."

He quickly hid his smile. "I know it's not. I think the fire was isolated to the kitchen, but they'll check the walls to make sure."

She moaned. "I can't believe I burned my kitchen down."

"Making my dinner," he said, shaking his head. "I bet the ribs would've been delicious."

Her gaze shot up again, narrowing.

He held up his hands. "I'm not making fun of you, I promise. I wouldn't do that." Pointing to his truck, he said, "Do you want to get inside? You can wait in there until the crew is done."

She smoothed her hands down the white shirt and nodded. "When do you think I can go inside? I'd like to get dressed."

"Tell you what... I'll get some things from your bedroom and be right back. Go ahead and climb into my truck."

She frowned at his bare chest then reached toward the console where he always left his straw Stetson. When she handed it to him, he raised an eyebrow in question.

She waved a hand at his chest. "Cover up something."

Shaking his head because she made no sense at all,

he donned the hat then waited as she opened the door. Then with one hand holding down the back of the shirt to keep her bottom covered, she stepped up. Benny reached over and held her hips as she turned to sit but quickly pulled his hands away when she was settled. "I'll be right back."

KELLY HAD NEVER BEEN SO mortified. Not only had she burned her kitchen up, she'd done so while in her underwear. A fact she hadn't been aware of until Benny had upended her over his shoulder to drag her out of her house.

Now, all his friends and many of her neighbors had seen her cheeks divided by a scrap of fabric that had the density of dental floss. She moaned and covered her face with her hands. She'd have to sell her business and move far, far away because she'd never live down the humiliation.

A tap sounded on the window beside her. Benny stood outside holding up the dress and sandals she'd laid out on the bed—the sexy, nearly sheer number she'd planned to tease him with.

The door opened, and he held out a washcloth. "You might want to wash your face first. You have some smudges."

Her eyes widened, and she turned his rearview mirror toward her and gasped. Worse than soot on her face, she was still wearing those stupid rollers. She quickly tugged them out of her hair then accepted the cloth and washed her face, hands, and arms, and then quickly finger-combed the fluffy curls around her head. When she was done cleaning herself up, she sat with her shoulders slumped. Could she have looked any worse?

"If you stand inside the door," he said softly, "you can take off my shirt, and I'll slide the dress over your head."

His voice sounded a little roughened, and she glanced across at him. There was no hint of pity in his expression. Instead, his cheeks were a little red and his eyes glittered. Was he still attracted to her? Was it possible she hadn't completely ruined her chances with the hottest firefighter in town?

He stood close, but didn't back away when she stepped down onto the running board then down to the ground. Only inches separated their bodies as she slowly unbuttoned his shirt. When she slipped it off, she turned to give him a view of her ass as she folded the shirt and set it on the seat.

A sharp intake of breath gave her courage to face him again. Lifting up her arms like a child, she waited as he placed the sandals on the floorboard then brought her dress over her head and smoothed it downward, his hands lightly grazing her breasts and hips before her head cleared the neckline.

"That better?" she asked.

"Better for whom?" he rasped. "I liked the pink…"

She wrinkled her nose. "I hoped you would."

Benny lowered his head. She raised her face

coming up under the wide brim of his hat. Their first kiss was a soft rub of lips, but then he palmed her cheeks and tilted her head, deepening the kiss. She came up on her toes and wrapped her arms around his neck. His hands dropped and cupped her ass, and he brought her closer to his body.

Reminded he was shirtless, if not hatless, she rubbed her fingertips in his chest hair and plucked at it then lowered her hand to tease along the line of dark fur that disappeared into his trousers.

Benny pressed on her ass as he ground against her belly. Then he jerked back his head. "They're gonna be a while. I could ask them to board up the door when they're done. Wanna come home with me?"

Truthfully, she wouldn't mind if they just popped into the cab of his truck and did it there, but she supposed she'd made enough of a scene for one evening and nodded.

Benny gripped her waist, lifted her into her seat, and slammed the door closed. Then he jogged over to the chief, who'd just arrived to supervise. Both men looked her way. Blaze grinned and gave her a little salute.

When Benny returned, he wasn't wearing a smile. No, his eyebrows were lowered, his jaw tight. She'd never seen him look sexier or more intense.

It was really going to happen. She, Kelly Lehman, was going to fuck a firefighter.

· · ·

BENNY DROVE out of town and along the highway for about a mile before turning onto his graveled drive. His place was still a bit of a work in progress. Some-day, he'd pave the drive and maybe bushhog the front yard, dump some dirt, and grow some honest to God grass, but he rather liked his little piece of Texas. His property was mostly undeveloped and host to a variety of animals that entertained him to no end. On any given night he could watch armadillos, deer, raccoons, and possums move about his front yard while he drank a beer on his porch. He liked the sounds of the birds that lived in the tree-lined ravine beside his house.

He wondered what Kelly would think, but it was too late to worry. At least the house was finished, if a little bare of decorations, like pictures and curtains.

Turning off the ignition, he sat next to her in his driveway, gazing at the white limestone house with its silver roof, the big square posts that held up the roof shading the porch. Inside, there were four bedrooms, two baths, and an open living room-kitchen area. When he'd chosen the floorplan, he'd hoped to have a large family one day that would keep that open space noisy and alive.

"This yours?" she asked.

"The bank's, for a few years, but yeah, it's mine."

"It's really pretty."

"Thanks. Wanna come inside?"

Her mouth pressed into a straight line while the light in her eyes danced with mirth. Benny grimaced.

"I did it again. I don't know why, but every time I open my mouth around you everything comes out like a line from a porno."

"Your words were perfectly polite," she said, then added, "but we're both dialed into the same porn channel. You ready to take this dress back off?"

Benny swallowed hard and reached blindly for the door handle, then jumping down to the concrete, he ran around to her door, opened it, and reached inside to pick her up. Only she didn't let him grab her up sideways, she faced him, pulled up the skirt of her dress, baring her legs, and made a space for him to walk right between them. Grabbing her ass, he lifted her against his body and sighed when she wrapped her legs around his waist.

"I really wanted to give you some great foreplay," he muttered.

Kelly grinned and flicked his nipple. "We've been doing that for months, big boy. I don't think I can wait another minute to feel you inside me."

Benny moaned and cradled her against him as he kicked closed the door then strode down the walkway, climbed the porch, then cursed when he had to pause to juggle her to get into his pocket to retrieve his keys.

While he finessed the lock, she nibbled on his earlobe and her hot little hands roamed his back and chest.

When the door flew open, he nearly stumbled inside. He'd never make it to the bedroom. He kicked closed the door then headed straight to the sectional sofa, bent and laid her back on the cushion, and then climbed right over her.

While his hands pushed up her dress, she grabbed his hat and flung it away then unbuckled and unzipped his pants. When her dress cleared her hips, he reached under her, tore the skinny strip that bisected her fine ass, and tugged the panties away. She shoved at his waistband and pushed down his trousers and underwear, just far enough his cock sprang free.

Then her fingers wrapped around his length. "Holy shit," she whispered, pulling on his cock and forcing him between her legs.

He gave a strangled laugh that morphed into a hiss when he sank into her snug, moist pussy. "Sweet Jesus," he gasped.

"Don't hold back on account o' me," she whispered and dug her nails into his backside.

Benny didn't need any further encouragement, but then froze and pulled away. "Just a second," he said, cursing under his breath as he dug out his wallet from his back pocket, slid a condom from an inner slot, and tossed his wallet away. "Don't know how old it is."

"Don't care," she said, taking the packet and opening it. As she rolled it down his length, she took some extra liberties, gliding her hand up and down his shaft and reaching below to cup his balls, bouncing them gently on her palms as though weighing them.

"Enough, Kel," he said.

"Yeah, I'm ready, too." Again, she pulled his cock to her entrance, draped one leg over the low back of the couch and the other around his waist. "Rock my world, cowboy." The words were sultry, but she followed them with a giggle and a roll of her eyes.

"Yeah, don't ever say that again," he said grinning as he drove inside.

All laughter faded as he sank inside her, burrowing through her slick walls in successive thrusts. Her hips rolled beneath his, and her fingers stroked, her nails scratched, and he learned through her sighs and groans just how to give her what pleased her most.

Soon, he was hammering at her, blessing his improved physicality for the stamina to extend their mutual pleasure. Still, he wished he could see her—all of her—when he took her the first time, so he pulled out and stood beside the couch. He quickly shucked his clothes then plucked the hand she was using to fondle her own breast through her clothes and dragged her up to sit so he could remove her dress and strip away her bra.

Good Lord, her tits were the finest he'd ever seen. Lush, full-bodied, round. He sat and patted his thighs. She didn't need much more of a hint and clambered over him, kneeing him in the belly in the process, but he didn't care because he had his hands on her glorious tits, and she was sliding down his shaft.

After she braced her hands on his shoulders and began rising and lowering, he lifted a breast to his mouth and latched around it, sucking on it hard like the thickest, richest milkshake then shaking his head and growling as he made it jiggle.

So, he was getting carried away, but again, she didn't mind, giggling and panting, and squeezing her inner muscles around him, giving him the sexiest of caresses.

When she entered a rhythm that allowed her to breathe, he plumped up her breasts and joggled them a bit. "Prettiest tits I've ever seen," he said.

"How many have you seen—outside your porno?"

"I don't really like porn," he said, wrinkling his nose. "I've seen some tits. Not a lot, but these, I know they're gold-ribbon. I mean, just look at them," he said, pinching a tip to see how it reddened from a pretty rose to deep cherry red.

"So, you're saying you would've asked me out sooner if I'd flashed them once in a while?"

Benny gave her bashful smile. "I might've been intimidated. You're still too pretty for me."

Kelly's mouth dropped open, and her movements stilled. "Are you kidding me? I've been hot for you for three years. Even before you went and got all Jason Momoa on me."

Benny chuckled. "You know, you're sitting on me."

Kelly narrowed her eyes. "I am. And I have something big and thick stuck up inside me. I wonder what I should do about that."

Benny lunged upwards, cupping her ass to keep their bodies locked together. "I'm thinking I missed my workout today. Maybe I should be doing most of the work. There anything you've never done?"

Kelly batted her eyelids. "I've never had a man handle me so easily. It's sexy. Think you won't get a hernia if you fuck me against a wall?"

"The woman wants to do it against the wall. We'll have to check that off your list of fantasies."

"You saying you want to *go down* my list."

He waggled his eyebrows. "I'm promisin' I'll go down on you as soon as I make you come against that wall."

Kelly pressed the back of her hand against her forehead and pretended to swoon. "I think I'm in love."

Grinning, Benny walked to a space where the waning sunlight gleamed through his picture window. If he was going to do all the work, he was going to see every bit of pleasure he brought her. When he had her firmly pressed to the plaster, he cupped her ass and bounced her on his cock. Up and down, faster and faster. He worked up a sweat as her legs clenched around his body and her head thrashed side to side.

"*OhGodOhGod!* Jesus, Benny!" she cried out and then her body went limp, except for her pussy, which clamped hard around him, and her channel, which convulsed all along his length in pulses that slowly faded away.

Benny wrapped his arms around her and backed away from the wall, sank to his knees, then lifted her and shoved her down, again and again until his own orgasm left him blind and shaking.

For what felt like a long while, they rocked together, holding each other tightly, savoring their connection. When they could both breathe again, they held each other's faces and kissed.

"I like this...with you," Benny said, knowing his words didn't begin to express what he was feeling. He was ready to let her choose the curtains and the throw rugs.

"I like you, Benny. And you fuck like a god."

He laughed because she blushed. She wasn't anymore used to sexy teasing as he was. He kissed her forehead then lifted her off his cock. Standing, he was surprised by how much his legs shook.

"Babe, I'm feelin' a little weak," Kelly said, pushing back her hair and reaching out to hold onto his arm.

"Do you want me to take you to go grab a bite?"

Kelly shook her head. "That would require me to get dressed again—and more to the point, I haven't stopped looking my fill of you."

Benny caught her hand and twirled her slowly around. "I won't ever tire of this view."

She lowered her eyelashes and gave him a flirty glance. "Maybe we can start another fire—one that only you can put out." With that, she turned and wagged her ass down the hallway, making straight for his bedroom.

Benny strode after her, musing he'd never felt this comfortable in his own skin, his cock bobbing as he followed a beautiful woman to his bed. Life was good.

THOROUGHBREDS AND THERMODYNAMICS

Sukie Chapin

"Lots more lube."

Not exactly the words I imagined saying to my sexy-as-hell Brad-Pitt-circa-*Legends-of-the-Fall*-channeling crush as we usher in Christmas day.

I can also think of more fun ways to be this sweaty and grunty than desperately trying to save a breach foal's life. However, we play the hand we're dealt, so I'm focusing on the horses and ignoring the way Boone's faded Wranglers hug his ass and thick thighs.

Boone's arms, which are total forearm porn, BTW, flex in a way that must be illegal in at least half a dozen states as he helps me pump Maybelline, the mare, full of lube. She gives us a murderous look and snorts indignantly, and I can't blame her—we didn't even buy her dinner first.

His panicked call came just after midnight, but it took me forever to get here in the sleet and snow. White Christmas, they said. It'll be great, they said. Yeah, until you're skidding down an icy two-lane highway in the middle of BFE, second-guessing your life choices. In three years of practicing, I've never wished for another vet's help this much, but I'm flying solo—the only veterinarian without Christmas plans.

If I'm honest, though, I thrive on this; work is my life. Working my ass off until I can't keep my eyes open anymore is all I've known, all I've had, since I turned seventeen. It's the way I survive. Although, sometimes, this whole surviving thing is exhausting, like I'm on autopilot, going through the motions but never feeling like I'm really here. Like I'm really *me*. Like I can breathe.

"That enough, Doc?" he asks. It's all he's ever called me, and I like the nickname. It's cute. But late at night, my vibrator and I get up close and personal as I imagine my real name rolling off Boone's tongue in that thick Texas drawl.

Get a grip, Adelaide.

"We're about to find out." I sound grim, even to my own ears. Dystocia is tricky, no matter what, but a breach presentation is one of the worst.

To save mama and baby, we'll have to push the foal back into the uterus and manipulate his legs until we can pull him out, hooves first. Then, the umbilical cord will be compressed, and we'll be racing the clock to deliver him before oxygen deprivation leads to brain damage...or worse.

"Hey," Boone stops me, placing a hand on my arm, and the skin tingles there. "I'm bigger, so let me help."

I crane my neck to look him in the eyes. He's got to be six-four, built like a Mack truck, quick and coordinated and capable. And thank God, because over the course of the last year, he's saved me from two rattlesnakes and a homicidal armadillo with that size and those reflexes. If I'm going to deliver this foal, I'll need Boone's help.

"Well, you *are* horse-sized." As soon as the words leave my mouth, I'm blushing. *Way to allude to horse penis, Adelaide.*

Boone smirks, and my body responds.

Ignoring what just happened, I push my arm inside the mare, again. I manipulate the foal painstakingly, getting him into the best position possible.

When I've done all I can, I don't even have time to say Boone's name before he's there.

"Let me help," he says softly.

He takes over the repositioning, and I walk him through each step. He's so damn big and intuitive; it barely takes any time at all before he's got two hooves out.

Go time.

We attach straps above the fragile joints, working

together like we've done this a thousand times, and within seconds, we're ready to pull. With every contraction, we provide traction, helping Maybelline get this little guy safely into the world.

When the black foal slips out of the mare's shivering body, Boone catches him in those burly arms and gently lowers him to the ground where I check vitals.

"Heart sounds great. So do his lungs," I say, and the look of relief on Boone's face makes my usually steely insides go mushy.

His gaze meets mine, and for the first time tonight, he grins, that huge smile that lights up his face, the one I can't resist. I feel my answering smile, and then he starts to laugh, the sound spreading warmth through my veins.

"I've seen a hundred foals born, but I've never been that fucking scared," he says.

I stand and attend to Maybelline, checking for damage from the rough delivery.

"May looks great. No tearing." I stroke her soft nose. "You're a good girl, Maybelline."

"Thank Jesus," Boone says, blowing out a breath.

"Why was this time scarier?" I ask, because I want to know things about Boone in a way that's completely foreign to me. A way that, frankly, freaks me the hell out. I don't usually indulge it, but tonight's different; we pulled off a freaking Christmas miracle.

"She was my dad's favorite, the last foal we delivered together. And this little guy's stud," he says as he runs a gentle hand over the perfect baby, "was my dad's horse."

"Brutus?" I ask, thinking of the gorgeous black Thoroughbred, a little unusual for a ranch horse. I remember how Boone always has a Honeycrisp tucked away for the stallion after his exams. How, when I mentioned that's my favorite apple, he started bringing an extra one for me. He does little things like that all the time.

"Yep," Boone says. "He's getting older. Never bred him before. But I wanted to have a piece of him when, you know, he isn't here anymore."

I swallow hard, my heart suddenly too big for the space it occupies. I know what losing a parent is like. What it feels like to hang onto any scraps of them you have left.

Boone stands and runs a hand over Maybelline's flank before catching my eye. "You're always damn impressive, Doc, but tonight..." He trails off, looks away. When his gaze meets mine again, his expression is so earnest, so intense. "Tonight, you were un-fucking-believable."

I have to play it off because I can't risk him seeing what he's just done to me. "You weren't too shabby yourself, cowboy."

"We make a pretty good team."

"Shoulder deep in horse pussy," I joke.

Boone's lips twitch. "Definitely not the pussy I'm interested in, but I can't think of better company."

"More of a goat guy? Or maybe pig?" I tease.

He laughs harder than I probably deserve, and I swear his gaze dips to my lips. But, running on adrenaline and the cold coffee I chugged on the way here, I don't trust that I'm not hallucinating. "I'd say I'm more of a smart, ballsy blonde kind of guy," he says, eyes dark and full of mischief, as he fingers the blond strands of my braid.

Yeah, definitely hallucinating.

Maybelline snorts, and we turn as the foal tries to stand but wobbles back to the hay.

"So close," Boone says, laughing, and while the moment has slipped away, there's something in the air—a charge that lingers, electric and inevitable as the sun rising in a couple of hours.

Boone watches the new foal, a faraway, soft look on his handsome face. "It never gets old," he says, "watching the beginning of life. It's like seeing a piece of forever."

We lean against the wall, arms close enough to brush, waiting for the foal to stand and nurse. His warmth seeps into my skin, and I don't miss how present, how *me*, I feel right here, right now.

"God or Gaia or some higher something at work," I say softly, and he nods. After a minute, I ask, "When did you lose your dad?"

"Four years ago, heart attack." He doesn't look at me when he says it, but I'm watching him, watching his big throat work on a swallow.

The foal gives standing another shot, but those

spindly legs aren't ready. We both chuckle again as he shakes his head furiously.

"It's been thirteen for me. Mom and dad. Car accident." I'm not even sure why I said it—it's not something I share with people.

Boone turns to face me fully. "No shit?" He doesn't need to say more than that; everything else is in his eyes.

"Nope," I say, and whether it's the late hour, the new life we just yanked into the world, or the fact that it's officially Christmas Day, there's a huge lump in my throat. Jesus, I haven't cried over my parents in a damn long time.

He raises a hand, like he's thinking about touching me, then shoves it in his pocket instead. He blows out a breath, and asks, "Do you believe in heaven?"

I shrug. "Maybe. I think there has to be some-thing…you know, after? Even if it's just like the whole thermodynamics thing."

He shifts closer to me. "What about thermo-dynamics?"

I duck my head, feeling sheepish. Here's Boone with his megawatt smile and the hottest body I've ever laid eyes on, and I'm talking physics. "Well, we're all made of energy, and thermodynamics says no energy is created or destroyed, so our energy, what makes *you* and *me*, will always exist. Even…after. It's still out there—just not organized the same anymore."

The blush starts as soon as I finish, but then rough fingers touch my chin, and warmth spreads through my veins, a low static hum under my skin that settles in my breasts and in between my legs. Boone lifts my face until I'm looking into those heated baby-blues, and when he speaks, his voice is full of gravel. "That's the most beautiful fucking thing I've ever heard."

That electricity in the air hums around us, more intense than ever, but a commotion in the hay drags our attention away.

The foal gets his shaky legs under himself again. I'm holding my breath, and I can tell Boone's doing the same. And just like that, the new baby takes his first wobbly step. We laugh softly together, and this time, I'm relieved the moment passed because all these Christmas-Day-new-foal-this-close-to-Boone feelings have me out of sorts.

I start to clean up, and Boone joins me. We work in companionable silence as May and her baby bond.

By the time everything's in order, the foal is nursing. "Well, mother and baby are healthy," I say. "I think you've got it from here."

If I could trust my radar, I'd swear disappointment crosses Boone's face, but, as it is, I know I'm too tired to trust anything.

"Thanks, Doc," he says.

He walks me to the barn door, but when he swings it open, we both freeze.

While we've been cocooned in the barn, the winter storm has turned into a blizzard. In Texas...

"Well, fuck me," Boone says, and I resist the urge to *that's what she said*. "I hope you didn't have any holiday plans."

I don't tell him that my Christmas plans are opening a can of Chef Boyardee and a bottle of "fancy" wine from the Piggly Wiggly, and then binge-watching *The Office* because that's not something you admit to a sex god.

I look at my Prius, half buried in a snowdrift. A freaking snowdrift.

"I can make it home," I say, but it falls flat. "Where's your shovel?"

Boone laughs. "You gonna ride it home like a broom, because you're sure as hell not thinking of digging your car out and driving in this. Crash at my place," he says, waving his big hand at the little white farmhouse up the hill. "You can check on these two tomorrow. Just in case."

Oh, he's good. I can't fight that reasoning.

And that settles it, because the next thing I know, we're picking our way through snow and ice. Boone helps me navigate the slick front steps to the covered porch. He holds the front door open for me, and we stumble across the threshold. It's after four, and he looks how I feel—like sleeping standing up is a valid option at this point.

He walks me to his bedroom and nods at the bathroom door.

"Shower's in there." He hands me a pair of boxer briefs and an A&M T-shirt. "I'll hit the other bath."

After our showers, Boone grabs a pillow to take to the couch. He's so damn tired, and way too big to sleep well on the sofa. It takes less than a second to make up my mind. "Hey, cowboy, we're both dead on our feet. Just climb in here. I promise I won't be a cover hog."

He swallows hard and raises a brow. "I snore."

"You could sing Queen all night, and I doubt I'd hear you," I say, crawling under the covers.

He laughs and slides in beside me. "Pretty sure I don't channel Freddy Mercury in my sleep."

"I don't know whether to be grateful or disappointed."

He laughs quietly and tucks the covers around me before settling back. My heart does that thing again, the one where it feels too big.

"You good?" he asks.

I sigh. "Better than I've been in a long damn time."

I say it without thinking, the truth of my own words hitting me like a punch to the chest. Boone makes a soft noise in the back of his throat.

Something deep inside whispers that I should want to snatch the words back, but for some inexplicable reason, I don't want to. Laying here, Boone's heat soaking into my skin, his smell all around me, his soft breaths a gentle reminder of life, I feel...like me. Present. Like I can breathe.

"Merry Christmas, Adelaide," he says, my name

like whiskey on his tongue, the words searing their way through my veins, burning the sounds into my synapses, making me drunk on Boone. Better than I imagined.

"Merry Christmas, Boone," I whisper back because it's all I can manage.

And as much as I don't want this moment to end, sleep is pulling me under before I hear Boone's first soft snore.

I HAVE no idea how long I've slept, but the sun is peeking through thick clouds when I open my eyes. That, and I'm using Boone's hard, heavy bicep as a pillow.

Okay. That happened.

We're on our sides, facing each other, my cheek cradled against his ridiculous pec, his left arm draped across my waist, hand *riiight* above my ass. One of my arms is wrapped around him, but the other...

Oh, the other.

God bless America.

My other arm is wedged awkwardly between us, and I say awkwardly because I'm 111% sure that's Boone's hard cock pressing against the back of my hand. I feel a little like a perv because my body responds instantly, my nipples tightening and everything low in my belly going hot and liquid.

I move, just a teensy bit, because if he wakes up in

this unfortunate, completely accidental, somnophilic moment, I'll legit die of humiliation.

But I don't consider the fact that, in moving, I'm now basically rubbing the obscenely large, rock-hard penis I'm trying to escape, or that said penis is attached to a living, breathing man, who groans, long and deep and sexy as hell, and then goes dead-still in a very much not-asleep-anymore way.

"I swear to God, I'm not feeling you up in your sleep," I blurt, but my hand is still on his cock, so there's that.

And at the exact same time, he says, "I'm going to be so fucking disappointed if I'm dreaming."

I pull my head back to look at him because... *What?*

His gaze is dark and hot, and it licks over every inch of my face before settling on my eyes. It's the same way he looked at me last night, no hallucinating. And the electricity between us? It's real, and it's here, and it crackles and burns along my skin. It tangles around me and makes every cell I have strain toward every cell of Boone's, as though I'd like to crawl right inside him because there's no such thing as *too close*. Undeniable and unrelenting.

"There's something between us, Addie," he says, so damn earnest, his voice a quiet rumble that I feel in every nerve in my body. Nobody ever calls me Addie, but the sound of it from his mouth is so perfect, like I've been waiting my whole life to be *Addie* to him. "And it's..." he stops and licks his full lips, "it's fucking strong, and it's there all the damn time. And I want to find out what it is, *need* to find out so fucking bad." The big, hot palm on my back presses me tighter to him. "But if it's just me, please tell me so I don't make an ass out of myself by kissing the hell out of you."

Holy hell.

I can't pretend anymore. Can't write it all off to an active imagination. This thing between us has been slowly heating for months, since the moment we met, really, and now, we're a couple of frogs who've failed to notice they're boiling alive.

My energy. His energy. Nothing created and nothing lost—but maybe always destined to intertwine in this moment.

He studies me like the entire world hangs on the next words out of my mouth.

The decision is made. So damn easy.

"You should definitely kiss the hell out of me," I whisper.

And then his mouth crashes into mine, everything I dreamed, soft lips demanding and coaxing all at once. He kisses me gently, lips just brushing mine, and then teasingly, with nips and bites. At last rough, with a rake of his teeth that makes me shiver, and deep, his tongue exploring, taking. And then he starts all over. He kisses me like he's imagined this a thousand times, made a list of all the ways he wants to do it, and now, he's trying each one out. I've never, ever been kissed like this before.

My pussy swells, and I'm so damn wet from just this little bit of him. But then Boone's knee nudges mine, and I'm spreading my legs so his muscular thigh can slide in between, hard muscle meeting my throbbing clit.

And, oh sweet baby Jesus, yes, right there.

My breath hitches as I shamelessly grind against him, and all hell breaks loose.

Boone's hand cups my breast, and I arch into the touch and swallow his growl. His rough thumb strokes across my nipple, and *Hallelujah*, it's bliss. It pebbles hard, and Boone notices. He makes another sound, deep in his throat, pinches the hard flesh between his fingers, and holy hell, the touch goes, bright as lightning, right to my clit. My hips buck against his thigh, and we both moan.

But Boone, the evil genius, has better ideas. In an instant, he's on top of me, and I spread my thighs, making room for his big body. He makes an adjustment in his shorts, then settles against me, his heavy cock resting, hot and hard, over my slit. And then he moves his hips, just a little, a question, and I see stars.

I gasp, my nails biting into his back.

"Good?" he asks as he finds his rhythm, his cock rubbing my clit with each push, but I'm too far gone to answer. Magic lips trail down my neck, biting along my jugular, making me shudder. And then his mouth is on my breast through the cotton of my borrowed tee, and it shouldn't be the hottest thing I've ever felt, but it is. Oh, it so is. He sucks my nipple hard, the wet cotton between us somehow making it even more exciting. He's not gentle, but I don't want him to be, and, in true Boone fashion, he *knows.*

When he nips at my flesh, I cry out, and my legs band around his waist, only making everything that much more intense.

"Too much?" he asks.

"Don't stop," I manage to choke out. His cock moving against me is driving me crazy, and to my utter shock, an orgasm coils low in my belly. *Can I... come like this?*

In the next second, his hands are cradling my head. "Open your eyes for me," he says softly, and I do, my breath catching in my throat.

He's looking at me like I'm the most precious thing he's ever held between his hands, and *damn...*

"Fuck me, you're beautiful. You know that?" he says.

I let out a soft sob. From his words. From what he's doing to my body.

"Are you going to come for me, Addie? Are you going to come just from dry humping like a couple of teenagers?"

And oh my God, I think I am. I didn't think it could really happen, but I've never been happier to be wrong. I whimper, but it's not like I can lie to him when my orgasm is *this close.* He's going to know the truth in about seven seconds.

"Because that's what you make me feel like. Like I'm sixteen, and everything's new and so damn exciting. Like this is my first time," he says, and I moan as he nips my bottom lip. "I can't wait to taste your pussy. To see how wet I can make you. To see the look on your face when I fill you with my cock. How pretty you are when you come."

Jesus.

"Let me see you come, sweetheart," he says, just as his fingers find my nipple again, and I go off like a rocket.

I cry out and stiffen as the orgasm pulses through me, robbing me of thought and breath, Boone's thick cock grinding mercilessly against my clit.

He kisses the side of my head over and over as I shake in his arms.

"Fuck me, that was so damn hot, Addie," he says when I'm finally still, holding me tight. "Even better than I imagined, and trust me, I have an excellent imagination and plenty of practice."

I pull back to see his face. Boone's bronze skin is flushed, and the look in his eyes...holy hell. He looks like fire feels. I swallow hard. "What else have you imagined?"

I didn't think his eyes could get any darker or any more filled with desire, but somehow, they do. "Every damn thing," he says and goose bumps break out over my skin. "I want to touch you everywhere. With my hands. With my mouth. With my cock. I want to know everything that makes you moan. Everything that makes you shiver. When you walk away from my bed, I want to know that your body doesn't have one fucking secret left." He huffs out a soft laugh and shakes his head like he can't believe what he's about to say. "Would I be too much of a cocky caveman if I said I want to ruin you for every other man? Because, Jesus Christ, Addie, I've never felt like this before. I've never wanted anyone the way I want you."

"I..." I stumble over my words, because *wow*. "Neanderthal looks good on you."

A wry smile tugs at the corner of his mouth, and I want to kiss it. "Really? Not too much?"

I shake my head. "Too perfect," I counter. "Now take your clothes off because we have a lot of ground to cover."

Now, he laughs outright and kneels between my spread thighs, grabs his tee at the nape, and whips it over his head.

"Merry Christmas to me," I breathe as I take him in, making him laugh again. And, God help me, I love making him laugh. My gaze skates all over him, and I know desire is written all over my face, because how could it not be? From his massive biceps, pale compared to his dark forearms, to his big, firm pecs, and down, down to the ridges of his cut abs, and the massive tent in his shorts, he's perfect. I sit up, and my fingers go all the places my eyes just went. Goosebumps erupt as I trace his muscular shoulders, and he shivers and sighs when I brush my thumbs over his nipples. But when I press my mouth to his flat belly, my fingers trailing to where his shorts ride low, his hips jerk, and his hand goes to my hair.

"Wait," he says, and I whine.

Nimble fingers pull the elastic out of my braid then work the strands until they're hanging in waves down my back. "Perfect," he says, his fingers tangling in them.

"You really did have a certain way you imagined this, huh?"

"Sweetheart, you have no damn idea."

"So, what am I supposed to do next?"

"Surprise me," he says, and it's like a shot of whisky through my veins.

I tug his waistband, and his cock springs free, legit smacking him in the belly with a meaty *thwap*. My mouth pops open. It's way more than I dared to dream; the guy's hung like a horse, and I'm a veritable expert on the topic. He's long and thick and heavy. I run my hands across his cut hips, down the massive thighs. He grunts, deep in his throat, and I feel the sound in my pussy. When I finally grasp that brutal cock, fist over fist because just one won't cut it, he makes a strangled sound and his grip in my hair tightens.

"Jesus, Boone, I won't walk for a week."

He laughs, and those amazing abs flex. "I'll carry you," he says, and I swear, my heart sighs.

Jesus take the wheel, I'm in trouble.

I run my nose along his length, breathe him in, and his smell is a dose of amphetamine to my libido.

Thoroughly hooked, I run my tongue around the thick, round head, slick over the slit where pre-come has beaded for me. Boone hisses out a harsh breath and gathers my hair in a fist. "Holy shit, Addie," he says. "Your mouth."

I go to work, reveling in his weight against my tongue. Never in my life have I had a cock like this, and I'm practically giddy with it. And it gets better when Boone moves his hips, cursing under his breath between groans and hisses, like he can't help himself. And I love that I've done that to him, this strong, stoic man. He's coming apart for me.

When I cup his heavy balls and roll them in my hands, his hips surge forward, and I gag. He pulls out with a "Fuck, sorry."

His face and chest are flushed, and he looks like it's just a thin wire of willpower keeping him together.

"I don't mind," I reassure him, going for his cock again, but he leans over me, forcing me back on the bed, and kisses the hell out of me instead.

When he pulls away, he grins that mischievous grin. "No rush, sweetheart. We can save you choking on my cock for New Year's."

"How romantic," I tease, but damn if I don't like the idea of ringing in the New Year with him, choking on cock or no.

"Hell, if you feel that way, we can even save it for Mardi Gras or President's Day. Let the anticipation really build." He says the last part with a wink, and I giggle.

"Washington would be honored," I say.

"Course he would. I bet Martha sucked cock like a champ."

I laugh harder, and Boone's gaze heats again.

"Of course, you keep laughing at my lame jokes, and we won't even make it to Boxing Day, sweetheart," he says.

"Me thinking you're funny makes you want to shove your cock down my throat?" I ask, trying to hide my smile and the way his *sweetheart* makes me feel.

"Addie, when it comes to wanting to put my cock in you, there's no limit to the places I want to put it, times I want to do it, or reasons why." He says it as serious as can be, and I feel my own gaze go as hot as his. "Now, get naked, sweetheart," he says as he kicks his shorts the rest of the way off, eyes like fire.

And to punctuate those hard, hot words, he grabs the waist of the boxers I'm wearing and yanks them off, as I get rid my T-shirt.

"Fuck me," he says, his gaze raking all over me.

And then his hands are everywhere. His fingers caress the inside of my elbow, the sensitive underside of my breast, the spot where my ass meets the back of my thigh. Lips seek out my neck, the ticklish spot just above the curve of my waist, my nipples, and finally the delicate skin of my inner thigh. I moan and gasp and sigh as he does his level best to memorize every inch of my body.

"Your pussy is so fucking pretty," he says, settling himself between my thighs, and I don't even have time to process that before he's making an absolute meal of me. I've *never* had a guy go down on me like this. This is Boone owning me. Boone showing me that when he said he doesn't want me leaving with a single secret, he means it. He's balls to the wall, and I'm on the verge of coming again in what seems like the breadth of a heartbeat. He sucks and licks, kisses and nips, while his beard chafes my sensitive skin in a way I'll never forget. There isn't a single millimeter of me that he doesn't toy with, that he doesn't explore, that he doesn't claim. His tongue teases my opening as his fingers play rough with my clit, and I'm a goner.

"*Sweeet*, oh my God," I blurt as I come hard, my hips bucking against his perfect mouth. The entire universe shrinks to a single blinding light that's throbbing behind my lids and in between my legs, as Boone relentlessly chases every last millisecond of my orgasm.

I think I black out.

When he climbs back up my body, his monster cock nudges the inside of my thigh, and he pushes sweaty hair off my forehead. He's breathing hard and his pupils are blown, and, despite the orgasm I just had, I've literally never wanted anyone inside me as much as I want him.

I hook my legs around his waist, whimper, and squeeze those hard abs between my thighs. Jesus, what is he going to be like moving over me? All that heft and power. I've imagined it a hundred times, and now, I'm going to finally get to experience it. It really is a very Merry Christmas.

"What is it, baby?" he asks, lips against mine, and I feel him smirk. "You want my cock now? That what you need?"

"Please," I say, and Boone runs his fingers through my hair.

"It'll probably be easier if you're on top," he says, then presses a soft kiss to my lips.

I don't have time to respond before Boone grabs me tight against him and flips us over so I'm straddling him as he sits with his back against the pillows.

"Time to cowgirl up, sweetheart," he says, and slaps my thigh, grinning. But then he's more serious when he says, "This way you control how deep." He caresses my pussy with the backs of his fingers, eyes trained on mine. "I don't want to hurt you."

I nod, because my throat feels tight, and it has nothing to do with how turned on I am.

As he rolls a condom on, I think about how he doesn't want to hurt me, how he holds me like I'm precious. How he was tonight with the delivery, the deliberateness of everything he does, the intensity and dedication he shows. I think about the time he brought in a dog that'd been hit by car, the way he cursed quietly when we told him there was nothing we could do, and then sat with the pup until it passed, stroking its soft brown ears. How he always hands me a couple of those little plastic hand-warmers when we're out in his fields because once I mentioned that my hands freeze out there during the winter. How he has an extra to-go cup of coffee, just how I like it in his truck if I have to meet him early in the morning. I don't think I've ever met anyone who watches so closely. Who makes remembering such a priority.

So, when he uses a thumb to hold his cock at the right angle for me to sink down on, I'm not only feeling him between my legs, I'm feeling this big, rough man in my heart. And it's like my entire body takes a breath for the first time in ages.

The broad head of his cock stretches me open from the first nudge, and an "Oh my God," falls from my lips as I rock my hips.

"Fuck, Addie," he says with a hiss. "Yeah, baby, go slow."

The next couple of inches of Boone take that stretch to a burn, and I whimper. But Boone is right there with me, reading every expression on my face. He shushes me softly, stills me with a hand on my hip, and then his fingers are on my pussy. He teases me; stroking my lips, circling the skin that's stretched obscenely around him, before finally going right where I need him. I cry out, my nails biting into his shoulders, as he fingers me, rough pads playing my clit the exact way I like best.

"Better?" he asks, pressing kisses to my closed eyes. I open them, and he's watching me so damn close, concern written all over his face.

"So good," I say with a sigh, moving my hips again, taking him inch by inch. Boone groans, long and low, and his fingers bite into my hips. His hips buck, barely a fraction of an inch, beneath me, and I know he wants to move, wants to take charge, but he's giving this to me because he wants to protect me, wants this to be good for me, and that just makes all these things I'm suddenly feeling even stronger.

"Addie," he says, and his gaze bounces from where we're joined to my eyes. "Your pussy feels so fucking good. I want to feel you come on my cock."

Boone's words. God, his filthy, fabulous words, are like the last push I need to get him all the way seated inside me, and we both moan as he bottoms out.

He kisses me again, this time slower, steadier, like he's proving this isn't something that has to be fast and furious, but can be savored for the gift it is.

"I've wanted this for a long time," he says, and his gaze strips me even barer than I already am.

"Me, too," I whisper.

It takes nothing to find a rhythm that has us both gasping. Boone grunts with each push, eyes hot on mine.

His hands find mine, and he laces our fingers together, and somehow this simple act, this seventh-grade handholding, makes this all the more intimate, all the hotter, until I can't pretend that I'm not walking away from this changed. My pussy feels so swollen, so full, but then Boone shifts his hips, changes the angle just a teensy bit, and now that big cock is rubbing some spot inside me that's making me see stars. My back arches until my breasts press against his chest, his hair rasping against my sensitive nipples. He meets me, move for move, his grunts, my whimpering, and the slick sounds of him filling my pussy only making me that much hotter. I can't believe anything can feel this perfect.

"Fuck, I love being inside you." He growls, the sound rough and feral, then grasps both my wrists in one hand, pins them at the small of my back, and his other hand goes to my clit. I cry out, a choked sound, so full of feeling, I'm about to blow apart. "Are you going to come again, sweetheart? Because it sure feels like you are. And, Addie, I wanna feel you come on my cock so fucking bad."

The orgasm takes me by surprise. It's in my head first, trickling down my spine, before it explodes in my pelvis in thick, rolling waves that seem to start fresh with every thrust of Boone's hips. I curl in on myself, the sensation so intense I can barely stand it, and Boone feels it too.

"Fuck, fuck, fuck," he says, thrusting, ruthless and frantic, up into my spent body, his mouth open, breaths harsh, and my orgasm starts all over again.

"Addie, fuck," he grits out, pulling me hard against his chest. He groans, low and deep, the sound vibrating against my nipples. His forehead presses against mine, and that huge body shudders against me, his cock jerking inside as he lets go. It's literally the hottest thing that's ever happened to me in my entire life.

Boone collapses against the pillows, taking me with him, crushed to his body. We stay like that, him still inside me, our sweat-slick skin molded together, both panting harsh breaths. He lets go of my wrists, and I wrap my arms around him, bury my head in his neck, as we process and come down. Boone strokes my hair, my back, my thighs.

Finally, he takes a shaky breath and pulls back, smirking.

"What is it?" I ask.

He shakes his head and cups my face in his big hands. "Just thinking that the night started with thoroughbreds and thermodynamics and ended with you, here, in my bed."

"Merry Christmas?" I ask, and bite my lip.

"Very fucking Merry Christmas. That was unreal. I think I left my body."

"Religious experience?" I ask, running my hands over his chest because I can't seem to stop touching him.

"Or maybe physics." He grins adorably, and his fingers sneak between my ass cheeks, down to where I'm still stretched around him, and I inhale sharply.

"Definitely chemistry," I say, then waggle my brows at him.

He laughs and kisses me, taking his time to taste and tease.

When he pulls away, I say, "And to think, Christmas isn't even over yet."

He strokes his thumbs over my cheeks, eyes so damn sincere. "No, sweetheart, nothing about this is over."

I know exactly what he means because I'm feeling all of it, too. All of this *something* that's between us. My heart feels too big for my chest, but even so, I'm 100% present in this moment, completely *me*, and I can *breathe*. Here, with Boone, it's easy.

His lips touch mine again, and it feels so right. He pulls back and says, "Stay 'til New Year's."

"You just want me to choke on your cock," I say, laughing.

He looks completely unashamed. "That's not a lie, but I want a lot more than that."

And I don't know what I'm doing. I think, over the years, I've forgotten how to be anything but alone, but lying here in Boone's arms, with his gaze on mine, his massive body holding me steady, present, his mouth breathing life into me, I'm ready to try.

Thermodynamics. His energy and mine. Maybe it really is that simple. And that beautiful.

"So do I."

ABOUT THE AUTHORS

Ava Cuvay writes out of this world romance featuring sassy heroines, gutsy heroes, passion, and adventure...set in a galaxy far, far away. She lives in central Indiana with her own scruffy-looking nerfherder, teenage kiddos, and two feline fur-babies. She loves writing, wine, and bacon in any combination or quantity.

Cindy Tanner grew up an only child in rural Indiana, relying on her imagination for entertainment. Starting at a young age she would read books to her animals and started telling her stories to anyone that would listen. Over the years her love of reading and telling stories grew into a career of her dreams.

Elle James spent twenty years livin' and lovin' in South Texas, ranching horses, cattle, goats, ostriches and emus. A former IT professional, Elle happily writes full-time, penning adventures that keep her readers begging for more. When she's not writing, she's traveling, snow-skiing, or riding her ATV, concocting new stories.

Izzy Archer writes erotic romance from sunny Southern California with a pen in one hand and a glass of Casamigos Reposado in the other. On the rocks, with a twist of lime. She has a fondness for both cowboys and cowboy boots. Not always in that order.

Jamie K. Schmidt is a *USA Today* bestselling author, known for her erotically charged romances. Jamie's books have been called, "hot and sexy, with an emotional punch," and "turbo-paced, gritty, highly sexual thrill rides." She is a #1 Amazon best seller and a 2018 RWA Rita® finalist in erotic fiction.

January George has been writing since she was a child and has always had a special love for happily ever after stories. She lives in upstate New York with her husband, children and two cats.

Jennie Kew writes contemporary slice-of-life erotic romance novels and contemporary and para-normal short erotic stories. Her books include *The Bennett's Bastards Series, The Brisbane Bachelors Series,* and *The Q Collection.* She lives in regional New South Wales, a stone's throw from Australia's capital, Canberra.

Kelly Violet is a born-and-raised New Yorker, living in a California world. She's four years into her writing journey and just getting started, so get ready for more angsty, flirty, and naughty reads. Kelly loves to hear from readers, so feel free to connect with her on social media sites.

Margay Leah Justice is the author of the para-normal romance *Sloane Wolf* and the MM romance *Strip Me,* winner of the Hot Books, Cold Nights contest and published by Pocket Books. She considers herself a multi-genre writer, writing whatever story hits her—you never know what comes next!

Megan Ryder pens sexy contemporary novels all about family and hot lovin' with the boy next door. She lives in Connecticut, spending her days as a technical writer and her spare time divided between her addiction to knitting and reading. Check out her Granite Junction and Redemption Ranch series on her website.

Michal Scott is the erotic romance penname of Anna Taylor Sweringen, a retired United Church of Christ and Presbyterian Church USA minister. She has been writing seriously since joining Romance Writers of America in 2003. Her erotic romances are published with the Scarlet line of The Wild Rose Press.

Natasha Moore is the author of more than thirty sexy contemporary and erotic romances. She believes stories of love and hope are important. Love can happen at any age, and she often writes about vibrant and passionate characters finding love later in life.

Reina Torres is an author for whom reading was always a way to escape, dream, and travel to different times and places. Writing was a way to discover new adventures and share those stories with others. Reina writes across a number of different romance sub-genres, remembering that those who wander aren't always lost.

Sukie Chapin has been a military wife, world traveler, almost-groupie, and preschool teacher. Naturally, the next logical step was writing erotic romance. She lives in Texas where she can be found reading, writing, mommying, and making a home-made chocolate pudding that will make you want to slap your mama.

ABOUT THE EDITOR

Delilah Devlin is a *New York Times* and *USA Today* bestselling author of romance and erotic romance. She has published nearly two hundred stories in multiple genres and lengths and has been published by Atria/Strebor, Avon, Berkley, Black Lace, Cleis Press, Ellora's Cave, Entangled, Grand Central, Harlequin Spice, HarperCollins: Mischief, Kensington, Montlake, Running Press, and Samhain Publishing.

Her short stories have appeared in multiple Cleis Press collections, including *Lesbian Cowboys*, *Girl Crush*, *Fairy Tale Lust*, *Lesbian Lust*, *Passion*, *Lesbian Cops*, *Dream Lover*, *Carnal Machines*, *Best Erotic Romance (2012)*, *Suite Encounters*, *Girl Fever*, *Girls Who Score*, *Duty and Desire*, *Best Lesbian Romance of 2013*, and *On Fire*. For Cleis Press, she edited *Girls Who Bite*, *She Shifters*, *Cowboy Lust*, *Smokin' Hot Firemen*, *High Octane Heroes*, *Cowboy Heat*, *Hot Highlanders and Wild Warriors*, and *Sex Objects*. She also edited *Conquests: An Anthology of Smoldering Viking Romance*, *Rogues: A Boys Behaving Badly Anthology*, *Blue Collar: A*

Boys Behaving Badly Anthology, Pirates: A Boys Behaving Badly Anthology, Stranded: A Boys Behaving Badly Anthology, and *First Response: A Boys Behaving Badly Anthology.*

Made in the USA
Monee, IL
26 October 2021